Beneath The Clouds

The Struggle for Truth and Justice

Can Turn Deadly

Christopher C. Black

BADAK MERAH SEMESTA

2016

Beneath The Clouds

Cover Design by: Rossie Indira

Layout by: Rossie Indira

First edition, 2016

Published by PT. Badak Merah Semesta

Jl. Madrasah Azziyadah 16, Jakarta

http://badak-merah.weebly.com

email: badak.merah.press@gmail.com

ISBN: 978-602-73543-1-9

"To Gail Zatylny, for her encouragement and patience."

"Yet, Freedom, yet, thy banner, torn but flying,
Streams like a thunderstorm against the wind."
~ Byron

1

The whine of the jet engines changed to a lower pitch as the 747 slowed and banked toward the city stretched out below. Johnny Eiger sat up in his seat, turned his head left to look out of the small window next to him, as the plane descended, and his ears began to pop. Below, Toronto appeared, disappeared, then appeared again, through the layers of grey, mystic, cloud. For several minutes, as the flight attendants made their busy announcements, and, all around him, passengers clicked their seatbelts, he had the sensation of floating down a river through a gentle mist, past flowered shores. But with the thud, the chunk of the landing wheels locking in place, the clouds broke with the illusion and the dirty, sprawled city lay spread out before him, like a broken puzzle. He searched over the city as the plane approached and flew over the scrublands on the northern approach. Nothing much had changed.

He saw scattered patches of snow ribboned along thin, black roads crawling with cars and trucks carrying the complexity of humanity along different paths to a single destination. He saw the lonely remains of once rich farmland, now fouled and corrupted by endless tracts of soul-dead housing, small factories and railways, the high rises and condos that sprang up everywhere nearer the city, like weeds. Here and there a small park blessed with a few trees wept for the forests cut down, beauty turned bleak, and, as the plane banked left again for the final approach, there appeared, on the horizon, the distant shoreline of the once pristine lake that stretched far into the distance, as if to escape it all.

"Going home?" the woman next to him asked. He turned his head slightly to acknowledge her. "It used to be home," he said quietly, then turned back to the window and thought about what it was now.

She hesitated to ask more but the air of melancholy about him made her curious. "You must have been gone a long time?"

He answered without turning his head, still looking out the window, as in a trance, "Yes, I was gone a long time."

"Europe?"

"No. Not Europe. East Africa. Tanzania."

He continued to gaze out the window, lost in thought. The woman looked at him curiously, but didn't press him further and began to pull herself together for the landing but murmured, "Africa, that must have been very interesting."

As if in a dream, he replied, "Yes, very interesting," then became quiet again as spectral images of the faces he had left behind haunted him and demanded to know just why he had left and what he was returning to.

Below him the great, cold city, on the great, cold lake, the city where the past lay heavy with his future expanded rapidly to fill the frame of the window. He pulled his head back into his seat as he wondered what he would find there, beneath the clouds. But he was not alone in his wondering.

~

Downtown, in the jagged maze of concrete and steel that is the center of the city, sits an old grey-stoned office building, a fashionable address in the 50's but now, just a sad icon of taste and functionality, overwhelmed by the dark menacing towers that surround it, that block out the sky, and crush the lake. On the 3rd floor of that building there is an old wooden door, in a corridor of wooden doors. On that old wooden door is a brass nameplate on which is inscribed, 'Budnick and Conway, Barristers'.

It's a nameplate like many others in the building, like many others in the city. The two men attached to the names are criminal lawyers, and, like all criminal lawyers in the city, they lead routine lives defending routine cases. But soon events were to happen in their lives, and the life of Johnny Eiger, that are not at all routine and which will have consequences that none of them could have foreseen.

Like all lawyers, Budnick and Conway advertise themselves as a 'winning' team and they do win cases, when a case can be won. But, otherwise, the word win has no right to be attached to their names. Winning means making a lot of money to most people, and that was something neither of them had managed to do for as far back as they could remember.

There were days when they had made good money, sometimes enough to buy a hundred dollar bottle of wine, a new suit, a fast car; the glory days back in the eighties and nineties when a down and out citizen could get legal aid and a lawyer was paid something one could live on in a little style. No one got rich but if you lucked out and a murder came your way or someone from Forest Hill or Rosedale needed to get out of some trouble then there was cash to be had.

In the late nineties it all disappeared, like snow before a warm March wind. The austerity boys came in to rule the roost and soon the usual culprits couldn't get legal aid or, if they did, it didn't pay enough for parking. Then the economy jumped off a cliff and the cash clients had the same problem. No money or, if they had it, they were tight spending it.

But fortune plays its games and sometimes a client would come into the office that had money and was willing to part with it; a businessman who couldn't afford to lose his licence on a drunk driving charge but could afford to pay a few grand for a chance to save it, another type of businessman selling marijuana by the pound, a Bay Street broker on a fraud charge, a high-end hooker evading taxes, enough to keep them going. But a lot of the time they wasted time chasing down money, money promised, money owed; haggling, sweet talking, sometimes threatening, anything so long as they got some cash in their pockets. So, the good times passed and the hard times came and it was all they could do to pay the rent.

But they have three things going for them; a fighting reputation, hard-won experience and a location right in the beating heart of the city. Their run-down office has seen more tragedy come and go than a Greek play and its worn carpets, scuffed furniture and yellowing walls reflect their self-image as hard-boiled defenders of the oppressed. There's a travel agency next door, a health clinic across the corridor and more law offices down the hall. It's very quiet except for the low hum of traffic outside and the slow elevator that struggles up and down eight floors. There's little activity at the health clinic and they wonder what really goes on in there. They've never seen anyone at the door, but they've never thought to go and check it out. There's no time. Too busy hustling, trying to get the clients before some other lawyer does or the clients decide to go it alone as more and more are doing.

The third person in the office is Susan Ash, the secretary, long, strawberry-blonde hair, longer legs, green eyes, a husky catching laugh and a smoky voice that grabs Conway every time he hears it. Beautiful and intelligent, she's anyman's dream. She and Conway had been an item at one time. The smoldering tension is still there.

The office is just off Queen Street, a couple of blocks over from the City Hall. Osgoode Hall and the Court of

Appeal are nearby. A block away from those old-world buildings is Bay Street, it's stock brokers and money lenders leading their miserable lives borrowing, buying, lending and selling in stuffy, ill-lit offices in the old office blocks that range down the street from Queen and merge with the new towers of golden glass and glamour near Union Station. Two blocks east is Old City Hall, where the criminal courts for the downtown area are located, and north of that, on Dundas, 52 police division. They're right in the centre of town.

Walter Budnick, a stocky, Ukrainian bulldog who could charm his way out of any situation, win any jury, is the older of the two. At 60 he's visibly tired, hates his wife, wonders at his daughter, and always has a joke. He has literary pretensions and is trying to write a book about a murder but he never gets past the first five pages, which he rewrites endlessly, hoping to catch that magic carpet ride that will take him to the end. But he's good at extracting money from the most hardened characters. Once he asked Conway and an actor they knew to pose as members of the Illuminati to make a Bay street fraud artist cough up the twenty-five thousand he agreed to pay after Budnick had made a series of very unpleasant theft charges disappear. Not sure what was happening, he wrote a cheque on the spot when Budnick speared him with a penetrating look and said, "It's ok. I can leave. My friends here will take care of it," and then just stared at him with raised eyebrows.

Conway is edging forty, divorced, tall, blonde, always wired. He smokes too much weed in his off hours but is one of the best trial lawyers around, sophisticated and sharp on his feet. Judges often compliment him on his presentation and juries believe him. He's sincere, but confused. One of those guys that always marries the first girl that's nice to him because no one ever has been before and then finds out he got it all wrong. He also finds it hard to ask for money, a big handicap in a ruthless profession. That's why he needs Budnick. And Budnick needs him.

The two of them compliment each other. Budnick complains to Conway about his life and Conway bitches to him about his. Budnick worries that time has past him by and the one big murder case, that million-dollar case, the one he could retire on will never come. Conway worries about the same thing; that he'll end up like Budnick, sixty and still broke, living on the edge, talent defeated by burnout and bad karma.

Susan Ash keeps them both balanced. She's street smart, country tough. She knows how to talk to the clients and everyone likes her. She's straight, knows how to keep things organised, keeps the books, makes sure they don't miss a court date. Conway fell in love with her when he first set eyes on her one night in a law class at the College.

A friend became ill. Conway agreed to take over his part-time job lecturing to law clerks. The trek out to the college in the winter snow the first evening was not encouraging. But an hour later, Susan was asking him questions, smiling, then insisting on walking him to his car. He offered her a lift when he heard her mention taking the bus. He felt electric in the car. They called each other the next day. For six months they exhausted themselves, drunk on raw passion, until, one day, she went to Calgary to see her father she said, and came back, a few weeks later, changed.

The night she got back the tension of their parting finally exploded with all the fury of two wild cats put in the same cage. It was violent and rough and she bit his lip so hard he bled. But, after she had done him like she had never done him before, lying in each other's arms, drifting on the heat, staring at the ceiling and all the dancing images they saw there, she turned to him, still in his arms, and said, "Look, I fucked another guy in Calgary."

She was confused, she said. She was sorry. She wanted to be honest. She confessed her betrayal in so sincere and contrite a voice that he felt very bad for her; until she left his apartment and he suddenly realised how desperately sad, how lonely, he felt. They hadn't gotten back together.

Not that way. They still scratched the itch sometimes, when they just couldn't help it, but the rest was on ice. She needed a job, so ever kind, and ever hopeful, he talked Budnick into hiring her to bring order out of chaos, and she stayed, Conway still wanting her but not sure where he stood and she wanting him but not understanding why she wanted that other guy too. The same old story, of love gone wrong, blown apart by the dynamite mixture of doubt and fear.

*   *   *   *   *

2

John Eiger, 'Johnny' to his few friends, walked off the plane at Pearson International and endured the customs officers' surly questions with a distinct chip on his shoulder and waited for his bags in ill humour. He was tired and he was bitter. He was tired from two days of travelling. Eleven hours from Kilimanjaro to Amsterdam. Eight hours to Toronto. No sleep on either leg or in between.

He was bitter because someone had told him he was a dead man if he didn't drop out of the trial and stop causing trouble. He'd had enough. He wanted out. He was tired of the threats, tired of the work, tired of the malaria, and fed up with the money. Only loyalty to the general and his own sense of honour kept him going. The trial was suspended for three months. He needed to change scenes, needed to get some perspective on what he was doing. The Tribunal was a swamp. It was swallowing him whole.

The cold winter air refreshed him as he stepped out of the terminal to find a cab. When he was down with malaria in Tanzania he thought he'd never see snow or smell Ontario air again. Sometimes he'd play The Band on his ipod just to get the feeling of the country, or Lightfoot or Young. 'There is a town in north Ontario...' would bring it to him. Trouble was, a few days back in Toronto, he would start to miss Africa.

He felt stronger as the cold air swept through his lungs as his body took in the oxygen. He stepped toward the line of limos outside Arrivals. He got in one and told the driver to head into town.

"Whereto?"

"Downtown. The Annex, I live around there. I'll tell you more when we get there."

The driver nodded and they drove along the 401 to Avenue Road down towards the university. Near Bloor, Eiger told him to pull onto a side street, then pull up in front of a modest row house.

"Wait here, I wanna dump my stuff, then go to Flo's. It's two blocks over."

"Sure thing."

Ten minutes later he walked into Flo's, walked straight to the bar and sat on a stool. Peter Lau spread his hands wide then laid them on the counter and with a wide smile said,

"Hey buddy, good to see you, my friend. It's been awhile. You been in Africa?"

"Yeh. Too long, man. Just got in."

Peter asked what he wanted. Eiger ordered coffee. Peter owned the place. It was called Flo's when he bought it and he had stuck with it. Best breakfast in town. It helped that Peter always had a ready smile.

Eiger looked wearily around, and said, "Yeh, too long, man. It's getting me down. The whole scene, the travelling, the bullshit."

"So, why don't you cut out. Do something else?"

"Cause I promised this guy I'd defend him. I try to keep my promises. But I've got a few months off. It's near the end. Need to take a break. See what the scene's like here again. I've lost touch completely."

"There's a couple of lawyers that come in here a lot.

Pretty cool guys. Always complaining about being broke but I hear they're pretty good. Maybe you should talk to them. Find out what's happening."

"What are their names?"

"Budnick and Conway. Jack Conway comes in the most."

"They're still around? I did a couple of trials with them ten years back."

"If you come back later tonight they may come in."

"I'm beat after that flight. But I'll hang around and have some lunch. Any place?"

Peter waved his arm at the tables, "Sure, grab wherever before the lunch crowd does."

Eiger indicated one booth and said, "That one has the right feel to it."

Peter led him over and then brought him a mug of black coffee.

"I assume you still want the usual," he smiled. Eiger attempted to smile back and said, "Ok, steak and eggs, as usual," while siting back, closing his eyes and breathing deeply.

The smell of jacaranda blossoms flooded his memory, the smile of a woman, dark skinned, holding a child in her arms. But then he saw the face of the man from the CIA at the Masai Camp bar. Heard again his matter of fact question, "Do you know how many people we've killed here, Eiger?", heard his answer, put just as casually as the question, "No, tell me."

"Ten, and I'll tell you who and how and why," and that's just what the guy had done.

"So why are you telling me all this?"

"It's very simple, Eiger. If you step across the line, you end up dead. You've been stepping over the line."

"Just defending the general. It's my job. Can't stop doing that."

"Then you're not going to live long. Step back or we'll kill you."

Peter hesitated as he put the coffee pot on the table. "Hey, man, you with us? You want an appetizer or something?"

Eiger sat up straighter. "Sorry. Yeh, sure, a salad or something. I was eating crap on the plane. Whatever's good, thanks. Bring me a glass of red wine too, would you? Yeh, I know it's early. Bring it anyway, man, bring it anyway."

Then when it came he took a deep gulp, relaxed a little, then thought about what he was going to do.

~

Susan lives in a highrise apartment a few miles north of the office in one of those upscale condos near Yonge and St. Clair, a ritzy part of town where she had taken over a cheap lease and somehow managed to hang on to it. She never has food in the refrigerator but she always has a couple of bottles of white wine. She never seems to be lonely and is friendly with everyone in the building. She's as charming, as beautiful, and both men and women have the impression she's in love with them when she talks to them. It was a common illusion. Susan has trouble loving anyone.

She fell hard for Conway, at first. But then she met that other guy in Calgary, with his pickup and sunburnt arms, the whole country music scene. Then she fell for him. She's not sure what she wants. A brief encounter with a woman, a doctor, at the hospital where she had worked the year before she met Conway, had confused her even more. The doctor had taken her by the hand one day while they were crossing the street to go to lunch. An hour later they were in the doctor's apartment sighing and moaning in unexpected ecstasy. Sometimes she felt she would climb the walls unless she tasted that ripe fruit again. She was very confused.

She arrived at 8 am, as she does every day, unlocked the door, made coffee, turned on the computers, checked the mail, and reviewed the day's files. She's very proud of being a legal secretary. She knows a lot about lawyers, she knows the law and thinks she could handle cases as well as they could if only she could appear in court. It's her constant frustration that she can't.

The office cat roamed through some files on the floor. She took him in from a friend who had moved, then she convinced the boys to let her have it at the office. Conway's allergic to cat hair but couldn't say no. Budnick welcomed it. He had several cats and a dog at home. His suits were always covered in cat and dog hair anyway. Susan tries to brush the hair off every time she sees him but it never does any good. The cat's name is Blackie because he's the colour of the blackest ebony.

Susan picked him up, stroked his fur, then put him in the window where he arched his back, stretched, and then lay down to doze. Susan poured herself some coffee, sat down at her desk and began looking at news on the net. Soon Conway and Budnick would arrive and the morning calm would disappear into a cloud of chaos.

Budnick takes his dog for a walk early each morning, partly to avoid his wife, who was a local prosecutor, partly for exercise, then he gets in his van and drives down to the office for 9. The courts don't really get going 'til 10 and he usually has time to check in, see if there are any calls, anybody arrested the night before, what court he's supposed to be in. This day, as he usually does, he stopped at a small café on Queen Street, drank strong black coffee, talked to the locals, read the paper and told corny jokes. After some other stops at another café, a newsstand and a Tim Horton's to get another cup of coffee he arrived at the office hyped up on caffeine and enthusiasm.

Conway, who Susan always calls 'Mr. Conway' when she's flirting with him or 'Jack' when she isn't appears at unexpected times. If he has no court he sleeps late, and comes in when he feels like it. He often takes the files to his apartment in the row house and works on them there. When he has proper files. Often all he has are disclosure documents and some scrawls in an old notebook.

But he's effective in court. He's quick and creative and polite to judges and police alike but he's never afraid to push a defence where it needs to go when there's a case to be won.

He developed a bad cocaine problem for a year or so. It started when a beautiful hooker he defended on an assault charge dropped off a small package for him one day as a thank you gift and both temptations proved too hard to resist. But both had become a problem. He finally dumped her after she pulled a knife on him in her apartment one night when he told her he didn't love her. But it was not so easy to stop using until one day he found white powder in his jacket pocket when he was sitting outside 102 court waiting for his case to be called. Several cops were standing around, making him paranoid, and he woke up to what a fool he was. He was luckier than Dan Headly, dead at 37 from overdosing on an eight ball. Everyone knew he was in trouble. Too much wine, too much cocaine, too much heroin. Had to be occupied all the time. Didn't want to think, but about what no one knew. Too many lawyers like that.

This day Conway arrived early, parked his old Jetta in the back lot and smiled when he walked in.

Susan looked up at him from her desk. "Good morning, Mr. Conway."

"Good morning, Miss Ash. You are looking beautiful today."

She smiled, "Uh-huh, so what's with you? Why are you

so happy this morning?"

"Just happy to see you sweetheart, just happy to see you."

He walked up to her desk and began looking at the pink message slips. "Any calls for me?"

"Nope, nothing yet."

He nodded but kept rifling through papers on her desk, anything to stay near her a little longer. With nothing left to rifle through he drew himself up straight, "I'll be you know where."

Susan glanced at him tenderly as she continued to read something on her computer screen, "Ok, sweetie. I know where to find you."

He felt his face flush. To hide it he walked over to the coffee machine. Poured coffee into a white mug then strolled into his office, sat down, put his legs on the desk, ran his hand through his thick, dark hair and drank from the mug while looking at Susan, as she moved in her chair, hiking up her skirt for comfort.

She was sorting through some letters but could see his look out of the corner of her eye, "You like something?"

He laughed, surprised that she had noticed his eyes, "You know what I like."

She replied with, "Down boy," and quickly swivelled her eyes over to see how he took it.

He threw his head back, laughing again, "Ok, sweetheart, let me know, you keep me on edge too much."

"The only way to keep you."

"You can be very cruel."

"I'm not the only one." She turned back to her desk as the phone rang. She answered it. There was a short conversation in which she said "Uh huh" a lot and then, "I'll let him know. Look I told you I'll pass on the message. That's not my problem."

Conway listened. When she hung up, he asked, "Nothing important?"

"No, you don't wanna know."

"I don't wanna know? What do you mean? Oh, a bill. Can they wait?"

"I think so."

"Good. Still waiting on those damn cheques from legal aid. They don't work for free but they expect us to. Pisses me off."

She raised her eyebrows, while shrugging her shoulders, "They don't want people to have lawyers. Gets in the way."

"Yeh. Every day it's worse. Saw a guy screwed the other day in court. Even when they read the charges it made no sense. Just the cops rousting a guy, but no lawyer, no money, no legal aid, so he pleads out and gets 3 months, for nothing. Whole thing is rotten."

~

At Flo's more customers were coming in and Eiger watched as the characters that made up the city came in and took their favourite tables. It was a popular spot. They served a great steak and eggs; home fries, fresh bread, top steak, free range eggs. The coffee was the best Johnny had tasted in four months. In Tanzania it was almost impossible to get fresh ground coffee. Every place served instant. Coffee plantations lay all around the town yet there were no beans anywhere. He savoured every sip. Midway through the steak he paused and put down his knife and fork and began to relax back into his seat to enjoy pleasant memories.

He was just cutting into the steak again when his mobile rang. It was his legal assistant in Tanzania, Claire, a twenty-eight year old American lawyer, from Rochester, graduated Stanford, smarter than he was, hard working and beautiful. Like many men he had often thought about her but tried not to since the prospects were absolutely zero. He was just not her type, too worn down and twenty years too old. She was usually upbeat, positive, but on the phone she sounded angry and frustrated.

"Hi Johnny. Hope your flight was ok. Listen, I didn't want to bother you. You must be exhausted but you won't believe this. They've changed the trial dates. It's going to be delayed for another six months. They're not saying why. Something's up, but no idea what. I got a message through to the general. But now I've got no job."

He could feel the despair on the other end and replied, as calmly as he could, "Don't worry. You'll be paid every month. I'll make sure of it. They wait until we all leave to tell us this. Real bastards. Ok, let me get back to you. I'll talk to them and see what's what. Yeh, I hear you. Don't worry. I'll make sure you're paid somehow. I'll take care of it. Ok, tomorrow. Take care of yourself. Let me know what you hear around. Ok, later."

"Problem?" Peter asked.

"Yeh. The Tribunal. More bullshit. Bring me another glass of the red, would you. Gonna need it."

"Take it easy, my friend, you travelled a long way. Maybe you should go home and sleep."

"Thanks, Peter, I'm ok, really. I'll sleep later."

"Same bullshit or different bullshit?"

"Delaying the end of the trial for almost nine months. What am I going to do for nine months? My practice here is dead 'cause of this gig at the Tribunal. I can't sit around and make no money for nine months. How am I supposed to live like that? They're crazy. Every day there's a problem, either screwing the guys they arrested, or screwing the defence counsel. And my assistant there, on the phone, great young lawyer, top, and she's broke.

Meanwhile the prosecutors are paid two hundred grand a year just drinking tea in the office all day while they think up every dirty trick in the book. Don't get me going," and he shook his head from side to side.

"Then I'm happy to have this place."

"Well, if you need a dishwasher let me know."

"I don't think you'd do dishes very well. You're too much in your head."

"Yeh, well these guys have ruined my life for six years. Told me it would be a two-year case and its never going to finish. Told me they pay well but they don't want to pay you at all and cut every bill I send them. On top of that I've had malaria five times, typhoid twice, typhus once and so many cases of food poisoning I don't know how my stomach can do anything with food. Mosquitos make me very nervous and then, and then, can you believe, sometimes they threaten to kill you unless you play the game their way."

"Man, I would step out of that if I were you and right quick."

"Yeh. But I promised to defend this guy and he's being set up."

"That may be man, but, if it's rigged, what can you do?"

*   *   *   *   *

3

The phone rang just as Susan stepped back to her desk from lunch. She picked it up and listened then said, "Sorry, we don't do family law, not unless you've been charged with something, good luck," then hung up.

When Susan joined the firm she had tried to get them to take on a few family cases for friends and relatives but Budnick always gave them to Conway and Conway hated them. Made him depressed. Always people phoning about petty squabbles over furniture, dogs, kids, visiting rights, support payments. Everybody angry, hurt, out for revenge, to put the knife in. It was a nightmare. He told her finally to stop taking the calls. She learned to agree with him. Criminal clients are always less of a problem. Leave you alone. An altogether better class of people.

Budnick tried to keep the practice open to all eventualities, to accept every buck offered, to be willing to do anything even if they had little experience at it. His theory was they were lawyers so they could do anything any lawyers could do. But Conway tried to keep it simple- criminal work or anything connected to criminal work.

Budnick agreed to drop the family stuff but still angled for the occasional big civil action they could make money on. Susan doesn't like civil cases. There's too much paper work. She had to organize it all. They take forever to come to an end. Criminal cases are quick and dirty. Civil cases, long and tedious.

As she hung up the phone she said loudly to Conway, "These people irritate me. When my husband and I split, we just kept it friendly and parted company."

Conway had taken his jacket off and was going through some transcripts for an appeal. He looked up from the page he was reading. "Yeh, me too but most people aren't as reasonable as you and I are."

"Would you treat me right if we split up?"

"Well, I thought we did already. Didn't give you a hard time did I?"

"Not out of bed," she laughed.

"Can I turn the radio on?"

"Sure, let's hear the news."

She leaned back behind her desk for the radio and pressed the buttons.

"This is the CBC, Good Morning, today's headlines..." Conway put down the file he was reading and picked up his coffee cup. He leaned back in his chair, listening.

The international news was the same as it always is, wars, bankruptcies, strikes, natural disasters. The Americans were promising to save democracy everywhere except at home, the temperatures in the Arctic were climbing fast, rumours of an asteroid headed toward earth proved to be true. Twenty minutes later the reader began with the local news and the headline that the mayor was making an ass of himself again, ensuring Toronto was a continuing joke around the world. Conway clenched his jaw thinking about how low life had sunk in the city since the eighties. He looked at Susan.

"How do we explain that buffoon getting elected? Tell me, please, tell me. What kind of people in a supposedly modern city vote for a mug like that?"

Susan shrugged her shoulders, "People are led by the nose and they seem to like the smell of garbage."

"Yeh. This city could have been something. Too late now."

The news ended with the 9 o'clock time signal, '.... a series of beeps followed by a long dash....' The long tone began just as the office door was flung open. Budnick walked forcefully in, shoulders and face twitching, carrying a brief case, plastic coffee cup in hand.

He was wearing his usual pin striped grey suit, rumpled, worn, but still making a statement, set off with a blue tie that was too wide for the fashion. There were some dog hairs on his pants and sleeves but he never thought to do anything about them except an occasional look down and a brush of the hand that never succeeded in dislodging a single one.

He stopped at Susan's desk. "Hi, cutie, how are you?" He looked at her with his green Mongolian eyes and smiled. It was one of those smiles that could be sweetness or a threat depending on the context but with her it was always sweet and warm. He never allowed himself to get mixed up with other women, even though he and his wife hardly saw each other, likewise his daughter, who was away at school a lot. He was loyal to his family. He was loyal to his clients, often against all reason. They were his world.

She smiled and said, in a very perky voice, "I'm fine and just how are you, today?"

"Oh, I'm ok, a little frazzled." He chuckled in his deep-throated way, as if laughing at himself.

He turned to Conway. "Jack how's the world today, anything new?"

Conway looked up from his desk, his tie already askew, pulled away from his throat.

"Nothing, Walter. Nothing at all. Need some interesting clients for a change. It's just dope charges the past two months and all the rest of that petty stuff. I'm tired of running to bail court for nothing. Need a good murder case, or one of those long biker trials, something where I can make some easy money, coast along listening to wiretaps, get to hang out with biker chicks."

Susan looked at him, shaking her head, "You know, sometimes I really wonder about you. You're such a straight guy but there is something very twisted in you."

She kept shaking her head as she stood up to get some more coffee, smoothing down her blue skirt to her knees as she made her way over to the coffee maker, one long leg caressing the other in the casually erotic style she had, tucking in her white blouse with her long fingers to accentuate her breasts.

Walter got distracted for a moment as she passed in front of him, then his shoulder twitched again. He quickly turned, walked into his office and began checking his phone messages. He paid close attention to one then picked up the phone and made a call while looking at the message slip.

"Hello, my name is Budnick, lawyer. Right, could I speak to Det. Sgt Morrison please? Uh-huh, well, just tell him I'm calling about the Zukov matter. Yeh, that's the one. Uh-huh. Ok just tell him I'm going to come in and talk to him this morning about that. Is Zukov still there? Or has he gone to bail court? No, no, the family called me. Uh-huh. Ok. Right give me an hour. Ok, see you," and he hung up.

He called out to Conway, "Looks like we've got a case. Zukov again. Got him at 41 division. Arrested last night. Say he assaulted his girl. Family called. Want me to go see him."

Conway stood up. Walked over to Budnick's office. "Anything for me in it?"

"Not unless he charges the girl," he chuckled. "But let's see if he has a defence."

"Bad assault?"

"Sounds nasty. But who knows. He's got a smack problem. Maybe he ran out, couldn't connect and took it out on her, or maybe she ran out, went after him," he laughed again.

"Witnesses?"

"So the desk sergeant says but we'll see."

Conway walked back to his office and sat down. Budnick checked through some more messages and then got back on the phone. Ten minutes later he called out to Susan, "I've got to be in 110 court at 10, can you get that held down while I go and see this guy at the station? Tell them I'll be there around 11."

She made a note and nodded as he checked his jacket, then moved toward the door. He opened it but stopped, went back to his office to get his plastic coffee cup, put the lid back on, then walked fast to the door. As he disappeared into the corridor he shouted, "Ok, see you guys later."

Susan shouted back, "Ok, See you, good luck."

The door closed behind him. Susan went back to listening to the radio now playing Mahler's 2nd Symphony. Conway opened up another file and looked at his watch as he settled in to read.

~

Eiger finished his steak and eggs. He sat back and looked through the window at the street. There was still snow on the ground. It was March and cold. Just two days before he had picked a mango off the tree in his compound and cut it open while he looked at the volcano that overlooked the town and the purple shadows the clouds cast on its steep sides. Now he was looking at dirty snow.

Peter came over and sat down. "So how's the trial going? You winning?"

"How do you win when the whole thing is rigged? I mean yeh, they have no evidence. We destroy them all day every day but it makes no difference. They just go on convicting these guys no matter what the facts are. What's in the newspapers, on TV, are the facts as far as they are concerned. The whole thing stinks. And they're not even charging the people that did the killing. Not one of them. Can you believe it?"

"How do you cope with it?"

"Everyone drinks too much or smokes ganja, me included."

"Ganja?"

"Weed. Powerful stuff there. One joint and you're paralytic."

"How much there?"

"You wouldn't believe it. A pound for 20 bucks."

"A pound? Wow, man. You should try to bring some of that back here and sell it."

"Thought of that. Yeh, you could make a killing, one container full of that and you're set for life. Trouble is how to get it back. Can't be done."

His phone beeped again. His girlfriend's name, Diana Larsen, and her number, appeared on the screen. He didn't answer it. The voicemail icon lit up. Diana's message was about what he expected. "Where the hell are you? You're flight got in two hours ago. I'm worried. Are you all right? Call me."

Diana was a junior manager at a big oil and gas company downtown but dreamed of being an artist. When he last saw her, months before, they had an argument about commitment, betrayal, lost time, lost chances. In other words she wasn't happy and she let him know it. Told him to go to Africa, never come back. But days after he arrived in Arusha she was texting him, asking to talk. She missed him. Why couldn't it work out? Was he fucking the local girls and throwing away his money? Same set of conversations they had every time he travelled. It was getting just a bit tedious.

His phone vibrated. A text message came in. Again from her. "Where are you? I called your apartment and no answer. Call me."

He didn't want to talk to her just yet. He had to adjust. She was always throwing advice at him, telling him what to do. She thought she was an expert in everything and had the answer to every problem, except theirs of course.

He decided to send a text back. "I'm ok, delay at the airport with baggage. Don't worry. I'll call you later."

"Sour face. Girlfriend?" Peter had come over in between new customers and sat across from him to chat.

"Yeh, she's ok but mixed up, pushy, ah, what's the point of talking about it I'll just bore you."

"Yeh, I hear you. Took me ten years of women 'til I found my wife. We have our problems but compared to the rest out there, well, she's ok. The sex is still good."

"We're dead in that department. Too much conflict, too many 'issues' as they like to say. She don't trust me. I don't trust her and we both have good reason."

"So why do you stay together?"

"A very good question. Need a shrink to figure that out. I sure as hell can't put my finger on it."

"Well at least you're making money."

"Right now I am but this gig doesn't pay me for losing my practice here, the malaria, the rest of the bullshit I have to put up with. Not by a long shot. Every bill I send in they cut by thirty percent right off the top. Then you have to fight them to get it back. In the end they give you a fraction of what you're owed. How may hours I've worked for free on this case I can't even begin to count. A big international criminal case, defending a general and I'm living on the edge all the time."

"You want some more coffee?"

"Yeh, sure, ok, guess I better slow down on this stuff," he said, holding on to his wine glass. "But I need it."

Peter smiled, and touched him on the shoulder as he got up from the table. "Ok, coming up."

A man in a long black coat came in, said "Hi" to Peter who was pouring Eiger's coffee, then sat in a booth. Peter nodded to him, returned the hi with a "I'll be right over, my friend." He walked back to Eiger, gave him his coffee then said,

"Let me take care of this guy. He's a bit weird but a regular. Used to be a big executive for a mining company. Drank too much. Got fired. Wife left him. Lost his shares. Living off his package. Not a happy man."

Eiger laughed, "The world's full of them."

Peter nodded in agreement as he walked away and went over to the man in the black coat. He exchanged a few words with him. The man looked dejected, haggard. He saw Eiger look at him. Made a small nod of the head, as if to a fellow sufferer. Eiger wondered what showed, but made a small movement of his head in return then watched Peter as he went to the bar, filled a long glass with red wine and took it over to the man who still sat in his long black coat. Eiger wouldn't have been surprised if he had been wearing gloves inside too. He had the look of the eccentric piano player.

Peter took a cup of coffee over to him, placed it on the table next to his wine glass as he exchanged a word or two and then moved over to the door to take care of another customer. Eiger leaned back against his chair, turning his eyes to stare out the window at the passing parade of people and cars. He was conscious of the man in black looking at him, was struck by his resemblance to Glen Gould, that eccentric Canadian genius. He began to hear, in his head, the rippling melodies of the Goldberg Variations. Imagined he heard the man in black humming to himself in accompaniment. He picked up his coffee mug. Took a long drink to break the spell but still he heard the music, the low humming, so gave up being rational and drifted off, once again, into memories of a Masai girl, dancing to a different rhythm while he held her in his arms. Until Peter came back, and abruptly broke the mood.

"So, what you gonna do if you don't go on with this case you're doing?"

Eiger resented the pull of reality but forced himself to be polite. "I don't know. Maybe I'll sit here awhile and think about it with the help of this elixir of truth." He turned back to the window, and became lost in another time and place, so barely heard Peter say,

"Be my guest, my friend, be my guest."

* * * * *

Beneath The Clouds

28

4

Susan picked up the phone, "Budnick and Conway. Uh huh, Yes, ok, just a minute, Jack, I think you'd better take this, some guy in the Don Jail, needs a lawyer, sounds weird."

Conway sat up and put down the letter he was reading and picked up the phone,

"Thanks, I've got it," Susan hung hers up.

Conway listened as a voice told him he was charged with murder, wanted him to be his lawyer, wanted to see him, didn't want to talk on the phone. Needed to see him today.

"Ok, I'll be there this afternoon. What range are you on? Uh-huh, ok, don't talk to anybody. No, I'll be there." He repeated, "I'll be there," with a little irritation but switched to a lower relaxed voice to say, "Ok, stay cool," then hung up.

Susan looked over at him and saw that he was puzzled. "What's up?"

"Don't know, sounded very sure of himself, like he was in control, not the usual voice you hear from inside. We shall see. Promised to visit him this afternoon. I've got nothing on today have I?"

"There's an appointment at 2:30. People named Bloch. Not sure what it's about. That's it." She walked over to him slowly. "But a murder, huh? I like it when things get mysterious."

"Don't tempt me. You might get under my skin again."

"Oh, can I?"

"You know it."

"So what do you figure?"

"No idea. Just got his name. Tommy Moore. Well, I asked for a murder and I got one. The gods must have listened. Check him out on the net for me. See what comes up. Must be a press piece on him."

She sat down at the desk, swung her long legs under the computer console, and hiked up her skirt again, exposing her knees and silk stockings. He knew she wasn't wearing anything else under her skirt and knew the stockings stopped at her thighs. He dismissed the vision in his head and tried to concentrate on what they were doing. She noticed the movement, pulled her skirt up a little more, acting the innocent and concentrated on the internet page she was reading.

"Tommy Moore. Yeh this is him. Boxer, middle weight champion, fought in the US and Canada, forced to retire when he tested positive for hiv but he says the tests were wrong and wants to box. Pissed off guy with a temper. Says he went to some friend's house with a shotgun and shot him in the chest when he opened the door. Police say he was angry with the victim over some business deal, respect, who knows, but nothing mysterious about it. Just another sordid story."

"That doesn't fit the voice on the phone. But a sordid murder case is the best kind. Anything else on him?"

"Just that he was arrested on the scene, denied being the shooter, denied bail two days ago, charged with 2nd degree murder, acted up in bail court, told the JP that it was a set-up and he wanted protection."

"Can't wait to talk to him." He smiled with anticipation and then walked back into his office thinking about Tommy Moore, and trying not to think about Susan's thighs.

An hour later, Conway was signing the counsel book at the Don Jail, the place where the last hanging took place in the country back in the sixties; an old, vicious Victorian pile of dirty granite and squalid, overcrowded cells. He flashed his ID and waited for an officer to come to take him to the range where Moore was being held. After twenty minutes a young woman in grey slacks and shirt came and motioned for him to follow her.

They went through a grilled door with a buzzing, clanging sound then over to an elevator. "He's on C," she said, hardly moving her lips.

He thanked her for the information and asked how she was doing. She answered politely, led him out onto the 3rd floor, showed him into one of the three small interview rooms across from the elevator and grumped,

"Wait here, I'll bring him," and she went to another door, and pressed a buzzer. When it opened, she called out, "Can you bring Moore out. Counsel," and waited.

Conway put a notebook on the small table as he sat back in the plastic chair. A few minutes later he heard the guard say "In there," and the voice he had heard on the phone said, "OK."

The guard pointed the way to a tall, muscular man in his late thirties, dark blonde hair combed straight back from his face. He was wearing the orange jump suit all the prisoners had to wear. Conway stood up and put out his hand, "Jack Conway, pleased to meet you, sorry it's in here."

Moore took his hand in a firm grip, looking at him with drilling blue eyes. "Thanks for coming." He held the grip and Conway replied, "Let's talk," then let his hand go, and motioned for Moore to sit down.

Moore took a plastic chair on one side of the white plastic table. Conway took the other, facing him. The prisoner started first. He leaned forward into Conway's face. "Look, I don't trust these rooms. So we write notes."

"You think they bugged this room for you?"

"All these rooms are bugged. They can listen to any of them if they want to."

"I don't know, but if they were, why you?"

"Notes."

"OK." He gave him his notebook and pen. Moore began to write. He wrote quickly. He turned the book. Conway read,

"I didn't kill my friend. The police did it. I wasn't there. They took me there. Said they found me there. I don't know what happened. They're trying to make me the fall guy. I need someone to help me. These guys are bad."

Conway had clients like this before. All lawyers did from time to time. Some guy who was probably schizoid, or a bullshit artist telling all sorts of fantastic stories, but sometimes...

He looked at the notes, then intently at Moore. "Why? Tell me why it happened, and no notes."

"I can't. I don't know anything."

"If you're a patsy they have to know something about you to make it stick. Who are you?"

"Can I trust you?"

"That's for you to decide but for what it's worth what you tell me stays with me and no one else. I keep my word. It's everything I've got."

"Ok, I'll take the chance. Look I don't know what's

really going down. I went over to his place a week ago. There were some guys there. Hadn't seen them before. I knew all his friends."

"What did he do?"

"For money? He was a computer geek. Had his own shop, repairing computers, stuff like that. He was good. Sometimes I got the idea he was into hacking, shit like that, but I never understood what he was talking about."

"And these guys?"

"Right, so these guys he's with, stop talking when I came in. I stayed an hour, had a beer, but it wasn't a friendly scene so I told him I was cutting out. That was it, I left. Never saw him again."

"So no idea what happened?"

"All I know the cops came to pick me up at my place at 3 a.m. Took me to his place by 3:30 a.m. Then I hear they claimed they got there and found me on the scene with a smoking gun in my hand. They're setting me up, man."

"For who? Why?"

"That's what you gotta find out."

"Well, it's interesting, so long as you aren't full of shit. Ok, I'll represent you but I need to know everything. Can't defend you when there are surprises. If you don't trust me, get rid of me. Ok?"

"Yeh, sure." They shook hands.

"OK, I want you to think about everything in your life from every angle. There has to be something that makes this add up. Write down names, places, conversations, anything. I'll try to get disclosure, talk to the cops maybe, see what we can find out. Give me a couple of days. If it's something urgent you can call me. But don't talk on the phone."

"I hear ya. And, do me a favour. Get hold of my girl, Marina, Marina Scozzi. Tell her what's going on. She's ok.

Here's her number." He wrote it down in Conway's notebook. "Thanks, man, don't forget dude."

"OK, and don't talk to anyone in here. See you later."

Moore turned towards the door and motioned for the guard. She pressed the door buzzer. With a loud click the heavy door opened and Moore walked through it into a corridor where other men in orange jump suits roamed around aimlessly, killing time 'til the next court date. He high fived a couple of them as the door slammed shut.

Conway waited for the elevator to take him down to the sign-out desk. Then he walked to his car up the street, parked near the small rehab hospital, all the while thinking what he should do next. He cursed when he saw the parking ticket on his windshield, ripped it off the wipers and stuck it in his pocket.

Half an hour later he was at 41 division. He parked on the street, hoping for the best, walked into the station and asked the Desk Sgt. if he could see Detective Bello. A few minutes later, Bello, smoothing his dark slicked back hair with the palm of one hand, came out from a corridor of small offices, walked up to Conway and shook his hand.

"Hi Jack, what can I do for you? We got one of your people?"

"Yeh, this guy Moore. What's the story on him?"

"You met him yet?"

"Hm-hhmm. Just for a look-see. Didn't get into anything but says he didn't do it."

"Of course. But not much to it. Pissed off with his buddy, takes a shotgun over there, the guy answers the door, he fires, stands there, stoned out of his mind, neighbours call us, we grab him. Anyway that's what the report of the arresting officers says. I don't know too much more myself. Another doped punk I'd say."

"Uh-huh. When did you get the call?"

"It's all in their notes. I'd have to get them and I'm not inclined right now. I got other things to do. But no problem, you'll get them in the disclosure package. These guys do a good job."

"Anyone I know?"

"Detective Sgt. Marko heads it up."

Conway's jaw tensed at that name but he said nothing except, "Ok, well, there's no point in wasting your time, thanks. Here's my card, again. Just in case. Ask Marko to call me."

"Ok, no problem but he's not too fond of lawyers. Especially you, if you know what I mean."

"Yeh, I know what you mean."

Conway shook his hand and left. They were being quiet on this one. Usually they bragged a lot. He wondered what was going down with a dirty cop like Marko involved. Maybe Moore wasn't so full of shit. His mood picked up with the mystery but he cursed again when he found another parking tag on his windshield. His mood turned quickly sour.

~

It was lunchtime. Eiger was still at Flo's. A man in black jeans, dark jacket and white shirt came in and went to a booth across from him. He had a round face and curly black hair. He was young. Peter walked over to him.

"What'll you have my friend? The usual?"

"Yeh, today is a usual day so I'll have the usual, no ice and a double."

"You need to relax?"

"You got that right."

Peter brought him a double whisky.

Eiger looked at him, caught his eye and said, "Anything serious?"

"No just the usual, like I said."

"A woman huh, yeh mine's texting me and I'm still sitting here."

"Ah, I don't wanna talk about it, just makes me angry. Treat them like gold and they got some one else on the side and he's dishing out the gold too. Women, sometimes I think I'll go the other way."

Peter laughed, "You think it's different with them?"

"Yeh, but really, it's too much for a man to take."

Eiger sipped his glass of wine then put it down and said, "You know among the Masai a girl is not permitted to look at a man when she's talking to him."

"Too good to be true."

"On the other hand, the Chagga are famous for poisoning their husbands and taking all their property."

"That's more like it is."

"All the things we suffer for love."

"I wouldn't mind if there was a little love, but six months into it and its bullshit, orders and whining and all you can do is wonder how you became the prisoner of a banshee. Then they cry, put on some sweet perfume, and it's like the day you met them. You love them again and then around it goes."

"Yeh, happy when there's money, on your back when there's not."

"Welcome to our club, gentlemen, the worldwide club of suckers."

Peter laughed again, "Come on, don't you guys believe in love anymore. I love my girlfriend. She's great. You guys just don't like women."

"More like they don't like us."

"There you go. I wonder why. Want another one Johnny?"

"Nah, still nursing this glass."

The young man in black sat quietly, his glass in his hand, studying the way the whisky moved as he turned it in his hand. He was reading the different colours and motions as the liquid rolled over the glass. He took a long gulp of it, put the glass down on the table, then leaned back in his chair and closed his eyes.

Eiger looked at him, wondering what his girlfriend was like. Probably beautiful, sexy. He began to daydream about his girl. How soft her skin was. How she tasted. How she moved against him slowly. He looked into her eyes, deep brown and heavy lidded. She kissed him. He held her back and moved his hand down to her waist, the tops of her legs, pulled her close. She moaned in his mouth and touched her tongue to his.

"Coffee ok?"

She dissolved into the sunbeam that streamed through the windows as the clouds suddenly cleared.

"Yeh, its fine. Sorry, I was day dreaming."

"Without them what dreams would we have? What was yours?"

"About a ride through a garden of pleasure and it felt real, for awhile."

"You get romantic on wine, don't you. Want another?"

"Sure, but I don't need wine to remember her. I can hear her voice, smell her."

"So what happened?" Peter was wiping down the bar.

"She died a few months back. Malaria. In four days she was gone."

"I'm sorry to hear that my friend." He looked at Eiger, staring down into his empty wine glass. "So you don't want to go home just yet. That's why you're here?"

"Yeh, something like that. To go home, call my girlfriend here, to have to talk to her, to sleep alone, when all the time I'm thinking about a brown skinned girl who set me on fire. Yeh, not up for that yet."

"She must have been hot."

"Yeh, she was, a lot of trouble too. Really I was crazy. She could do anything and I was still there. Sang beautifully, wrote poetry, angry about the state of the world.... Anyway, that's over now, she's gone and I'm here. It's all fucked up," and he raised his glass to ask for more wine as the man in the long black coat who sat silently in his booth, staring down at the table, raised his head almost imperceptibly after a couple of seconds and said,

"Nietzsche got it right, when he said God is dead but he got it dead wrong when he said happiness is a woman, dead wrong," then turned inward again and continued to stare into his whisky.

*　　*　　*　　*　　*

5

Diana arrived at Flo's a few minutes past noon. She was angry because she was worried. She needed to see Johnny, to be with him. But he seemed to want neither. So, when she left the taxi and walked in she walked in with determination and flair. Her dark blue coat swung against her long body, caressing her long legs. Her dark brown hair hung past her shoulders with a curl over one eye, like a dark Veronica Lake. The whole effect made her look taller than she was and she was tall. Her lips parted when she saw him in the booth. She forgot her anger for a second and drew a deep breath when she saw his blond hair flung straight back like a Norwegian skier. She approached him slowly. "So, you don't want to see me or what?"

Eiger raised his face and greeted her demanding blue eyes with his. He slowly stood up,

"Hi, Yeh, of course I do. I'm sorry. I'm... Ah never mind. Here, sit down." He took her coat, hung it on a hook near the booth, then sat down as she did. "I'm just pissed off. Had to think. Couldn't talk. How'd you find me?"

In response she adjusted the shoulders of a small flowered jacket she was wearing, put her clutch purse on the table, looked at him in mock disbelief and, cocking her head said,

"Just guessed." Then she changed. A look of frozen anger reflected the light from her eyes as she continued, "So you wanted to be alone like Garbo, huh."

She said nothing else except to call Peter over to ask for a glass of wine. She stayed silent until the wine came, all the while looking at him, his face, his hair, the darkness in his eyes and wondered how much Africa had chewed him up this time. When the wine came she drank from it deeply, sat back in her chair, looked at him again, more softly, and almost whispered,

"Anyway. I'm glad to see you. You ok, Johnny? No malaria or anything? You look pale. You're girlfriend give you problems?"

Eiger's eyes turned cold and his lips froze for a second, then he said, "Yeh, she gave me problems. Don't know what I'm doing anymore."

"You're burned out."

"No, I'm fucked up. There's a difference. She's dead."

"Oh." Diana's eyes opened, startled. She looked at him more closely, saw his throat constrict "I'm sorry. HIV?" She didn't want to hurt him but it felt good when she made the jab. She wondered where that came from as Johnny glared at her.

"No. Malaria. That's what they all die of, that and TB."

"I'm sorry, Johnny, I hated her but —well I won't say anymore." She paused as he took a drink from his glass then stared down at the tabletop.

"How long you going to stay here? You must be exhausted. Come to my place. I'll cook you something real and you can sleep." She touched his arm. He relaxed a little more into his chair.

"Maybe, I don't know, let me see how I feel. What have you been up to?"

"Oh," she tried to sound normal, chatty, "Trying to handle the office politics, trying to stay together, trying to find a guy that wants me but meeting crazy people. Wondering about the future."

Diana had a nordic name but oriental eyes. She'd heard it had something to do with a great grandmother's liaison with a Burmese prince in 1885. The story never did make sense but explained a lot. She looked Chinese when she wore no eye make-up and always felt embarrassed by it so constantly tried to make her eyes look round. Johnny preferred the Chinese look. More exotic.

They met by chance at a party. He wanted her as soon as he saw her. The first time he kissed her standing against a door, he touched her leg with his hand and moved it slowly up her skirt, moving in response to the kiss. Their kiss deepened so he moved it higher and felt her naked and wet. He touched her with his fingers and she collapsed onto him. He began to remember how she smelled...

"You're not listening to me. You're off somewhere else." He blinked a few times quickly and apologised, "Sorry, jetlag."

She leaned forward toward him and grasped his hands, "Anyway, what's going on with you?"

"Aside from her? This trip was the worst. The trial's a farce, I've got a co-counsel who's probably a spy, no electricity most of the time, no water, and I spend my nights drinking too much wine at Stiggy's to stop from going crazy." He paused to watch her reaction. She sat still, blank faced, waiting for him to continue.

"She was seeing other guys. I knew that all along but most of the time I could forget it, like it wasn't happening but then it became too obvious. I was crazy. She did it and I still wanted her. Then, still wanting her, she dies on me. It's pathetic."

Diana sat back and raised her shoulders in a tired shrug, "Well the guys I've been seeing aren't much better.

They're all strange. None of them can hold a conversation. I miss our conversations sometimes. We argue but we sure talk about interesting things."

"Yeh, that's true." He sipped on his glass, looking at her.

"You look pretty today. What are you wearing?"

"I can't tell you in public." She looked down shyly, smiled, then looked into his eyes and slowly licked her lips with her tongue. "But you know."

"I missed you sometimes too. Don't know why."

"Just sometimes? She must've done you good."

"Most days I was caught up in the trial, preparing witnesses, all that jazz. No time to think about anything except how to stop them from framing this guy. They play dirty. It's not a trial. To them it's a game they're playing and the deck is marked, so they win." He paused, took another gulp from his glass, then continued,

"Last weekend some guy, who says he was CIA, threatened to kill me. I'm sitting in a bar. Just comes over and sits down. Then I found out he really was CIA. Just talking like this. I couldn't take it in, that it was real. It was like a conversation about flowers. But every time that door over there opens I'm nervous. I was nervous on the trip, in Amsterdam, I'm nervous here. The General told me they were just trying to scare me. Maybe, but they got to me, that's for sure."

She leaned forward and put her hands on his. "I think you should get out of this game. Why don't you do real estate or something? You can't deal with all this and the travelling. You've never been the same since you first had malaria and what do you get for it? They hardly pay you enough to survive and our relationship hasn't gotten any better."

"That's what I'm thinking about. I've got a nine-month break now. No idea what's going on. So nine months of no money but plenty of boredom. I've to got to look around, think outside the box, see if there's something else."

She sipped her wine. "I'm hungry."

"Peter, Diana would like something."

"Be right over."

He brought a menu and Diana ordered some fettuccine.

"How's the portrait going?"

"Don't ask. Some days I work on it, other days there's no energy. I need to be loved to paint. I need to be fucked to be creative. Otherwise I'm all dried up."

"You have to be able to paint no matter what your mood or you will never finish anything. Use your frustration to paint. Don't let it stop you."

"You don't know what you're talking about. I'm a woman. A woman needs to be fucked."

"Oh, you don't think I do?"

"Not apparently."

He sat back in astonishment. "Really? I fucked you 'til you were out of it and you know it. It wasn't me that stopped that."

"Ok, let's not go there again. It's pointless." There was a long pause.

"So what you going to have? I can't eat alone."

"I already ate but ok, so you feel comfortable. Say, Peter, a club sandwich here. Still hungry. Thanks." Peter acknowledged him with a movement of his head and went into the kitchen. Eiger turned back to look at her and thought how attractive she looked sitting there waiting for him to say something else.

"Anyway good to see you."

She relaxed into her seat a little more, flipped her hair from her face and said, "You too, Johnny. I really missed you."

~

Conway walked back into the office. Susan was checking her lipstick in a hand mirror.

"You still look beautiful."

"Thanks, but gotta keep it that way." She checked herself again in the mirror and put it in her purse.

"So what was he like, the guy at the Don?"

"Interesting. Acted mysterious. Says the cops set him up. Says they shot the victim. Made me write notes, wouldn't talk in case the room was bugged. A little bit crazy I would say. But you never know. And some bad cops are involved. So, who knows, anything's possible. Phone the Crown's office and see if we can get some disclosure on him. See what's what."

"Ok." She made a note in her diary and turned back to her computer.

The phone rang and she picked up the receiver. "It's Budnick, says he's stuck in court 'til around 3."

*   *   *   *   *

6

It was 2:30 precisely. Susan looked up as a man and a woman walked in. The man was in his fourties, tall, greying dark hair, square solid face, gold wire rimmed glasses, good looking, taller by a head than the woman who was petite and blonde, elegant, once beautiful, still attractive.

"Can I help you?"

"We need to talk with a lawyer. We called yesterday about an appointment. Our name is Bloch," she said.

"Human Rights lawyer," he specified.

Susan said, 'Yes, of course, it's in my diary here. Certainly, please, take a seat," indicating a set of chairs and a coffee table just inside the door.

Once they settled into the chairs the woman said to Susan, "I'm Emma Bloch. This is my husband, Richard. He can tell you all about it. They've treated him very badly and something has to be done about it. They have no right to treat people like that. It's...."

The man interjected, "Emma, let me tell it and to the lawyer. The secretary doesn't want to hear all this," and to Susan said, "I'm sorry she gets carried away trying to help me sometimes."

"We're in this together, darling. I'm entitled to get carried away."

The man nodded, looking at her proudly. "Yes, I suppose you are."

Then he began to speak in a low voice, almost to himself,

"I've been a professor at the university for 20 years, professor of philosophy. The academic rules committee has told me I'm dismissed for speaking at a meeting and publishing articles opposing the wars. Said I was acting erratically, that I'm a danger to the students, that I'm irrational. But I'm not and they can't."

He stopped, leaned back and looked at Susan who looked back at him with sympathy and some admiration. He then sat back in his chair, withdrew into himself and held his wife's hand.

Mrs. Bloch leaned forward, "How much do you charge here?"

Susan became professional, "You'll have to discuss that with the lawyer involved. It depends on the amount of work, what they have to do, the time involved, the responsibility involved, but civil actions are never cheap. A human rights complaint can take a long time to get anywhere. Maybe it's a wrongful dismissal case. We don't really do labour cases."

"Well, we're not going to let them get away with it."

Conway, who had been listening through his open door while he finished working on a document rose from his chair and entered the waiting area.

He put out his hand to the man, then his wife, "Pleased to meet you. Jack Conway, please, come in to my office. We can talk more comfortably. I am sorry I kept you waiting. I had something to attend to."

The professor said, "Not at all. It is a pleasure to meet you. We heard good things about you from a friend of mine you helped a couple of years ago."

Conway asked, "Friend of yours?"

The professor took hold of Emma's arm as they walked into the office following Conway. "Yes, Professor Childs. His son got in some trouble with the police. I'm not sure what it was all about but anyway, he thought very highly of you."

The three went through the door to his office. It closed behind them. Susan turned back to her desk, took out her mirror again to check her hair, then began typing on her machine.

Conway held out his hand to two chairs that faced his desk and said, "Yes, I remember. You'll have to say hello to him for me. Please, have a seat."

They sat down. He adjusted his jacket and went behind his desk and lowered himself into his leather chair. He looked at both of them carefully, trying to size them up from their clothes, the way they sat, how they moved. He was impressed. Some clients called for a rough familiarity. These people demanded formality. He leaned forward with pen in hand ready to get to work. In his practiced voice of concern and authority he asked,

"So how can I help you, professor?"

The professor told him what he had told Susan. His wife remained silent aside from the occasional murmur of agreement and expression of anger against the university.

"What was the reason they did this to you?"

"I can't be sure but I think it's my opposition to the wars and talking to the students about it. I heard some students complained that I wasn't patriotic or some nonsense like that. There was an allegation I acted strangely in class but it's nonsense."

"Was there a hearing?"

"They called it a hearing. Invited me to a meeting, never warned me what it was about, leveled accusations at me, no witnesses, never gave me a chance to reply or call witnesses of my own and instantly made the decision that I was not fit, that I was no longer competent. They said they were suspending me indefinitely. Suggested I needed psychiatric help. Me, of all people." He stopped talking and looked to Conway, "What can be done?"

'And your union or association?"

"I asked the Dean of my department and the association to intervene. They said they would protest and put a stop to it, but they've done nothing. Now they won't take my calls."

"Well, you've got a case that's clear. It can't stand. But to fight it we have to take two routes at the same time-a wrongful dismissal action including damages for defamation of character, and an action for review of their decision in the Divisional Court and reinstatement. Maybe an action against the association too. That's not going to be cheap. And we don't really do dismissal cases. I can refer you to someone who..."

Professor Bloch stopped him, "I heard you were fighters and I'm sure such a matter is well within your competence. But I would like to know how much you charge for your services."

"I can charge you at $150 an hour. Most lawyers charge two and three times that but we don't think it's proper. I have to tell you no lawyer can guarantee anything. Based on what you have said, you've got a very good case. But it's going to take a lot of work and time. Like you professor, I can't work for free, however much I'd like too. Not on every case."

"How much do you need to start?"

"Let me have $5,000 to start and then I'll bill you each month. If you think I'm unfair a court official can review it for you. But I'm fair, and you need someone to fight for you and that I will do."

The couple looked at each other then the man turned

and said, "Ok, so how do we start."

"Well, what I can do for nothing is to write them a letter demanding reversal of the decision and telling them that you have counsel and mean business. Another one to the association to get them to take a position. Just that alone might be enough to solve the problem." They looked at each other and back at him. "Very well, please proceed."

Conway took a long yellow legal pad, picked up a pen and said,

"Very well, let's start with your full name, address and so on and go from there. Tell me everything about yourself. What I'm missing, I'll ask for. Take your time professor, first consultation's on me." And so, as Emma Bloch looked on, the two men began their duet, the professor talking, Conway, stopping him and asking questions, while Emma listened with tightened lips to every word.

~

By mid afternoon, Flo's was almost empty. The lunchtime crowd had come and gone. The young guy in the other booth had gone, a bit more dazed than when he came in. The man in the long dark coat was still there just staring into space.

Peter came over to top up their coffee. Johnny asked, "He come in much?"

Peter looked over at the man and then turned back to them and, with raised eyebrows, and a frown on his face, said, "Yeh, most days. Losing his wife and being fired has fucked him up but he's ok usually. One of those guys who's lost 'cause he was too rich, you know, had everything he wanted. Took it all for granted. Now it's all gone, and all he can do is sit and brood all day."

Diana looked at her watch. "Look I've got to do

something at the office. I'm supposed to be at a meeting at 4. You coming to my place or not?"

"Yeh, ok, sure I'll come over later. Let me take my things to my place first. Have a shower. I'll be ok, but maybe I'll just crash at my place tonight. Starting to feel it."

She stood up and kissed him formally on the cheek. "Ok, whatever, see you later," and she turned quickly and walked out onto the street without looking back.

Peter walked over and poured coffee into his cup as he followed Diana with his eyes. "She's very attractive. What's the problem? I could take her anytime."

"Yeh, well just remember that every girl you see is some other guy's trouble."

He laughed and walked back to the bar. "Yeh, you never know what's in their mind."

"What can be said at all can be said clearly. What we cannot talk about we must pass over in silence."

"Meaning?"

"Meaning that women never talk straight and we can never know what they are thinking."

"Nor they us."

"I guess."

~

Conway set down his pen and leaned back in his chair.

"Ok, I have the facts. I'll write a letter to the university stating that you have a solid case and demanding the association act on your behalf as well. You still being paid?"

"So far, but I think they will move fast to terminate that."

"That is going to be complicated for them. You have your pension with them and all that, I suppose? Ok we'll figure it out." Conway stood up. They acknowledged the signal and stood up with him then hesitated until Conway took their hands to shake, and reached into his jacket pocket.

"Here's my card. Try not to call me with every whim but if you really need to talk, call me."

They shook hands. Mrs. Bloch also took his hand. "Don't let us down Mr. Conway. This is our life."

"I'll do my best."

She curved her lips in a shadow of a smile, stared him in the eye, then turned to join her husband as they both walked out.

Susan caught his eye as he turned back to his office.

"Well?"

"Nice people. Like to help them. Really getting screwed just because he had the guts to speak his mind. We live in a democracy. What a joke."

*   *   *   *   *

7

"You know it's past 2 now Johnny. If you want to meet those two guys later you should go home and get some rest and come back."

Johnny looked up and over at Peter. "Yeh, right, ok." He took out his wallet and gave him his credit card. "Sorry, my friend, have no Canadian cash left, just Tanzanian shillings and euros."

Peter took his card, swiped it on the machine and gave it back, "Ok see you later. Get some sleep."

Eiger raised his hand in salute, then turned and walked out onto the street. It was suddenly warmer. The sun had come out. The buds on the trees promised beautiful things. People were walking with their coats open and spring in their steps. He decided to walk onto Bloor Street to get a sense of the city again.

He walked slowly down Yorkville Avenue then Bellair on the west side past the small restaurants, high end clothing shops and art galleries. He found himself on Cumberland and stopped at Sassafrass on the corner. He hadn't been in there for a long time and decided to step in for another glass of wine. Why not? He was met by a young girl in a low cut black evening dress, with hair pulled back, bright brown eyes, a sweet smile and hips that thrust forward in just the right way.

"Would you like the bar or a table?"

He asked for the bar. She sat him at a stool at one end so he could survey the rest of the café. There were the usual types in there. Businessmen from the film and fashion business, a couple of lawyers, some Americans who had a Ferrari parked outside with Florida plates and kept bragging about it, a couple of bartenders. Nick was a guitar player in his off time, had a couple of recordings out. Maria was an American girl up for the year from San Francisco to be with her boyfriend. Had a tattoo across the back of her neck in Chinese calligraphy. He asked her what it meant. She responded that without the right Zen spirit he didn't need to know. He decided it was just her name.

He ordered a glass of wine and while sitting there opened his phone and searched for Budnick and Conway. Several Google responses came up, a couple with cheap web ads for their services and a listing of their address and phone number. He noted down the address in his notebook then, suffering the effects of the wine mixed with fatigue decided to drop in and say hello, just for the hell of it.

~

After the Blochs left the office Conway dictated a letter to Susan to send out to the university. As she was doing that, Budnick came walking in the door with a Tim Horton's coffee cup in one hand, an oatmeal muffin in the other and entered into his office. Conway got up, walked in after him and told him about Tommy Moore and the Blochs. Budnick gulped his coffee and ate his muffin while listening, dropping coffee and crumbs on his shirt.

"Uh-huh, uh, huh," he said to every fact. "That's got me

going because I finally got a chance to talk to Zukov at the detention centre and he also says he's been set up by the cops. Says they got his girlfriend to lay false assault charges on him under threat and says they don't like him cause he's white with a black girlfriend and they think he deals drugs. Of course he's right about the drugs and maybe the girl. Probably have a wrongful arrest case. Make some money."

Conway shook his head. "We never make money on those cases. It's a lot of work for nothing if you ask me."

"Well, somebody has to help people against the crimes of the state."

"Fine, I'm all for that, just don't tell me we're going to make money."

Budnick hauled a file out of his briefcase. "You ever hear of a drug called Aldarizine."

"No, never."

"Well, you have now. It's going to make us a lot of money. There's a class action suit against the manufacturer in the States for damages. They settled in the millions. I got someone who's affected. We're going to do the same."

"Who's paying for this?"

"We do it on a contingency basis."

"Convince me."

Budnick shoved the file towards Conway. "Here, read this, its all about it. The drug was designed as a treatment for arthritis but people using it suffer all sorts of damage to body systems and immune function. Terrible stuff. We need to get hold of their files, their experts, their claims everything you can find. If we can get in on this we can get rich on one case."

"Did you ever read a book 'Civil Action'?"

"Don't worry, that isn't going to happen to us. We're

smarter than that."

"Are we? They lost everything."

Budnick laughed, "Yeh but they had lot of fun losing it."

"Must have been a different book."

~

Eiger finished his wine, paid and went back onto the street. He went down a set of stairs near Harry Rosen's men's shop where he bought all his Zegna suits and headed along the underground shopping complex towards the subway.

It had been several years since he had taken the subway. He was not prepared for the seedy squalor of the place. It had never been a showcase but now every wall was falling apart, exposed wires hung in every ceiling, advertising covered all the walls, the subway cars were covered in scummy ads for low-slung jeans, bad movies and fake universities. Inside, the cars were no better. The passengers looked more miserable than he remembered them. Everyone looked dead tired. Many were nodding off in their seats. There were beggars laying down on the platform. People wearing badges identified as subway security walked through the throngs of people who all edged away at their approach.

But it was still a fast ride. Within ten minutes he had arrived at the Queen Street stop. He went up the escalators, entered the street on the north side near the Sunlife Building and the Federal Court, crossed over, walked past Osgoode hall, then crossed south at the City hall plaza to the Sheraton Hotel and walked into the lobby.

The hotel hadn't changed. Men in dark suits and sexy women in high-end office clothes walked past each other in different directions. The shoeshine man was still at the corner near the stairs to the lower level. He remembered the days when he had worked in one of the tall towers nearby on the 54th floor.

He cut through the lobby to the street on the opposite side and turned right to enter the building where the Budnick and Conway office was. The March light was beginning to fade again as clouds came in. He walked through the lobby door. The elevator didn't come so he slowly walked up the three flights of stairs, down the hall, saw the sign 'Budnick and Conway, Barristers', turned the handle of the door, and went in.

Susan looked up. Her eyes widened. "Hi, can I help you?"

"Hi, yes maybe, I was wondering if Mr. Budnick or Mr Conway were in. I have no appointment. I just took a chance and its not urgent so..." and he began to withdraw, but slowly because he couldn't help taking in Susan's full lips and flashing eyes.

"Do they expect you?"

"No, and the name is John Eiger."

Susan waved her hand to a chair, "Well, come on in. I won't bite. Have a seat."

"Thank you," he sat down.

As he did Budnick came out with a paper in his hands, looking down, reading it as he walked. He looked up when he noticed a body in the waiting area, saw Eiger, looked puzzled briefly, then his lips formed a smile and his eyes opened as he walked up to him quickly.

"Johnny Eiger, well, this is a surprise. Long time, my friend." He put out his hand. Eiger stood up, took it and said, "Right, Walter, I think since we did that robbery trial in Brampton about ten years back for that gang that knocked over a gold dealer. You remember? We had fun on that one."

"That's right. You know I had completely forgotten that

case. Yeh, we had fun on that trial. I guess it was the last one we did together. But, here, take the weight off your feet and we can talk. Like some coffee?" He let go of Eiger's hand and invited him to sit down again.

Eiger, relieved at the reception replied, "Thanks but I've had too much coffee today. I just flew in from Africa, actually. I'm sort of wired." He paused and realised how very tried he was and began to wonder why he had come. But he continued, "That was about the last trial I did in this country, and that's my problem. Frankly, that's why I came to see you."

Budnick's face took on a serious aspect as he looked at Eiger, taking in the remark about Africa. He sat down next to him. Looked at him closely. He sensed fear and wondered of what.

"Africa? You must be exhausted. Shouldn't you be home sleeping? Yeh, we heard you were doing war crimes trials all this time, or something exotic but it was never clear where. Thought it was The Hague or somewhere. We all envied you. Lot more interesting than the stuff we get around here."

Eiger spoke more slowly as the jetlag began to kick in. His face lost some of its colour. His lips were beginning to feel thick. "These trips always mess me up. I was on a plane a few hours ago staring at the clouds as we flew in, wondering what I was coming back to, even why I was coming back at all. I guess that's really why I wandered in here."

He looked down at the floor for a moment as if he was falling asleep but then quickly raised his head and continued, "To answer your question, yes, I was at The Hague for the President's case but most of my time was spent in Africa. And yes, it was interesting all right. Just a bit too interesting."

"Burned out?"

"More like turned off."

Budnick looked concerned, frowned a little and watched Eiger closely. "So, Johnny, you're looking for what exactly. We're not hiring and...."

"I don't know what I was thinking. Just want go get back to doing the cases I had before. But I've been away a long time. I need a place to hang my hat, get back in the game...."

"A place where there's some work."

"Yes, that would be ideal...I've got nine months free, so I thought I could try something...."

"After nine months?"

"Well, I've gotta make the final arguments in this trial-take a few weeks maybe-then that's it. A couple more witnesses."

Conway came out of his office to satisfy his curiosity. When he saw Eiger he called out "Say, I thought I recognised that voice. Been a long time, my friend. A long time. How you doing?" He walked over to shake his hand, then, without waiting for a response asked, "Any experience in class action suits or damaging medications?"

"Long time ago I worked for a big civil litigation firm downtown-did a lot of that kind of thing. Experts are the key."

Conway looked at Budnick. Budnick looked at Conway, lifted his eyebrows and shrugged his shoulders.

"Tell, you what," said Budnick, "we could use some help on this case. Couldn't pay you, but you could take a percentage of the win like us if you can live like that for a while. Same with any other cases come your way. We split 60/40 our way."

Eiger smiled, "Sounds great to me, really. I'd love to work with you. What's the case?"

Budnick stood up, "Come on in to my office and we can talk. I'll show you a small back office you can use later."

All three went in and sat down. Susan walked in right behind them, close to Eiger, "Need any coffee?" She turned her body close towards his. He stood his ground. The air became charged.

Budnick broke it. "Good idea, thanks, for me anyway. I think Johnny's had too much caffeine already." Susan looked Eiger over once more as her eyes met his and, as mesmerized, he said, "I really have had too much but why not, thank you," then followed her with his eyes as she slowly turned and left the room, extending her legs just a bit longer than she usually did.

The paralyzed gaze of three dreaming men froze their thoughts until Conway nervously moved and cleared his throat, "Anyway where were we?"

"The case."

Budnick said, "Yes, you ever hear of a drug called Aldarizine?"

"No."

"Well, it's an arthritis drug but has really bad side effects. Lots of people damaged by it. We have a client and we want to get a class action suit going and we need help to build that."

"Yes, those cases are difficult and cost big money. You gotta have the best experts and real damages, you gotta have doctors, you need to know your science. You gotta have patience and patients." He smiled at his own joke. "That's why you need me. But you also need money."

Conway walked closer to him and shook his hand. "That's the kind of stuff we need. Welcome to Budnick and Conway, Johnny —you're back on the streets again."

Just then, Susan walked in, bent low and put down a tray of coffee cups and a large pot of coffee. Her hair fell off her shoulders as she bent down. She looked at Eiger and softly said, "Your very welcome," slowly stood up, and walked, even more slowly, back to her desk.

Eiger began imagining a scene but quickly brought himself back to the conversation,

"Well, gentlemen, I have to thank you, really, I didn't expect ... I mean I just came in here on spec..." he slightly lowered and raised his head then looked at them with drooping eyes.

Budnick opened his eyes wide and laughed, "Serendipity. That's what it is. But more on that later. You have to tell us about the work you've been doing."

Eiger's face began to contort in pain but he suppressed it, "That's a long story I think left for a better time." He sighed involuntarily as exhaustion overwhelmed him. He looked down at the floor as if his head had become too heavy then he sat back up against the chair, shook his head slightly. "I'm sorry. I think I've hit the wall. I should go home and crash."

Conway stood up, "I'd say so, Johnny. You look wiped out. Go home. Take your time to recover. Whenever you're up for it. Just give us a call or come on in. Anytime."

Eiger slowly stood up, braced himself, accepted Conway's hand and his card, gave him one of his then shook Budnick's hand. As he turned to leave, Budnick gripped him for a second on the shoulder. He smiled quietly at Susan, left the office and walked out onto Queen Street. It was getting dark. The streetlights were coming on. Streetcars rumbled past. Taxis dropped passengers. He hailed one. "The Annex." He lay back in the seat and closed his eyes.

Conway turned to Budnick, "What do you think?"

"Maybe its synchronicity," he said, in a matter of fact voice.

* * * * *

8

The next morning Eiger woke up slowly. His unkempt hair hung in his opening eyes. His long body twisted slowly in the bed, his arms reaching out to the air. His lips held back a yawn, then failed. He groaned, still floating on a fading dream of sex with a stranger, then came to his senses, turned in the bed, and reached for the phone on the floor where he had dropped it the night before. He picked it up, touched the screen. The lights came up and he saw the time-8:30 am.

He tapped the email box but there was nothing worth looking at; just junk ads and messages from people asking for money or promising to send a few million if he could just get to an offshore bank and meet a crippled lady whose father had died at the hands of a foreign government, and one email from Diana, demanding that he call her.

He got up, and went to the small kitchen to make coffee. While the coffee was brewing he turned on his computer to check the news. BBC first. Things continued the same; wars in the Middle East, wars in Asia, wars in Africa. Europe was paralyzed by strikes. The economy was bad. The temperature was still rising. Stockholm was on fire. The world was on edge.

He went back to his emails. He saw a message from LinkedIn–someone asking to connect with him, Patrick Rice. Didn't know him but he connected with the site anyway to check it out. He accepted the link and went back to his inbox. Ten minutes later he received an email from Rice asking if he would be interested in defending Mahmoud Mahmoudi, the Prime Minister of Libya, the African country NATO had attacked all summer. It looked like a fake message. Mahmoudi was in a Tunisian jail. Had lawyers there. But you just never know.

The message asked Eiger to call a number. He got up from his desk, got a cup of coffee and wondered what it was all about.

He replied to the email saying he was interested and asking for more information and whether it was serious. He got back a message from Rice, stating that he was a Toronto lawyer, that it was serious, giving his phone number, asking Eiger to call.

He checked Rice out on the internet. But there was nothing about him except a listing with the Law Society that said he worked for small firm in town. He checked the latest on Mahmoudi too. He was still in a Tunisian prison. But it was too intriguing to ignore. An hour later, coffeed and showered, he took the bait and made the call.

Rice was hushed, said he couldn't say much on the phone but confirmed he had been asked to put together a legal team for Mahmoudi. Said his contact was a friend of his who worked at the UN, also a friend of Mahmoudi, said he had thought of Eiger because of his defence of the President and the General. The stroke of flattery overcame his suspicions and he agreed to meet in two days, Friday, at a restaurant downtown.

He called in to the office right after he hung up with Rice. He wanted some one to know, just in case. He spoke to Susan.

"Hi, yeh, I'm fine, still getting over jetlag but look, I got a strange call about something interesting. I've got to a meet a guy in two days, Friday. Like to talk to Conway or Budnick about it."

Conway came on the phone. Eiger filled him in.

"Yep, right, ok, I'll let you know what happens. Really, no idea what its about. Thought I might need some backup. Thanks, Jack."

Then he hung up and called Diana. She didn't answer. He left a message telling her he would sleep another day or so then they could go to dinner Friday night and to call him back. He got some more coffee and stood drinking it, staring at the old houses across the street as dark bands of rain swept across the sky.

Friday came faster than Eiger realised. He had slept most of the time. The rest of the time he was punchy with jetlag. Hadn't even called Diana. The restaurant was just east of Yonge on the north side of Eglinton. The sort of upscale place that always has a sexy hostess. Eiger got there early to have the advantage. The place had just opened for lunch. He was the only customer. The hostess, walking in a cloud of exotic perfume, invited him to sit at the bar and have a drink while he waited. Ten minutes later, right on time, Patrick Rice walked up to him. He looked like an Irishman, tall, swarthy, with dark hair, a chiseled face. A grey cloth coat covered black jeans, and an Irish tweed jacket underneath. His blue eyes and quick smile were engaging.

"Mr. Eiger." He put out his hand.

"Mr. Rice, nice to meet you."

"Let's sit over there, we can talk more easily."

He indicated a table in a small alcove and waited for Eiger to proceed ahead of him. They sat down and ordered coffee.

"The food here is very good, the buffet especially. Perhaps we can settle that and talk while we eat."

Eiger agreed. They walked over to the buffet. Rice greeted some of the staff. "I'm in here all the time," then pointed out some of the best items, "especially the Portuguese beef".

They chatted as they took their food, about the weather, about the times, about Toronto. Rice told him that his office was at the corner of Yonge and Eglinton. He had just walked over. They made their way back to the table, plates in hand.

Eiger put a napkin on his lap, picked up his knife and fork and was cutting into a slice of beef when he hesitated, put his hands down and said, "Ok, let's not waste time, what's this all about exactly?"

Rice appeared a bit surprised by the abruptness of the question but he recovered his poise. "All right, it's like this. I work for a small firm here but a friend of mine works for the UN. He's in Africa now." He picked at his food and took a bite of his beef, said, "Excuse me, we forgot wine, you would like some I understand?"

"You know me well."

"Pretty well, we have, how shall I put it, researched you. Excuse me," He signaled to a waiter, asking him to bring two glasses of burgundy. He continued eating while they waited for the wine, occasionally asking about Eiger's experience with malaria but as soon as the wine was brought and they had each toasted the other's health and taken the first mouthful, he put down his knife and fork and leaned forward.

"Ok, this friend, through his work, got to know the Mahmoudi family. They trust him. They asked him to put together a legal team. He simply called me to ask if I had any ideas and I thought of you because I've followed your career, your defence of the President, and the General. So, I thought I would contact you. See if you would be interested in taking it on."

"But I checked him out and he has lawyers in Tunisia

acting for him there."

"Yes, that's correct. But he's worried the International Criminal Court will try to grab him and those lawyers are ok for the immigration charges he faces in Tunis. They aren't your calibre. Can't do a political trial. The family's looked around. They decided on you. One lawyer in London wanted seven million pounds to act for him, which they are willing to pay, for the right lawyer of course, but he wasn't it; too close to MI6, and all those British Secret Services. I told my friend about you. He told the family. So are you interested?'"

"But he faces no charges right now. It's not clear to me what I could do or would be expected to do for him. Why were you following my career?"

Rice examined him for a beat then said, "Right." He picked up his wine glass again, put his nose to the top of the glass then drank, "Not bad, you agree?" He took some more then began toying with his food, as he continued,

"I did a paper for my masters on the Balkan wars. Your role in the President's case when he was sent to The Hague got a lot of attention. You claim he was murdered and I don't doubt it. But let's leave history. What they want is for you to prepare for any charges and to do what you can with his situation in Tunis."

"Uh huh, well, in principle yes, I am interested, but how serious is your friend? Does this have the approval of Mahmoudi himself? I have to tell you I really wanted out of this international swamp. It hasn't been a positive experience. But if the money is that good I can get over it."

Rice laughed and said, "I thought you would see it that way. No, Mahmoudi hasn't yet approved it himself. But our contacts assure us that if they give him the word, then you are in and the money really is that good."

"Your role?"

"Well, right now I'm just a go-between, but if I could be on the team somehow, make some money, I wouldn't refuse either."

"That is a very large sum of money for nothing."

"They're very rich. Its small change to them as long as they get the right type of lawyer to help."

"Who is your contact at the UN?"

"A friend of mine. We were students together at Laval and stayed in touch. He's worked for international organisations for years. Now he's in West Africa, with the UN."

Rice looked at Eiger like he was waiting for a revelation but Eiger just nodded, took a bite of beef, then asked if they could get some more wine, as he drained his own glass.

"Ah, of course, yes, sorry." He looked over at a waitress placing cutlery at another table and beckoned with a movement of his head. She came over.

"More of the same, please."

"But there are other lawyers around and Mahmoudi was or is prime minister. He must know many lawyers and important people he could call on for help. But really, how do you know so much about me?"

"To answer both questions at once, and, like I said, there is no one with your history, your experience. Naturally your defence of the President drew my attention. I have made a hobby perhaps of following your career since. Your defence of the General has been nothing if not tenacious. But I heard you had threats?"

Eiger took his wine glass and drank deeply. He put it down, leaned back in his chair, looked straight at Rice and wondered just who the hell he was and why he had followed his career. He decided to talk straight.

"Who are you exactly? I mean, how seriously do I take this? I don't know you yet you know all about me and suddenly you're offering me millions of dollars for I don't know what. Yes there were threats. How did you know that?"

"You have a cautious mind, but no matter, in this world it's a requirement for survival. I salute you for it. Nevertheless, this is an entirely serious offer. So my contact informs me. I trust him completely. The threats? Well you made it public in the trial. Very prudent. Good way to protect yourself. It was another factor in your favour."

"This contact, who is he exactly and what's his connection with the prime minister?"

"Like I said, he works for the United Nations. Right now he is stationed in Senegal."

"What is his position at the UN? What does he do?"

"I'll leave that for you to discover when you talk to him. I propose we go to my office. I agreed to Skype with him at 3 p.m. I would like you to be there. You can talk to him yourself, that is if you have the time."

Eiger looked at Rice carefully. "All right. I'm game. But you knew that already?"

"That's right," he answered, and looked amused. "But, let's enjoy the wine. Then we shall go. So, tell me, how are things with the General?"

Eiger sat up straighter in his chair. The question was more like an interrogation, but he answered,

"He's fine. Stuck in prison when he should be free. But fine."

"I never thought you could win that one but it's clear that you will. He's a big fish. You really gave them a fight.'

'It's been difficult. But we work together. Had to. Can never trust anyone, never know what was really going on, who was who."

"What do you mean?"

"Intelligence people everywhere. They planted agents in our team several times. Passing information to the prosecution.   Some of the defence counsel for the co-accused stabbed us in the back. There have been threats. They spread rumours about me. Tried to get me off the case. Anything to stop me, to stop the General from telling what he knows."

"Why did you continue under those conditions?"

"I don't like it when people try to push me around. But sometimes I wonder why. Vanity maybe. Got me in the limelight for awhile."

"Vanity, yes," he laughed, "Gets us all in the end. Thinking we're important when we're not. And the President?"

"Meaning?"

"How did you get involved with him? You got a lot of press. It's too bad he died before the end of the trial."

"They murdered him."

"So you claim. Can you prove it?"

"We've got information." Eiger stopped talking, picked at his food, took a gulp of wine and looked at Rice.

"Why do you ask?"

"He was winning his trial, from what I read, making fools of them so his death came at a very good time for them-saved them from having to acquit him. So I assume your thoughts are in line with mine. Just wondered if you have any information on what happened."

"Poison."

"Any idea of the poison they used?"

"If I did I couldn't tell you, sorry, but I know who. That much is obvious."

"The CIA?"

"When they threatened to kill me they tried to impress me with how serious they were. The guy who approached me said they had murdered people at the Tribunal with a poison that was undetectable. Said they had used it on some important people and they could use it on me. I took him seriously. He didn't appear to be joking. He mentioned the President by name."

"They were that direct?"

"Yep. Very nice guy, just telling me they were going to take me out of the picture."

"So, what do you do next about that?"

"The CIA? Or the President. What can I do? I'm still involved with the family so can't tell you what we're thinking."

"I understand."

"I just agreed to work for a small firm here for a while. So you're call came sort of out of the blue. But I don't think it was a coincidence it came just after I got back in the country."

"Interesting speculation but I assure you my call just happened to occur when it did because I myself just got the call. But can you really go back to the routine stuff after all this? Forgive me but I do not see that happening. You like adventure too much."

"That depends on whether you're full of shit or they are. These guys are small time but they do the stuff I used to have fun doing. This war crimes gig is more trouble than it's worth. But I'm no fool. I'd like the money. But I'd still like to know what it's really for because I have to tell you I'm not buying your story."

"Ok, finish your wine and we'll go to my office and connect with my contact. Perhaps that will reassure you."

~

While Eiger was meeting with Rice, Diana was looking

for him. When she walked down the hallway the first thing she noticed was the health clinic next door to Budnick and Conway and wondered why its office door window was curtained. Eiger had called her and left a message telling her about Conway and Budnick, then mentioned a meeting but she hadn't heard from him again and decided to take a chance and see if he was with his new crew or if she could at least scout them out, see what he had gotten himself into.

She had called ahead and was told he wasn't there yet but she was welcome to come in. She had detected a distinct air of curiosity in the secretary on the other end of the line.

She liked the look of the office, classy, but old fashioned. She had expected something a little seedier. It was almost 5 p.m. when she walked in and Susan was cleaning up her desk. Diana's heart sank as soon as she saw her and Susan became more intrigued by Eiger when the tall woman with the curl of hair over her eye and the long coat caressing her legs swept into the room.

"Hello, may I help you?"

"I'm looking for John Eiger. I'm a friend, Diana..."

"Of course, please have a seat. It's a pleasure to meet you."

Susan got up and walked to the door of one of the offices, "Mr. Eiger's friend is here to see you." There was an "OK" from the other side and Susan returned to her desk, all the while looking Diana up and down, figuring out where she bought her clothes.

Conway walked out of his office. He paused for a moment when he saw Diana. It was almost imperceptible, but Susan noticed it.

"Diana?"

"That's me." She blushed as she took his hand. She felt it and was surprised she did.

"Jack Conway, it's a pleasure to meet you." He found himself mesmerized by very big, blue eyes that seemed to have an honesty about them that was childlike. Her jet-black hair curled around her neck. She was almost as tall as he was. She kept his gaze until Susan shuffled some papers and deliberately slammed a drawer of her desk shut. The spell was broken.

"Have a seat. Johnny said he would be here soon. Something about a meeting and lots of money. It wasn't clear exactly. Anyway, he's an interesting guy. Would you like some coffee or something?"

Diana sat down in a chair facing Susan's desk and slid her coat off her shoulders showing her long neck circled by a string of pearls. She crossed her legs and asked if it was all right to smoke as she pulled a pack of cigarettes out of her purse she kept by her side.

Susan gave a questioning look at Conway but he didn't answer. He was locked onto Diana's black nylons that disappeared under her skirt at the knees. She answered for him.

"Sure, honey, go ahead, I'll join you, to hell with the by-law," and thanked her when Diana offered her one of her Gitanes. After she lit up and Susan was enjoying the pungent french smell, Diana blew a ring of smoke into the air at Conway who seemed to be in a trance and asked,

"Is he all right? He called and told me he had met you and decided to work with you. Frankly, I'm confused. He doesn't usually do things spontaneously like that. But he told me some of the things that have happened to him. I'm worried it's affected his mind. He drank a lot at the cafe when I met him the day he arrived."

Conway shook himself a little, asked Susan to bring them some coffee, then asked Diana to join him in his office. She followed him in, aware of Susan's eyes drilling into her back and sat down in an armchair as he sat down at his desk. Susan brought them two cups of coffee, smiled at Diana, winked at Conway who was nervously playing with his tie, then walked back to her desk swinging her hips provocatively. Conway saw Diana follow her and thought he saw her tongue touch her lips just briefly. She turned back to him. They each took their cup and sat there sipping it for a few minutes then Conway asked what she did in life.

"I'm really just a secretary in an office but the title is junior manager. The rest of the time I work on my art, painting. I'm doing a portrait now of a friend. If I can get the energy, I'll have it finished soon. I can't seem to deal with it. It's good but I'm always changing it. So, mainly I like to paint. But I have to live. So the office job keeps me paying the bills."

"Yeh, wish I had done something more positive with my life. The law is a tough business. Everything about it is negative. But going back to Johnny. It was a whim on his part to come here, a whim on ours to tell him he was welcome. We can't afford to pay him. But it may be we can help each other. He's looking for a place to hide I think. A refuge."

Diana didn't respond to that but asked, "How many lawyers are there here?"

"Just the two of us. We do mainly criminal, but anything interesting."

She looked around the office. The cat came walking into the room and walked against her leg. She stroked it.

"Well, it has a comfortable feel to it."

"Thank you." He smiled. "More coffee?" She politely refused. "I'm ok for now, thanks."

"Does he usually drink a lot? Just like to know."

"No, never before but he tells me he was drinking a lot in Africa. Smokes too much pot though."

"No coke problem or anything?"

"No, he's never used that, or anyway not that I know."

"Just curious. We've all had our problems. It isn't easy to be a lawyer and stay sober. I got into some problem with coke myself awhile back. Managed to get over it. Took up yoga instead." He was starting to look distant. He took a deep breath and sat up. "Anyway, all of us must go for dinner some night and get acquainted."

Diana smiled but was a bit worried to hear about Conway's cocaine problem.

A few minutes later as they exchanged views on life in Toronto they heard the front office door open and in walked Eiger, his blonde hair a bit windblown, running his fingers through it to calm it down. Diana noticed that Susan straightened her back and raised her breasts when he walked past her and smiled. She narrowed her eyes and drew on her cigarette as she watched the interaction. Then he suddenly saw Diana and his smile softened almost to a question but he showed his teeth again quickly and walked up to her and kissed her on the cheek.

"Hi, a bit surprised to see you here."

"She was worried about you," said Susan coyly from her desk. Conway saw the interplay between Eiger and Susan and sized up his chances with Diana in seconds. "Very charming friends you have Johnny. Anyway fill us in."

Eiger took off his coat, sat down next to Diana, then took a cup of coffee from Susan who brought him a mug but pretended not to look at him and said, "I'm ok." He settled into his chair and sipped on his coffee taking in the feeling of sexuality in the room. It seemed to come from everyone. It unsettled him a little. His hand trembled as he put his cup down. He looked at them in turn and watched Susan go back to her desk, then shrank bank as he saw Diana look at him coolly. Conway rescued him. "So, you were saying?"

His face relaxed. He picked up his cup again and drank some coffee, then held on to it as he said, "This meeting was something else."

"What happened?" Conway leaned forward. Eiger had suddenly become tense.

"Well, ..." And he went on to tell them what had happened at the meeting, that he had talked by Skype to the UN man who confirmed "they" wanted him to do the North African case and had mentioned another big fish at the ICC.

Conway asked how much they were offering.

"14 million."

He stared blankly ahead of him. "That smells bad to me."

"Yeh, something doesn't feel right about this whole approach and just after I get back from the General's trial."

"I think we better talk to Budnick. What was this guy's name?"

"First name is David, very ordinary. Last name Owens, but from Montreal. I don't know. I'd like to see how it plays out. What they're really after."

Conway tightened the muscles in his forehead as he frowned at the suggestion. "You better think twice about that. I'm telling you it stinks. Tell you what. Go home. Or better take Diana to dinner. Try to forget all this for a bit. Go see a play. Have a good bottle of wine. I'll get our investigator to see what they can find about this Owens guy."

A few minutes later Diana kissed Conway on the cheek good-bye, said 'Ciao' to Susan, then she and Johnny were in a cab going uptown. She took his hand and said, "Let's go to Jacques place." He nodded and allowed her to hold his hand but she felt the lack of feeling and let his hand go as they watched the scenes of the city flash past. She felt sad, almost like crying, as the car drove around Queen's Park crescent, under the yellow lights, past the museum and crossed Bloor St. into Yorkville

9

Susan came in earlier than usual on Monday. She hadn't slept well and was awake by 5:30 so got up, made coffee, had a shower, put on her make up, then smoked one of the Gitanes Diana had given her, all the while thinking about Johnny Eiger. Diana's lips kept popping into her head too. She drew on her cigarette while she thought about them.

Susan never ate breakfast, except for a Danish at work. She didn't listen to music in her apartment, rarely watched the television. There were no books anywhere except for a collection of erotic photographs and some poetry that she read when she felt too lonely or down. She finished her cigarette, drank a last cup of coffee, threw on her coat and left the apartment. She said hello to the distinguished older couple that got on the elevator with her, passed Charlie the concierge with a nod and a smile and walked across the street to the subway.

It was milder than the day before, so she left her coat open as she descended the stairs and waited on the platform with all the other people gathered to begin the trek downtown to work. Ten minutes later, relaxed by the rhythm of the train, she was back on the street headed towards the office. A man carrying an expensive briefcase gave her an up and down as he walked past her, making her feel good for a second. She was thinking about what he would be like when she opened the door and was surprised to find Conway there before her and said,

"Wow, what got you up and in so bright and early?"

"Couldn't sleep."

"You and me both."

'That's because we weren't together. The things we could have done waiting for sleep to come."

"The thought crossed my mind but not with you." She went over to the coffee machine and poured herself a cup. He came up behind her.

"You don't need to be cruel about it. What's with you? Before you got messed up with this guy out west you were all over me. I didn't do anything to deserve the digs."

"You're right. I'm sorry. I don't know. I'm just messed up. Pushing you away makes it easier. Sorry, don't mean to be mean." She kissed his lips, walked away, and said,

"But I have to tell you that this new guy bothers me."

'Yeh, I wonder if he'll turn up. Budnick thinks so. Was acting a bit desperate. Probably change his mind next week and cut out."

"That's not what bothers me. He excites me."

"I did that once. You really are fickle."

She laughed, sat down at her desk and turned on her computer.

"I can't help it if I'm made that way."

"You could be a bit more discriminating. We had a good thing going. But what's the use. You've turned me into a monk."

"We didn't play out that role. I should have stayed around a little longer."

Conway shook his head in frustration as he walked into

his office. "Enough."

He stopped and turned. "What did you make of his girlfriend?"

Susan's look expressed her jealousy. "Impressive woman. Beautiful. Smart. Ambitious but insecure. An underachiever I'd say but full of herself. I can see why they have a problem."

"She was hot all right. I wouldn't mind…"

"You wouldn't have a chance with her. She wants class and money that one. Now she's nervous cause he's having a crisis or something and wants to give up all that high end international life, all the traveling and fancy hotels, meetings with important people. She's a climber."

"Anyway," he said, "she played it cool while she was here."

They both went silent for a few seconds. He was thinking of Diana and how she was wasted on a guy like Eiger. Nice guy and everything but clearly on the edge. Then he glanced over at Susan remembering how much fun it was to make love with her. The whole experience with her was always surreal. She liked to play games. Once he had gone to her place and she answered the door in a man's suit and tie. The game had gone from there.

Susan was thinking how Eiger was wasted on Diana. She was very aware of the tension in the air.

"Yes, she's very cool. Do you think he'll stay?"

"Hard to say but he could be useful in that drug case if it gets going. Talking of which, how many names do we have in out data base, emails, numbers, all that?"

"Several thousand I guess, why?"

"I want a mass mailing to everyone asking them if they've ever been affected by this drug or know anybody who has. We need to get some clients to put together a class action suit. There are big law firms in the States all over it. But no one in Canada has picked up on it yet, or so

Budnick says."

"But most of those people probably never heard of it and never used it and some of them don't even like us or owe us money-you're not going to get clients that way. You should put out a press release or run some TV ads like those other guys do."

Conway made a face. "That is one thing I will never do."

"Well, you were just going to do the same thing on a smaller scale. What are you talking about?"

He dictated a letter for her to send out while muttering and rubbing his hands together, then pacing up and down talking about the big fees they could make, even a couple of million he dreamed. He bathed in the light of the happy illusion he built in his mind of immense riches spent on a villa in Venice. Susan had her own vision.

"Ok, I hope you're right but if you make big fees I want a raise, a big one."

He leaned over to kiss her quickly on the lips. It surprised her so she forgot to reject him and let him linger, tasting him, their faces touching, then he pulled back, smiled and said, "A deal."

Budnick came in at the usual time and asked what was up. Susan said, "Hi Walter," then gave him a quick rundown.

He looked pleased as he stood there and began to flip through the document she had prepared. "Great, you're way ahead of me. I told you this idea was a good one." He said more loudly, "So, Jack, I've convinced you to fight the good fight on this one?"

Conway heard him and meandered out of his office, his look expressing amusement, and sat in the chair next to Susan's desk, legs splayed out, arms akimbo, looking very relaxed.

"Ok, Walter, Maybe there's a case. But how are we going to finance it? It's going to take a lot of time, a lot of work and a hell of a lot of research and as Eiger said, experts, and they cost plenty. And we'll have to get them in the States. There aren't any up here that can do that. I have one in mind though, a professor at Vanderbilt I used once a long time ago when I worked on a case for CN Rail. Spraying pesticides along the tracks. Sprayed houses too. Long before I ran into you. We won that one. He's still around. I checked him out the other day. But he won't come cheap and he's gonna demand all sorts of documentation to do a report."

"Well, we have to find a way, we can take out a loan, or…"

"How are we gonna take out a loan, from who, and how much? Our credit wasn't so good last time I checked."

Budnick clapped him on the shoulder, "Well, it would be great if that money they offered Eiger is real."

"Yeh, you checked into that?"

"I got Pierre Morin to do some checking over the weekend. The lawyer is odd because he can't find a history on the guy more than a year old. Very odd. The other guy, this David, has intelligence officer written all over him. Before he worked at the UN drugs unit in Africa he was an intelligence officer for ISAF in Afghanistan in the American zones. So, I suspect the other guy is Canadian intelligence as well or something like that."

"Which means?"

"Which means someone is trying to set Johnny up. He said the CIA threatened him in Africa. Wasn't sure if he was exaggerating but this approach smells bad to me. I'm going to tell him to break off with them. I don't know how the set up is supposed to play out but a set up it most definitely is. Pierre is certain they're spooks."

Susan listened intently with some excitement. "It's like a movie."

Just then the front office door opened and Eiger walked in. He shook hands with Budnick and Conway, poured himself some coffee and sat down in Budnick's office.

Budnick asked him about the meeting with Rice and his Skype friend. He listened intently, without saying a word as Eiger described the scene. Then he told Eiger about Pierre's quick investigation. Eiger nodded. "Yeh, it had to be too good to be true, maybe they'd accuse me of laundering money or something or aiding the enemy, like those two they arrested last week in Mexico."

Budnick leaned forward and leaned on his arms. "They're spooks, anyway they smell like spooks. You have to break off the contact. Tell them you're not interested. Tell them you smell a rat even. Let them know you know."

"They're making me nervous, that's for sure. And I told him. But if it's real, the money is..."

"You can't let them get to you. The cops are always playing games. They can just go fuck themselves and it's a good thing you're with us." He put his hand on his arm and gripped it in assurance.

"Ok, Ill contact them. See what happens."

"Good," Budnick said and stood up, "Now we have to figure out how to attack this class action case. That'll take your mind off all this spy shit and maybe they'll decide you're not worth the bother anymore. The first thing we have to do is find the clients and the money."

*   *   *   *   *

10

Monday morning Eiger sat in his new office, a room seven feet square with no window. He had a small desk, an old lean back chair, a credenza behind it with some old law reports laying on top and a number of dusty old files stacked underneath.

It wasn't much different from his office in Africa except there he had a small window and the office was shared with his two legal assistants. He was used to a small space. But there, when he walked out into the street, he was greeted by the street boys, calling out his name, trying to get him to buy one of their batiks, or two-day old newspapers. Now when he walked out onto the street no one knew him, no one bothered him, no one even looked at him.

He sat thinking about Africa, about Arusha, about Miriam. He shut his eyes and drifted. His cell phone buzzed. It was a text message from Rice, wanting to talk. Rice had said he would get a phone number for Eiger to call and check things on his own. He returned the call. Despite what Budnick had told him he was intrigued by the game. He couldn't resist letting it play out some –just to see.

Rice sounded tense, "It's ok, but the contact wants you

to promise to pay ten percent of the 14 million to him as a finders fee. If that's ok, they can transfer the money to you in a few days. You can call them on this number in Geneva." Eiger wrote the number down carefully.

"Switzerland? I thought your contacts were in Tunisia or Algeria."

"Yes, some of the family are in those countries but this guy is in Europe now. People move around. It's a dangerous situation for them. Call him and talk to him yourself."

"Ok, but if this contact is not a lawyer referring this case to me I can't pay a finder's fee. The Law Society forbids it. Get me disbarred. Sorry, can't promise that. But we can work something out I'm sure."

Rice was quiet on the phone for a minute or so, then said slowly, "You astonish us Mr. Eiger. Really. But very well, we'll work around that."

Eiger hung up, looked at the number and began to wonder. But he didn't get to wonder long when Budnick came in and asked him if he wanted to go over to the Old City hall courts to take a look around. "Might see some old friends. Get the feel of the place again. What's up, you look a bit tense."

"I called Rice back. He gave me a number to call in Switzerland. Wanted me to pay a ten percent finders fee. I refused. Said I astonished them. What, they think I'm bent? Or it was a test? Bizarre."

Budnick stood listening twitched his left shoulder a couple of times, a small little tick, and said, "Told you. They're spooks, trying to set you up. Cut it loose. No good playing games with those guys. But forget that. Let's go."

 They put on their coats, walked out, down a side street, onto Queen Street, crossed Bay St and over to the court house in the Gothic old city hall topped by its clock tower.

"You're girlfriend is beautiful."

"Diana? Yes, but difficult. We're not having a good time."

"Be careful I think Conway likes her."

"Married?"

"He was, got divorced. Usual story, married a woman who had no idea who he was, ditto for him, so in three years they were at each other's throats. Then he falls for some secretary at another firm. Met her hanging around the courthouse. Fucked his brains out, made him crazy, leaves his wife for her, then after he's lost the house, the car and everything else worth having the secretary leaves him for a fat guy who has a gun and feeds her cocaine. Conway's not seeing things too positively these days but I could see he likes your friend."

"Left him for a fat man?"

"Yeh, must be the security thing. Conway was a lawyer so for her he was the gravy train, make life good, but he couldn't do it for her. So she went for the gun and the coke. Hear she's totally miserable. But to hell with her."

"You never been divorced?"

Budnick laughed, "I wouldn't give her the satisfaction." He laughed again.

They walked up the courthouse steps, through the doors and the security check and entered the main lobby where the wings of the building divided into corridors with courtrooms and offices. It had been ten years since Eiger had been there. It all looked the same except for the security check. He followed Budnick to the left and down a flight of stairs.

"Where we going?"

"To the cells, to see Zukov. Then to bail court. Gotta try and get Zukov out if the surety shows up."

They walked up to a narrow steel door in a wall. Budnick kicked it with his feet. A guard appeared at the small glass window, looked at them, then opened it. They both walked in to the holding cell area. Eiger could see prisoners walking aimlessly around or sitting listlessly on a few benches. Some looked at them with angry faces, others looked hopeful.

"Long time since I've been in here."

Budnick looked around. "This hasn't changed." They signed their names in the register. Budnick asked the Sergeant for Zukov.

"OK, cubicle C," he said, and waived them away as other lawyers crowded round the register, all looking harassed, and mouldy under the yellow lights, desperate to talk about deals before their case was called, looking at their watches, frantic, since most of them had to be in two courts at the same time.

Budnick motioned to Eiger to follow him. They went into the small set of cubicles with thick glass windows. There were several lawyers and prisoners talking already. It was difficult to think in the babel of voices.

They went along to cubicle C. It was just a chair up against the window with a partition shielding it from the next interview area on either side.

"Here he is," said Budnick, and waived as Zukov walked into view. He was dark haired, swarthy, looked Italian, but was also Ukrainian. "Hi, Walter. Can you get me out of here?"

Budnick pulled himself forward in his seat, put his face closer to the glass and the sound holes cut into it, "They say it was a bad assault on your girlfriend, want you to stay in. You've got a record for assaults. What gives?"

"Yeh, I know man, but that's old stuff. They can't look at that now can they? Look, she's a lying bitch. I came home the other day, found her blowing some biker type. He comes at me, I deck the guy, he runs out the door, so she gets on the phone and says I beat the shit out of her. But she's got no marks I tell you. The cops just wanna nail me. I think that biker was undercover. I swear they wanna nail me 'cause he's a cop."

"Uh-huh, ok," Budnick kept saying to each statement. "Well, don't worry we'll get 'em." He waited for Zukov to react. Zukov scowled, then leaned close to the glass, "So, how we gonna do it, Walter, I can't afford to lose my job. If I don't show up today I'm fucked, man." He slammed his hand against the glass.

"Calm down. I want you cool up there. Ok, I'll do my best. You know the routine when you get up in the court. Your mom's there. Maybe I can swing a deal with the Crown. Get you released."

"OK, thanks man, see what you can do for me, man." He quickly turned and walked away.

Budnick and Eiger went out the holding cell door and down the hall to the lower bail court. There were lawyers standing talking to families, girlfriends, to each other, or to some cops in uniform, some in suits. Clerks came and left. People walked around in the hallway looking lost. Most of them were poorly dressed and had dark circles under their eyes.

They walked into the small courtroom. There were ten rows of benches either side of a centre aisle. There was a small judge's dais at the end of the room and below that the clerk's desk. On the left hand side, a long bench against the wall with a glass partition. On the bench were three men. A fourth was on his feet being questioned by a prosecutor.

The room was full. It felt claustrophobic but Budnick walked to the front. He and Eiger managed to find two chairs near the counsel table. Budnick whispered a few words to the Duty Sgt. who gave him a file. Budnick looked through it, then asked for Zukov to be brought up from the cells next.

They waited for twenty minutes as the other three cases were dealt with. All three detained; no fixed addresses, all had prior records, no friends to act as sureties, no lawyers.

Duty counsel who handled them had time only for perfunctory remarks in their favour.

Finally Zukov was brought in.

The clerk called the case. Budnick stepped forward.

"Mr. Budnick," the Justice of the Peace said as he signed some papers and gave them to his clerk.

"Good morning, Your Worship, I represent Mr. Zukov here. I wonder if I might speak to my friend briefly. Perhaps we can resolve this."

"Very well. Speak to her now, counsel. We have a busy list. Stand it down," he said to the clerk, "Who do we have next?" and the clerk called another case.

Budnick walked over to one of the two prosecutors, a young lady in a black pin-striped pant suit, attractive, long hair thrown to one side, stylish black glasses. She looked like Maria Callas. They stood close. Budnick talked to her in whispers for several minutes. Sometimes she shook her head and said something to him. But he began gesticulating with his hands, then showed her something in the file he had been given. She looked at it, then nodded her head, broke off the conversation, walked back to her place and began speaking, breaking into the case that had the JP's attention.

"Your worship, the Zukov matter again, if we may." The JP nodded and told the prisoner in the box to sit down and the duty counsel to step aside, then calmly asked, "You have an agreement, Madame Prosecutor?"

"Yes, Your Worship, we have. We've agreed that Mr. Zukov is to be released on a $3,000 dollar surety, cash bail, to be his mother, Maria Zukov, usual no contact clause regarding the alleged victim, to report once a week, report change of address and so on."

"That ok, Mr. Budnick?"

"Yes, that's fine Your Worship."

The JP then issued the order. Zukov spoke to Budnick

for a few seconds, shook his hand and was then taken back to the cells. Budnick and Eiger left.

Eiger asked where the surety was.

"She's waiting by the clerks' office I hope so we can get him released. Let's go see."

"How'd you work it?"

"Oh, she owed me a favour. She's ok. I told her the biker might be a cop. She didn't want that to come out in court today." He laughed to himself. "There's always a way to finesse it."

They found Maria Zukov standing alone in the hallway on the main floor near the bail office. She looked like she wanted to cry. She was wearing a smart blue cloth coat, sensible shoes and though in her forties, she looked younger. They both walked up to her. Budnick asked if she had the money. She gave him an envelope full of cash. He turned and went into the bail office. Eiger smiled at her. "Your son will be out soon."

"Yes, thank you. Are you working with him now?"

"Yes, just started, I used to be around here a lot but I've been away for a long time."

She smiled weakly and turned her head away as he looked at her. She said quietly, "He's a good man." Eiger smiled in agreement but to avoid the awkwardness he pretended to be drawn to a heated discussion going on a few feet away between two young men about who was to put up bail for their father.

Five minutes later, Budnick came back out, then took her in to sign the surety papers. Ten minutes later they watched as Zukov was brought up, released and went to hug his mother. Budnick told Zukov he would talk to him on the weekend, that they had to be in 101 court to set a date the next Monday and not to forget. Maria assured him she would get him there. Budnick smiled, chuckled a little and as Zukov turned to walk away, called out,

"And try and get me some money, I'm broke."

Zukov nodded his head and gave a thumbs up, "You'll have it Monday. Thanks man."

"Attractive woman, that Maria."

"Hey, Johnny, don't you have enough problems with Diana? You have a girl in Africa too?"

Eiger hesitated a second before answering, then said, "There was a girl." He turned his head away, unable to say anything more, cutting off the conversation. Budnick knew when not to press someone. He let it be as they walked across Queen Street, both lost in thought, looking at the crowds of people walking past, all buried in their own jumbled worlds.

*   *   *   *   *

11

"Where are we going now?" They were driving along the Gardner Expressway west, out to the endless tracts of housing and strip malls where once there had been orchards and blossoms.

"Out to see a client's mother. She's our first Aldarizine case. Anyway, it's always good to pay attention to the families sometimes."

Eiger rested his head on the seat back and looked out the window at the ugliness and the dirt, the travelers alone in their cars, the 'for lease' signs that littered the malls, the industrial parks.

"Fuck, it looks like shit here. It looks worse than Africa. At least there's life on the streets there."

Budnick squinted as he drove, "Yeh, its ugly made by ugly people. Nobody cares about beauty anymore. This ain't Europe that's for sure. It's all white trash here in control of everything. Anything for a buck."

Eiger murmured, "A slaughterhouse of the spirit. A city of flattened souls."

Budnick chuckled as he drove. "Whoever said that got it right. But they're not gonna crush me. Not yet anyway. I still got spirit," then he swore under his breath, "Uh-oh, goddam. Look at that. That's enough to crush you, right there." He adjusted his body in his seat as Eiger looked ahead of them to see what was happening.

The traffic was quickly slowing down. They could see rows of cars stretched out far beyond the horizon. "Gotta take this cut-off, something's up ahead. Last chance we'll have." He pulled to the right and exited down an off-ramp and through a residential area full of split-levels, manicured lawns and speed bumps.

Twenty minutes later they pulled into the driveway of a house on a cul-de-sac. The house looked well kept, its white clapboard and paint box of flowers welcomed strangers with a smile. They got out. Budnick walked up to the door, Eiger following, and knocked. Anna Morello came to the door. She looked happy at seeing them, smiled, stepped back and asked them in.

"Thanks Anna," said Budnick. He kissed her on the cheek as he walked through the door, "Won't stay long. I just wanted to say hello and say that I saw your husband last week and he's ok, considering."

She looked down and stayed quiet for a few seconds. "Thank you, it's a problem to know what to say about it."

Budnick took on the look of a sad spaniel as he spoke to her, "Well, you didn't know he was involved with fixing the books. He'll be out in a few months. Things will get better after that. He's changed in there. I can see it. Depend on it." She smiled wanly but continued to wring her hands as she sat there. Eiger looked quizzically at Budnick who cleared his throat and said,

"But I would like to talk to you about something else."

She raised her head and with trusting eyes, clouded by melting tears, replied, "Something else, I don't understand. Is he charged with something else?"

"No. No. Nothing like that." He touched her hand with his. "No, He mentioned that you had been taking a drug, Aldarizine. That you had bad effects."

"Yes, I took it for my arthritis but now I find I can't remember things, and sometimes I am nauseous, and then agitated, like panic attacks, then headaches come, very severe headaches. They can last for hours or days. I didn't think much at first because the doctor said they would have some effect but I've been taking them for nine months until I stopped last week. These things are still happening. My doctor thinks it may be the drug."

"Would he be willing to sign a statement to that effect?"

"I don't know. You can ask him."

Budnick pulled some documents out of his briefcase. "This is a retainer. You need to sign it before we can do anything. You're not the only one that has this problem. There is a big case in the States about this. It could be worth a lot of money. But we have to act now, start investigating and build a case for damages."

"Well, that's fine but I don't have any money to pay lawyers. I mean..."

"You don't need to worry about that. We'll do it on a contingency basis so we carry it. If we win, we take a percentage."

"How much of a percentage."

"We can talk about it. But we get our expenses on top too."

"Oh, yes, naturally."

He handed her a pen. She slowly signed the paper.

"What do I need to do?"

"You don't need to do anything. I'll write to your doctor, who is...?"

"Dr. Rodanski. He's very intelligent, very good-looking."

Budnick looked over at Conway. "OK, I'll send him the release and ask him for a report. If he has something useful then we'll go from there, ok?" He looked at her, waiting for her to say yes, but she simply shrugged her shoulders, clasped her hands together on her lap and said, "I'll leave it to you, Mr. Budnick. Thank you."

When they walked back to the car Budnick stopped and turned to Eiger, "You see. That's how you do it. Now we have a case. Maybe we can make some money. It's up to us. A bit different from taking a pay check from the UN every month."

"That wasn't so different. Most of the time you had to hustle to get paid."

Budnick, nodded, "Yep, this world is full of petty people. No one has any imagination. Look at what you see on TV these days, absolutely nothing. Nobody sane watches TV anymore. They charge you to stare at ads all day and all night. At least when we were younger you didn't have to pay them for the privilege. It was free to anyone with an antenna. Now, they're just ripping us off every day. We get back shit."

Eiger looked down at his phone.

Budnick looked over. "The spooks?"

"How'd you know?"

"The look on your face."

"Yeh, Rice is asking if I called the Swiss number yet."

"Ok, lets pull in for a bite to eat. It's past my lunchtime. I'm starving. Call while we're there."

They pulled into a steak and burger joint parking lot, locked the car and went into the restaurant. They sat at a booth by the window.

As they gazed at the menu a gum-chewing waitress brought over, Budnick's mobile rang. He mumbled a few words into it, laughed, then closed it. Eiger looked up from the menu he was holding, "Jack?"

"Yeh. Jack. Feeling lonely. Wants to know what's up."

"You been together for ten years or more haven't you?"

"Fifteen now I guess. Wasn't' thinking it would last so long. We're very different. But it works. His divorce got him down though. Started into the coke for a while. Couldn't reason with him. But I think he's coming out of it."

"And Susan?"

"She's gorgeous isn't she? She sure likes you. She gets irritable if she doesn't see you."

"She is that. I like her. But there's Diana and there was, ...I'm like everyone, complicated."

"Not me, I keep it simple. I've seen too many of you guys go down to the pits of Hades for women and be willing to slay dragons, and you're burned to cinders every time. Not me, I've learned to accept my fate and forget about it. No other choice."

Eiger tried to forget the girl who walked on the beach at Bagamoyo while the wind caressed her face while she splashed her naked foot in the silver surf. He could hear her voice calling out, "Darling, it's so cold," tugging on his arm to come and play. He caught Budnick looking at him.

"Sorry, let's order, then I 'll make this call."

*   *   *   *   *

12

Budnick took a bite out of his hamburger as Eiger made the call. He chewed methodically and took one bite after another as the conversation began and finished.

"And…. I didn't hear you say much."

"I don't even know who it was. When I asked if the guy that answered was the guy he says 'yes', then goes quiet. So I asked the questions and all I got was yes or no or 'uh'huh.'"

Budnick kept munching, nodding, "Just a number they gave you. Told you this thing is fake. But anyway, it's very strange. I wasn't sure whether to believe your story about the CIA, but this is strange."

"Didn't believe me?"

"Hey what do I know? Haven't seen you for years, then you pop up with all these dramatic stories. It was fun to hear them but no, wasn't sure what to think. But now? You better watch your back. And now us too."

He stabbed a couple of french fries with his fork and looked fixedly at Eiger. "One day you're going to have to tell us more about this trial you've been doing."

Eiger looked out the window, "Sometimes I think I

have it all figured out, other times, I wonder if I know anything. But one day I'll tell you. I need about two hours."

Budnick nodded, took a bite out of his hamburger, dropping relish from his mouth as he chewed and replied, "Did you know the Americans have a base on Mars?" and stared at Eiger waiting for his reaction. Eiger just looked at him. His head down, eyes up, mouth open.

"I'm not joking. Ask me about it some time," and he went quiet, looked very serious and went back to chewing on his hamburger. When they finished eating they called for the check, left the waitress a handsome tip and drove back downtown to the office, Eiger wondering all the while whether his leg was being pulled or Budnick knew something. He finally decided it was impossible and it was his idea of a joke, but doubts lingered.

It was nearly 4:00 pm. when they walked into the office. Conway was with Susan at the scanner arguing about how to insert a document. Conway greeted them and asked, "What's new?" Eiger told him about the meeting with Anna Morello and the phone call to Switzerland, then added,

"We forgot Zukov. Walter worked magic and got him out. Really attractive mother."

Conway nodded. "Met her once. Very sweet. Wonder why she's alone?"

Budnick walked over to the scanner. "Why are they all alone?" and laughed mysteriously. "What you trying to do?"

Susan sighed, "Trying to scan in some data we pulled off the web about that drug, trying to put it on the computer and the scanner won't cooperate."

Eiger stepped forward, "You using one of those trial programs to organise information? I had to use one of those. They're great on output but scanning material in is a nightmare."

"No kidding," said Susan, "and we haven't even got any

client yet so I don't know what we're doing this for."

Budnick held up his briefcase. "You're misinformed, we do have a client. We just need more."

"How you going to do that?"

"We file this action first, issue a press release, get it out there, people see it and everybody and anybody that ever took any medication whatsoever will be pouring through those doors demanding we take action against the companies that have callously poisoned them."

Susan looked at him skeptically. "Uh-huh, that easy huh? Well I sure hope so but if any of that happens we have to have a new scanner."

"The insurance boys will make an early offer to make it go away. You'll get a new scanner."

Budnick was always optimistic. For him problems and obstacles didn't exist. But Eiger was quiet as he listened, then said,

"You haven't thought this through, if I can say so. They won't pay and they'll fight it all the way. Unless you get some solid evidence, they are going to bankrupt you with legal costs. You're starting the case the wrong way round."

"I've got the client."

"You need the evidence. Where is it? Her complaint?"

"Her doctor."

"You haven't got his report yet and he's just a GP. Specialists will chew him up."

Budnick put his hand on Eiger's shoulder. 'I leave that to you.'

Eiger was about to answer him when the office door opened and a small, delicate girl walked in wearing a long camel coloured coat and a blue scarf framing her blonde curls. She looked to be about nineteen or twenty, and shyly hesitated when she saw them. Conway said, "Hi, can we help you?"

Her voice sang more than spoke. "I'm Tommy Moore's friend, Marina."

Conway went to her and took her hand. "Miss Scozzi. I'm Jack Conway, Tommy's lawyer. He wanted me to call you. I'm sorry. You beat me to it."

She smiled sadly and asked if she could sit down and took off her scarf.

Susan showed her a chair. She sat down carefully, and pulled her skirt to her knees where her coat opened and fell to the floor.

"I didn't know if I should come. I don't know what's going on. But I'm frightened."

"The police paid you a visit?" Budnick sat down next to her.

"Yes, two detectives, the same ones who took Tommy away, when they arrested him. Wanted me to make a statement saying that Tommy had a shotgun. That he wasn't with me that night. But he didn't have a shotgun, least I never saw one and he was with me. They said if I didn't say so they were going to fix me. They asked me what I knew about Frank. What he did."

Susan brought her a cup of coffee. Marina took it, thanked her and sipped it, then let it rest in her lap, "Tommy couldn't have done what they said. He was with me at the time they say the shooting happened. But they've got it in for him since he was fighting. Once he got in a bar fight with a cop, he told me, and beat the guy pretty bad. He got off with a few months. They're still hot for him. He was with me at some demonstrations too...maybe. But I don't know who did this shooting. It can't be Tommy."

Budnick looked grim. Conway looked at Budnick. Susan sat down on her other side and held her by the shoulder.

"You have relatives you can go and stay with for awhile?"

"No, no one in the city. I have some friends at the university. I take some courses there when I can. But they can't really help me with this. That's why I came to tell you so you'd know what to do."

"So Tommy's set up, you're pressured, but for what?" Eiger began to pace. "She needs a safe house."

He looked down at Susan, who shook her head no but he looked at her again and she offered Marina a cigarette, which she took, and waited as Susan lit it. She sat there inhaling and gazing into the floor until Susan said, "Well, you're welcome to stay at my place."

She looked up and held the cigarette down by her side, "No, thanks, really. But maybe Mr. Conway can talk to them and call them off. They need to know some weight is around."

"What were their names?"

"One was Randall. The other one was Marko or something."

Conway raised his head. "Marko again. He' s one of the two guys who told me to drop a case last year. Remember I did a case for Charlie Baxter, the black lawyer? He was busy one day, so he asked me to take a small robbery case. Some black guy in the Black Action Committee the police set up."

Budnick nodded. Eiger asked what happened but before answering Conway took Marina by the arm, "Was Moore involved in anything else? This guy Frank who was shot, what's your connection with him?"

Marina looked startled. Her voice became tight and higher pitched.

"Sometimes I went to demonstrations, anti-war, peace, things like that. Tommy would come with me, sometimes Frank, but there were lots of people at those events. That can't be anything to do with it."

She swung her head from one to the other and began

to talk more quickly, as if she were in a hurry, "Frank was a friend of Tommy's. But he was different from Tommy. Serious I guess you would say. It was difficult to know him but he was very determined to stop the wars. Frank was in the army at some time so he'd seen things. He said so many things and I....well I don't see how that's connected to what happened. They were friends, Tommy and Frank. It doesn't make sense. Why are they doing this?"

Conway replied that they would take care of it and would call her later in the day, indicating the conversation was over. She stood up, put out the cigarette in the ashtray on Susan's desk and moved toward the door. Conway approached her, held her hand affectionately and told her to call at any time if she needed them. She smiled sadly, lowered her head, then turned and left, leaving behind a very faint scent of Chanel No. 5.

He watched her as she made her way to the elevator and waved to her as she turned her face toward him before she disappeared into the elevator. He turned to the others and said, "A classy lady. Think there's a political angle to this?" and looked at Budnick who was rubbing his chin with his hand.

"It could be. At least we have a link between Moore and the dead man. Let me think," and he slowly rose and, still rubbing his chin, wandered back into his office.

Eiger picked up the ball. "Ok, Jack, so you were telling us about this cop Marko and the black lawyer, Baxter. So what happened? About the two cops I mean."

Conway took a deep breath "Right, Well, I'm just standing around in the hallway on the second floor over at Old City hall there when these two guys walk up to me and ask me if I'm doing this case for Baxter. They told me that if I knew what was good for me I better drop it and walk away and don't do anymore work for him. So, I said or else what?' and this guy Marko gets in my face and says, if I don't they're going to fix me. I told them both to fuck off. They just walked away and said, 'Remember.'"

Eiger looked worried. "You know guys I had hoped I was getting away from this bullshit not walking into more of it. Man." He shook his head. "So did they ever try to fix you?"

"Yeh, they tried to fix me. Picture this. I've got a guy in the Don. Charged with armed robbery. Stuck up a variety store for 50 bucks to buy some crack. Nice guy. Married. But the crack got him. Lost his job. Started sliding fast. He walks in with a zip gun, scares the owner to death, takes the money and walks right into a police bike patrol. The prosecutor's asking eight to ten. I'm doing a slow plea, trying to talk it down to two years. Keep putting it over for trial. Get some character evidence. Sob story. The time comes for the plea to take place. I visit, tell the guy I've gotta be in a different court at 10 the next day, but I'll be there by 11 so if his case is called to hold it down 'til I get there. No problem."

"The day comes. I get rid of the case in the first court then go to the Hall for 110 court for his case. As soon as I walk in I see my man already standing up in the prisoner's box and he's talking to the judge. I walk in announce myself and the judge tells me that I'm too late, he's pleaded and been sentenced to 2 years and I was fired. I'm confused so I go over to the client and ask what's going on. He looks very nervous. Can't look me in the eye. Says 'sorry, man I had to do it, you're fired.'"

"So ok, I've been fired before. Just have to retire with grace. So I leave. I'm outside the court wondering what happened when a detective comes out, the one on this case and tries to console me, saying its weird. I had done such a great job for the guy, he's an ingrate and don't let it get you down and all that jazz. He leaves. For two weeks this bothers me. I can't figure it out. But then I get a phone call from the client telling me he has to talk to me. So I pay him a visit. He comes into the interview room shaking like he's got the dt's. His whole body is vibrating."

"So I ask him why he's so nervous? What's up? He tells me, "Look, Mr. Conway I don't know what you're up to but the cops want you inside real bad.""

"I say what are you talking about? And he says, "Ok look, I'm sorry I fired you. You did a great job for me. But two weeks before that date two RCMP guys and that Toronto detective came to see me and told me I have to sign a statement that you've been smuggling drugs into the jail. If I sign I get two years. If I don't, I get eight. I told them to go fuck themselves. They came back twice. Same thing. Finally, on that day the detective comes down to the holding cells and tells me its my last chance, they like that I'm not a rat, they can respect that but if I won't sign a statement they want me to fire you, to put the word out you're no good, kill your practice. I had no choice. It was two years or worse. That's why I fired you in court and went ahead without you.""

"So I leave the Don and now I'm wondering what's going on but then I got calls from two other detention centers from clients who told me the police had been to see them for the same thing. I was lucky. My clients are loyal to me. Told them to go to hell. But the cops were really trying."

Eiger sat down and shook his head. "What did you do?"

"I've been nervous ever since. Every time I see a patrol car I wonder if I'm going to be pulled over and they are going to search my trunk and find a kilo of coke or something. But I confronted the Don's superintendent and asked if I was being investigated. He asked me why I thought I was. I told him just a hunch and he denied it. But I let them know I knew. I talked to Budnick and a couple of judges I know to cover myself. But this is a dirty world we work in."

*   *   *   *   *

13

Tuesday morning Susan brought in the latest report to Budnick about his campaign to drum up clients for the Aldarizine action. He looked at the single piece of paper.

"This it?"

"That's it."

Budnick frowned, stood up and walked into Conway's office. Eiger was talking to him about the drafting of the claim, how it should be set up, what damages they should go for.

"It's gotta to be economic loss. This isn't the States. You're not going to get big damages here for pain and suffering. We have to prove loss of income, psychological harm, disability. These cases take a lot of resources."

Budnick sat down, "And we haven't got enough clients to make it work. My contacts aren't producing anything. I think we may just have to stick to the bread and butter."

"Then what can we give Eiger to do?"

"There's a smuggling case that needs looking after. Client's a guy named Paul Gabrieli. Him and his buddies were buying bourbon in the US, shipping it to the Czech Republic, putting it in containers labelled glass and then shipping it into Canada without paying the duty. Went on for two years. Somehow the feds got an informer in the bonded warehouse. Tipped them off about the shipments. The whole operation came crashing down. They're looking at big time and fines for smuggling and tax evasion. Too detailed for me. Too much paper. You interested Johnny?"

Eiger shrugged his shoulders. "Sure. Let me have the file and I'll take a look. What's Gabrieli's story?"

"Ah, he's really just a cheap hustler. Likes to make out he's mafia. Used to have a contracting business that went bust a few years back. 50. Married, Two kids. Hangs out with a black hooker named Janet sometimes. Getting money out of him is not easy but I've done a few cases for him before. So far kept him out of trouble. He'll cough up, eventually. His partners all have different lawyers. There are six of them involved."

Eiger said, "Ok, let me have the file and I'll give him a call."

Budnick said "Ok," then went back to his desk and asked Susan to pull out the file and then asked to see what Conway and Eiger had drafted up for the Aldarizine.

"We're going to file this action anyway. See if we can drum up some business."

She brought him the file and left him reading their notes and the statement of claim. He penciled in some changes, crossed out some paragraphs, inserted new ones. He wrote fast. Three hours later he called Susan back in.

She was wearing a tight black skirt that ended two inches above the knee and a snug pink blouse. Budnick didn't usually notice these things but his adrenalin was flowing and it made even him stimulated. He tried not to look at her as she stood to one side and leaned over as he went through the changes in the document with her. He couldn't take it long. He coughed a little and suddenly put the file back together and gave it to her.

"Here, type me up a draft. We can do this." He watched

her as she walked slowly back to her desk. He got up and closed his door.

The phone rang. Susan answered then called to Conway. "Jack, disclosure's ready on Moore."

"Can you pick it up?"

"Can't. Walter wants me to do this statement of claim."

"Like I've got time to go over there. Johnny do you mind?"

"Sure, where do I go?" Conway gave him directions to the disclosure office. Eiger put on his jacket and coat. He stood near Susan. "Like what your wearing today."

"Oh you do, do you?" she smiled and winked at him. "You're cute too. Too bad about Diana."

Eiger looked chagrined and laughed as he walked out the door. "Later."

"Later."

Eiger, high on Susan's energy, walked across the street to the Hall and found the disclosure office. While he waited for the clerk to bring the file a couple of other lawyers turned up he hadn't seen in years. Anderson, tall, lanky and now going grey bellowed a loud "Hello, my friend, long time." Kudaz pretended not to remember him and said nothing.

Anderson continued to bellow in his over the top voice, "Where you been all this time Eiger? Thought you were dead or in the crazy house or something. Kudaz been telling me you were doing war crimes, that must be all bullshit, eh, I can just imagine."

Eiger replied it was then let Anderson babble on while he waited for the clerk to bring the file. Eiger signed a receipt. All the while Anderson kept telling him he hadn't missed much except things were worse, the judges weren't as eccentric or as much fun, the weather was wild and his kids were costing him a fortune to go to university. "It's only for the rich and we ain't getting rich. Terrible what's going on, really," and he pounded Eiger on the back.

Eiger took the file, shook Anderson's hand, took his card and said, "Really great to see you again. Let's do lunch."

Kudaz continued to ignore him and stood to one side as Anderson continued to go on speaking to them both about the problems with his kids, his wife, his practice, and didn't seem to notice the freeze coming from Kudaz. Eiger stifled his anger at the snub, said good-bye to them both and walked out onto the street, wondering 'what the hell was that all about?'

~

Later that afternoon, on the outskirts of town, way up north, beyond the miles of identical houses, clustered in identical estates, laced with identical treeless streets, beyond the boredom, beyond the depression, the family squabbles, beyond the strip malls and small, impoverished shops, up in the country where the trees began and farms still graced the land, where horses ran across the fields, up in the ancient beauty that heals to see, a dog lay lazing in the pale March sun, its cold nose resting on its paws, its eyes half-closed dreaming of younger days. It was just one of those yard dogs, part shepherd, part hound, part many other things.

He was lying on the porch of an old farmhouse. It lay among a stand of oak trees that were just beginning to bud, about a hundred metres in from the road. The driveway was gravel and dirt and rutted from use. There were no curtains in the broken windows and the only paint on the walls hung in dead faded strips from the doors and eaves troughs.

The only sounds were the wind in the treetops gently brushing branch against branch and the sudden calls of blue jays and crows. The house and trees were surrounded by acres of fields, fallow and ruined. Rusted farm tools littered the yard and the ancient barn was bent to the ground, its roof collapsed in sorrow. No plough had turned the soil for many years.

The dog lifted his head. His ears perked up straight. It was the noise of a car engine, very faint but increasing. He stretched his neck to look down the road. A cloud of dust and dead leaves followed a dark van that came towards him at high speed. He stood up to watch as it stopped where the road ended, between the barn and the house. The driver's door opened. A man with a tanned face in a dark grey suit got out and scanned the area with care.

He motioned to someone in the van then opened a side door and said, 'Ok, bring her out.' A girl was pushed out violently. She stumbled and fell hard to the ground, moaning. The tanned face roughly dragged her to her feet and shoved her up against the wall of the barn. A second man got out, taller, dressed the same as the first, but his face pale, like it never saw the sun. He was wearing black gloves and holding a pistol.

The girl stood up against the wall, frozen, her eyes wide open. The tanned man held her by the throat. She was wearing a camel coat that fell away from a rose-flowered blouse and a blue skirt. He shoved his hand under her skirt and touched her. 'You like that, huh? 'Cause that's the last good thing you're going to feel.'

She tried to twist her body away but he just gripped her harder as she struggled and tried to scream. He nodded his head and the man with the black gloves, in one silent movement, walked over, put the pistol to the side of her head and pulled the trigger. Blood splashed the wall of the barn and the crack of the shot sent the crows and jays into chaos. The tanned face relaxed his grip. The woman slumped to the ground.

The two men looked at her for a second then turned to the van, got in, and quickly drove away. The scattered birds gradually stopped their calls and began to settle down. The wind was all that could be heard. The dog walked slowly over to the girl and sniffed her gently, and then, one leg at a time, stretched out next to her and rested his face by hers. She was looking at him. But she could not see.

*   *   *   *   *

14

The next day, Wednesday, Eiger was sitting in Flo's, at the bar, having lunch, swirling the Johnny Walker Black around in his glass, staring at the TV screen. He hated TV screens in bars. If he wanted to watch TV he'd stay at home and figured everybody else should too. But the place was empty, he had no one to talk to, Diana was late and the news was on, so he watched.

Peter looked over at the TV as a weather girl, who had more curves than the weather map she was pointing to, babbled on excitedly about a late season snowstorm in the States. Eiger was watching the girl and didn't hear much of what she said. A picture of farmland flashed on the screen as she talked about some local flooding. Peter turned his head to Eiger,

"Johnny, did you hear about that girl they found this morning on that farm up near Bradford? Whoever killed her is gonna need a lawyer. Maybe it'll be you."

Eiger looked at the screen. "Yeh, heard something in the car. Shot? Maybe. Who was she?"

"I don't know. Young they said. Maybe nineteen or twenty or so. Marina, or something. Can't remember."

Eiger put down his glass. "Marina?"

"That's what I think it was, yeh."

Eiger opened his phone and called the office. "Conway,

you heard about this girl being shot up north? News reports say her name's Marina. Any connection with the Moore girl?"

"Uh-huh, uh-huh. Ok, look, I was waiting for Diana but we should meet and talk. Uh-huh, ok, sure, I'll be here." And he closed his phone.

"What's up? You know this girl?"

"Maybe. Not sure. Did they give a description or a photo?"

"I don't know. Wasn't really paying attention. Just said she was young."

Eiger stared at the mirror behind the bar and watched as he put the glass to his lips, then put it down and saw the faces of the girls in Arusha, Rose, Janet, Comfort, Nehema, all of them dead. Their voices had chattered in the night, happy, laughing, teasing each other, as if they didn't have a care in the world. But they each had the same care, the daily hunt for a man that night for some money so they could eat, instead of starve, in a town without mercy or jobs or hope. The hopelessness had killed them, one by one. Eiger looked at his face in the mirror mixed in with theirs and wondered how long it would be before it got him.

~

Conway walked into Budnick's office and shut the door. He sat down and adjusted his jacket. Budnick stopped eating a sandwich and wiped his hands on an old napkin.

Conway asked, "You heard about this girl shot up in Bradford? Johnny thinks it's Marina. Any word from Moore about his girl, anything more on the news?"

Budnick nodded. "Yeh, when I heard the news on the radio I put a call into the jail to get him to call you but I doubt they passed it to him. Never do. We'll have to go to see him. He hasn't called you yet?"

"No, so maybe it's a different girl."

Budnick nodded but his lips were turned down more than usual and his shoulder twitched a little. He picked up the phone. "Susan, anymore on the news about this girl they found this morning? Uh-huh, ok, let me know."

"Well, we don't know. But I don't like it."

Conway rubbed his jaw with his right hand slowly, "Yeh, nor me. Johnny's having a liquid lunch at Flo's. Said I'd go over and meet him and we could both go down to see Moore together."

"Good idea, maybe I'll go with you. But I have to get going on this civil action. We're filing the claim today against Crixos Pharmaceutical. Asking ten million in damages."

"I still think you're crazy. You're going to end up broke after this I tell you."

"You know the problem with you is your too cautious. This drug has problems. They don't know we don't have what the big firms have. They'll assume we have the same ammo they got in the States. They'll settle in short order and we my friend, will make a tidy sum."

Conway just shook his head. "Well, we shall see. I better get going before Johnny gets gone," and he walked out. He put on his coat and as he walked past Susan said to her, "Going to meet Johnny at Flo's then we're going to see Moore at the Don. Give us a call if anything comes up about this girl."

"You got it." She made a mock salute and winked.

~

When Conway walked into Flo's, Diana was sitting at the bar with Eiger. Both were sitting silent, staring at the TV screen. Both of them looked tense. He walked up behind them and put his hands on their shoulders, "So, what's up, you two fighting or something?"

Diana flinched at his touch but relaxed when she heard his voice and turned to him, "Or something is the phrase. I guess you two want to talk. No point in me staying." She started to put things back in her purse.

Conway touched her hand with his and held it until she looked at him, smiled, then sat back down on her stool. He sat next to her.

He turned to Eiger. "Any news?"

"Nothing new yet on the girl but it's her I just know it." He touched Diana on the arm just so Conway could see he did it. Conway smiled and ordered a glass of wine as Diana watched them both and smiled at the desire of the one and the jealousy of the other.

Diana sat up straight between them, called to Peter for another drink, then looked up to the TV screen, "Johnny tells me this is the girl that came to the office?"

Eiger looked up at the screen too. "Tell me I'm wrong." Conway looked up and nodded. "Can't do that. Not sure yet but I also have a bad feeling it's one and the same. So what do we do about it? We're now witnesses to a murder."

Diana turned her face sharply to his and looked hard at his eyes. "What do you mean?"

Conway turned to her and met her gaze. "She was killed because she came to us. We know a reason for the cops accusing Moore, to protect themselves. The trouble is we can't call the police because the killers are the police. So we have to go to the Special Investigations Unit, and hope we can trust them. Or...."

"Or what exactly?" Eiger clenched his teeth and stared down at the bar. "She was an angel, Marina. But you don't explain why Frank was killed so you don't know very much. If you know that you'll know the reason Marina is dead."

Conway took a sip of his drink, "We have to talk it over with Budnick. He knows everybody. If this is a couple of bad cops then we can deal with it but if it's something bigger then we don't know what we're dealing with or who, then we need contacts at the minister's level."

Eiger began laughing quietly to himself, "You know, I really have to congratulate myself, here I was thinking I had found a safe haven from bullshit and death threats, from government agents, and all the while I've crawled into a world filled with every type of crime and corruption. Is there no escape?"

Diana said, "You want to spend the rest of the afternoon discussing philosophy and escapist dreams."

Conway became grim and replied, "That's the problem. Everyone's trying to escape from reality when we should be trying to change it."

Conway's mobile buzzed. He took it out of his pocket and put it to his ear, closing his eyes as he listened.

"It's Budnick. Tommy Moore got a call through from the Don. It's his Marina all right. The police went to see him and showed him the photographs." He turned back to the phone, "Uh huh. Yeh, ok, sure, we'll be there. Right. Ok." He closed the phone. "Budnick wants to meet at the office. Things are getting out of hand."

Eiger waved his hand to Peter, "Tab, we gotta get going."

Diana shuddered, "Johnny, maybe the African case is safer, I don't see how this situation is going to be better for you and, sorry Conway, but the money has stopped coming and," turning to Eiger, "Well, how are you going to live."

Eiger nodded his head, "Yeh, I didn't really bargain for this."

Conway pulled some cash out of his wallet and put it on

the bar. "Well, there is a difference. First of all the CIA isn't threatening to kill us, it's just a couple of crooked cops likely working on their own for what we don't know yet, but the state isn't on our back and there are still laws here. Not like that crap at the tribunal."

Diana sighed, "I don't know how you guys put up with this. Ever think about teaching or something?"

"Ah, but where would the excitement be?"

The three of them stood up and put on their coats, said good-bye to Peter and walked out into the cold rain of a March day. It was raining so hard that it was difficult to see in front of them and they held on to each other as they walked to the parking lot and their cars.

~

Tommy Moore paced up and down his cell, muttering to himself. Jackson Johnson, a thin black man about 30 with a thin moustache, and a record for break and enters, lay on his bunk watching Moore and the background parade of prisoners passing back and forth on the range.

"I heard that's your girl on the TV."

Tommy glared at him and stood still. "And?"

"Nothing, just wanted to say I'm sorry to hear it, man. Pretty bad to do that."

"You working for the cops? What's your problem, was I talking to you?"

"Hey man, cool it. I meant nothing by it. I hate the cops."

"That makes two of us. And they're going to pay for this. I guarantee it."

"Yeh, well they got you in here, my friend. I'd be worried if I was you," and went back to watching the parade.

Moore glared at him then walked up to the bars of the cell and gripped them hard with both hands. He knew Johnson was right and beads of sweat began to appear on his face and neck.

~

Susan was typing a letter when Budnick came out of his office and asked her if she had seen the Zukov file. She handed it to him and turned away but then turned back, "What's going on with the Moore girl?"

"I don't know. Conway knows more than I do. It's his case. But I think we have to go and see Moore together. This file smells. He and Eiger are coming back to the office soon. If we get time we can try to visit Moore this afternoon or this evening. Conway mentioned going to the Mayor's office and chief of police but the system's as crooked as they come and everyone's in everyone's pocket. I don't think we can trust any of them."

"So what can we do? They can't just murder people like that. They could do it to anybody."

Budnick nodded and took a breath, "No law any more. No rules. Anything goes."

The office door opened suddenly and the shadow of a man swept over the carpet as he walked into the office and extended his hand.

"Hello, you must be Mr. Budnick. I'm Professor Bloch. I met with Mr. Conway a few days ago about my problem at the university and I was just wondering if I could talk to him or you about it. Something has happened that I..." He looked down at the floor as if he was looking for the words to continue but he didn't find them. He looked up at Budnick and Susan and seemed puzzled.

Budnick stretched out his arm and took him by the

shoulder and invited him into his office, "Come on in Professor and tell me what's bothering you. Susan, can you get the professor a coffee?"

"Tea, please, I would prefer it, thank you."

Susan smiled, "Certainly, black or green?"

"Jasmine would be very pleasant."

She smiled again and walked away. Budnick sat down behind his desk. Professor Bloch sat down in an armchair facing a bookcase lined with books on law and history. He was wearing a long coat and a suit and tie. He looked even more distinguished without his wife present. More sure of himself. He looked at Budnick who was clearing some papers to one side so he could lean his elbows on the desk. When he saw he had finished and was settled in to listen said,

"Yesterday I was visited by two men who said they were from the Committee of Public Safety. They said they wanted to talk to me about my views on the government's position in the war. They were very nice, very polite really but it was clear they were trying to intimidate me just by their presence. They left after about an hour and thanked me and that was it. But they were sent to give me a message and I don't like the message. I thought you should know about it."

Budnick replied with his usual "Uh-huh," then went quiet as Susan walked in with a tray with glasses and a grey Chinese teapot and two small grey porcelain cups and put them on Budnick's desk.

When she left Budnick poured a glass for Bloch and handed it to him and then poured himself one. 'He sat back in his chair.

"Did they leave a card?"

"No, they told me their names but frankly I didn't pay attention. The whole thing rattled me."

"Well, what is it they don't like about what you're

saying exactly?"

"That's just it, they didn't refer to any one thing they just asked me what my views were and I told him the same thing I tell my students-that the war is illegal and immoral and against the interests of the citizens. It was clear. There wasn't one thing on their mind-it's my whole point of view."

Budnick nodded, "So they want to keep you quiet."

"They seem to prefer that yes, but they also asked me something curious about a former student of mine, Marina. They wanted to know what I knew about her."

"Marina? Marina Scozzi?"

"Yes, do you know her?"

"Just a little, the girlfriend of a client of ours."

"They told me she was murdered."

"That's right, her body was found this morning."

"That's very disturbing in many ways. She was a very sincere woman, sweet, very intelligent, pretty, very against the war. She was active with a small group of students against the war."

"She mentioned to us yesterday that she went to demos. She never mentioned you though. She have a boyfriend named Tommy?"

"Yes, she was involved with a man named Moore I believe, a rough character but that was her, always thinking she could save people and the world."

"She said to us that she was threatened by the local police. They think she can finger them for a murder they're putting on Tommy."

Bloch blinked his eyes and drew in his breath and pursed his lips.

Budnick continued, "So now we have two motives for her murder, one criminal, one political and they have to be connected. Mentioning her to you was a warning."

"But how can this be in a civilised country?"

"You're the professor, professor. You explain the state. All I can do is make it jump through hoops."

*   *   *   *   *

15

Conway and Eiger came in together while Bloch was still in with Budnick. Budnick heard their voices, excused himself and walked out to meet them.

"The professor is here. I think you should here this." He turned and they followed him into his office and shook hands with Bloch as Conway sat down and Eiger introduced himself, then leaned against a side credenza and put his hands in his pockets.

Budnick tossed his head towards Bloch and pointed his finger to emphasise what he was about to say.

"Dr. Bloch just told me the Committee came to visit him. Looks like they were trying to shake him up a little bit, keep him quiet. But he told me something else interesting, that Marina Scozzi was a student of his and politically active, same as the professor. They mentioned her. Asked what he knew about her. But they already knew all that. It was a message-it could happen to you. And he knows Moore."

Bloch looked at Budnick as he talked and then turned to Eiger and Conway and raised his hands as if in supplication. "Why would they do such a thing? I find it difficult to believe that the government would murder a young student just to frighten me. I can't think her death is connected to my situation."

Conway answered, "This is not exactly the government. This is the Committee. No, they didn't kill her for that. Whoever killed her wanted her quiet permanently, and likely it is connected to this murder Moore is accused of. But they decided to use her death to get at you. They must know something about the cops being involved in the Moore case. There has to be a connection between the cops, and Moore and this girl that we don't know yet."

Eiger nodded, "Walter, we need your investigator to start looking around. And we have go and see Moore. He's holding something back."

He moved away from the credenza, balancing on the balls of his feet like a fighter springing into action. "Well let's go. The suspense is getting to me."

Budnick nodded his head while looking at the professor who was looking from him to Eiger and Conway and back to Budnick again who reached into his pocket and began playing with some coins.

"Dr. Bloch, stay in touch, let me know immediately if anyone contacts you about anything, don't answer anybody's questions anymore, tell them to speak to your lawyer. Think about any connection between Marina, and you and Moore or anybody else. I don't know what I'm saying you should look for but anything could be important."

Bloch nodded, slowly stood up, put out his hand to Budnick, expressed his thanks and then turned to leave. Conway took him towards the door. Susan smiled at him and said, "Nice to see you again. Say hello to your wife."

Bloch nodded, bowed almost imperceptibly, smiled and said, "I will, thank you, good-bye."

Later that day the three of them drove in Budnick's van through the still heavy rain along the grey, dingy Toronto streets and signed in at the Don. They were escorted up to Moore's range and put into an interview room. There were only three plastic chairs around the small table so Eiger stood waiting for Moore to be brought in.

Conway looked up at the light fixture, "Think they have one in there?"

Budnick looked up from where he was sitting with his arms crossed and chuckled, "Oh yeh, I don't know. Maybe."

Eiger looked around the room and shook his head. "I don't think so. It's a matter of chance which room we get and they can't listen to everything despite what everyone says. But then again, you just never know."

Just then, there was the loud sound of a clanging door and a heavy electric buzz and loud voices, of prisoners shouting to each other or at each other, guards telling them to shut up. Then the door clanged again, the buzz stopped and Moore walked into the room in front of a guard who pointed him to a chair, then left.

Moore looked more tired than Conway remembered him. There were dark circles under his eyes and he looked stressed out and older. He sat in his chair quietly, looking at each one of them slowly, then he leaned back in his chair, looked at Conway and asked "So, what's up, counsel and who are these guys?"

Conway introduced every one. Moore was pleased to see Budnick "Yeh, heard some good things about you too counsel."

Budnick smiled tightly then Moore looked over at Eiger for a few seconds, then turned back to Conway. "So, where do we begin?"

Budnick took control. "When and where did you meet Marina Scozzi?"

Moore stared back at him, looked down at the table for a second then straightened up.

"In a bar one night. Over on College. One of those upscale places. Went to meet a couple of guys I know, just for a beer, see if I could pick something up. You know. Anyway, Marina comes in with a group of people, all young and they sit down at a table near us. I noticed her right off. I saw her look over at me a couple of times while she was talking to her friends, so I'm not shy, I caught the drift of what they were saying, something about the situation in the country and what to do about it, politics, economics, that sort of thing, so at the right point I put myself in the conversation and said I agreed with what they were saying and how we're all getting screwed and her eyes lit up. So I knew, that was it. That was about a year ago."

"Uh-huh, and so, how did it develop?" Budnick's left shoulder twitched a little and he hunched over the table leaning towards Moore.

"Ok, so I found out they were students at the university, belonged to a protest group, Rebel Youth or something, and most of the conversation was about the wars the corporate boys had dragged us into and what to do about it. I'm a fighter but I'm no dummy. I follow the news. But I hadn't heard what they were saying before. And she was one pissed off girl. Really angry about it all. So I left my buddies and joined her group at their table and got into it. There were a couple of guys there and about three other girls. But they seemed to be with these guys. So we talked, she and I. She asked me what I did. Told her I used to be a boxer but now I'm just trying to figure out what to do next. Told her about the problems I had. She was real nice. Paid attention. Made me feel like she was really interested. I think the boxer thing got her going a bit. Some women like that."

Budnick nodded, "Did she ever talk about any of her teachers or classes?"

"Not too much but there was one guy she did tell me about, someone who spoke out against the situation and the university's laying down for it and letting it happen. Said it was like the Germans when the Nazis took over. Forget his name, something like Blake or....."

Conway said, "Right, like Bloch?"

Moore tightened his eyes and looked into the distance, "Yeh, that rings a bell."

Budnick tightened his lips again, "This guy who was shot. You say by the police. Who was he and really, no bullshit."

"I'm not sure I like the tone Mr. Budnick. I told Conway all about that. You calling me a liar 'cause we can part company right here."

Budnick held his ground and his stocky body solidified in the chair. "I'm not calling you a liar but we have to know what is going on. You're in prison, Marina is dead, we're all now involved as witnesses and we have the Committee involved as well. So we need to know more than you are telling. This guy was shot for a reason. What's the reason? Why did the cops threaten Marina-they could have left her alone-they didn't need her to get you. But they brought her into it or was she already in it. You see there are other things going on connected to this. That teacher she talked about, he's in trouble too. Did you ever meet him?"

'Yeh, Marina got me to a few demonstrations. Not my thing really, but I went. That professor spoke to the crowd a few times and she introduced me. Hadn't met a guy like that before. Pretty tough for a book lover."

"This guy who was shot, what was he into? No, let me ask you this, you can't box anymore, you have no job I know about, so how have you been surviving the past couple of years?"

Moore went quiet and looked at all of them. "Look I told you I don't like talking in these rooms and....."

Budnick interjected, "Well, we can't use notes. That's impossible. You're just going to have risk it and talk."

Moore, "Look Mr. Budnick, no disrespect or nothing but you guys don't know what you're dealing with 'cause I don't. They've got no evidence against me, they can't prove a thing, so you can get me out of this with what you know

now."

Conway shook his head, "You're cooked if the cops stick to their story. You expect us to break them down on cross-examination. Maybe we can, but maybe we can't and we can't do that unless we have something to work with so, what's going on?"

"Look I really don't know. This guy they shot, Frank, used to be in the army. Signals or something like that. Technical stuff. Computers and shit. I met him at a gym around the same time I met Marina. Got to talking. Interesting guy. Said he was in some special unit and was in all sorts of places. Not a bad boxer. So we started to hang out. He introduced me to some other guys, all ex-army, cops, tough guys, all of them. Some of them knew my name, 'cause of the boxing. Asked me if I had done any security work before. Which I had, you know, a lot of boxers have to survive being bouncers and shit, so I'd done that. But they wanted to know if I had done any personal body guard stuff or taking care of people."

Budnick nodded, "Had you?"

"A couple of times yeh, I had some work for some corporate clients who were in town for meetings and stuff, mainly from the States. Anyway, I hung out with these guys and I got some work through them and then one night we went to the airport and met two men. I don't know who they were. I was just told they were businessmen who needed protection. We took them to a hotel downtown and watched their backs for a few days then they left."

"Where were they from?"

"Figured they were Americans, but I don't know-they spoke good English, for Americans."

Conway put his arms back on the chair in an open question. "And so what's this got to do with anything?"

"Because while we watched their backs, they met with people. Including Frank. They went to see him at his place and had a meeting. They were there for a couple of hours and it seemed intense, you know, a lot of heat in the air. Me and the other guys outside wondered what they were doing and who they were. But, we never found out much. Everyone was tight. That's all I know."

"When was this?"

"About a month before Frank was shot."

Conway rocked back on his chair, "And Frank never told you anything?"

"I asked, but he wasn't talking. Told me it was nothing. Not worth talking about. But he smoked a lot more after that, weed that is, was pretty hyper. Paced up and down a lot, wasn't really a drinker but began drinking a lot of tequila and wine."

"So what is it we don't wanna know as you put it?"

"Look, the only thing Frank told me was that he had to finish some computer work for them and he was late and they were pressing him. He never said anything directly, but people drop clues when they can't talk and he kept dropping words like secret files and secret services, secret this and secret that. Sometimes when he drank a bottle of wine he'd tell me he wished he had never been in the army, they wouldn't leave him alone. So I got to thinking he was connected to spooks and the government in some way, and then he ends up dead and I'm fingered to take the fall, so the only people that can make that work –well who else can do that? So, I'm just saying, I appreciate the help, but watch your backs."

Budnick thought for a minute or so, "Did Frank have a girlfriend, anybody we can talk to?"

"Off and on. No one whose name I can remember. But he knew Marina. He came to a few demos with us. He was real gung-ho on the anti-war stuff. Said war was all bullshit."

Eiger, standing against one wall, looked at the other two and raised his eyebrows, then shifted his feet back and faced Moore, "So Frank knew this Professor Bloch and Marina?"

"Yeh, that's right. But so what, they're just college people. They killed Marina cause of me."

Eiger continued, "Are you so sure? There wasn't some other reason? Why is Frank dead in the first place?" He tensed up in frustration, then caught himself and consciously relaxed. "Anyway, what did the cops tell you?"

"Two of them came, homicide squad, same two that arrested me. Asked me if I knew Marina and showed me photos of her body. It was her. No sympathy from them. Cold as ice those two. Then they asked me if I knew why she was killed. I didn't answer them —just said 'You tell me'. They didn't like that. Then the lead guy, the heavy, he said that if I didn't get rid of you guys as my lawyers they were going to make sure I never came back on the street. I told them to go fuck themselves. They left."

Budnick stood up, "Marko and friend again. Ok, well, we're running blind here. Marina was your alibi and now she's dead. Her prof's being leaned on. Now they want us out of the picture. Think harder. We'll be back in a few days. Have to do some digging. Those cops will be back. Stay cool. Think about Marina and Frank. They have to be connected more than you're saying."

Moore angered a bit at the suggestion but controlled himself. "Don't worry Mr. Budnick, I can stay cool but Marina was very cool, man, very cool. They shouldn't have done that too her. Fucking worse than animals. But don't worry Mr. Budnick, I'll stay cool."

As they were driving back to the office through the rain drenched streets and listening to the wipers move across the windshield, Eiger's mobile buzzed. He took it out of his jacket pocket. "It's that guy Rice. Asking to meet again. Wants to meet tomorrow downtown."

Conway sitting in the front seat next to Budnick, looked back at him, "That's pretty strange. We leave the prison and then you get a message from those spooks."

Budnick laughed, "What next? I told you the Aldarizine case is better, no cloak and dagger and lots of money." He beeped the horn at a truck that overtook them fast and covered the windshield in water. "Now they're trying to drown us for god sake. No goddam courtesy anymore." He shook his fist as the truck disappeared into the rain.

~

Susan picked up the phone on the second ring. "Hi, Diana, no they're not back yet. Ok, I'll get him to call. Ok, take care."

Diana put down her mobile phone on the table next to a glass of red wine. She was drifting from one image to another, in a kaleidoscopic fog. She wanted a cigarette but wasn't going out in the rain to smoke one. She was on her second glass when Eiger called.

"Yes, took the day off, wanted to paint, told the boss I was sick. But couldn't do anything. You weren't around so I came to Flo's, yeh a couple of hours ago, Drunk too much. Came to have some wine, think about the world, just float in the moment. Yeh, get some sense of being with you."

She smiled, laughed lightly and tossed her head. Her hair fell over her eyes. "Tonight? Yeh, ok, your place or...ok, your place. Where are you now? Uh-huh. Ok. Ok you too." She closed the phone and sat back in the booth and sipped on her wine.

As she did, a tall man walked in through the front door. He was wearing a long grey coat, had a strong face and dark curly hair. He was older than thirty-five but still young.

He walked over to the bar, ordered a glass of wine and

129

then took it to a table near her booth. He sat just a few feet from her. She watched him as he put the glass down, took off his coat and sat, as if it were a performance for her. She kept looking at him, partly out of curiosity, and partly because she thought he was attractive. He looked intelligent and sophisticated. She was taken by surprise when he locked his eyes on hers in return, leisurely drank from his glass and then, his eyes still fixed on hers, said, "Hello, Diana, may I talk to you?"

She put her glass down, a bit taken aback by the bold approach but tried to act as nonchalant as he was and asked him, "How do you know my name?"

"If we can talk I can tell you."

*   *   *   *   *

16

"That depends on who's doing the talking."

"I'll take that as an invitation," and he stood up and carried his glass of wine over to her booth, sat down opposite to her, and, while smoothing his hair and adjusting his jacket, said,

"My name is not important."

She looked at him closely and realised this wasn't a pick-up. She felt he was examining her like a specimen under a microscope instead of a woman. She leaned back against the booth to distance herself, looked him over again and replied, "I think it's important. Who are you, and what do you want with me? Are you a policeman?"

"A type of policeman I suppose."

"Then I don't understand why you're sitting here talking to me."

"Let's say we require information and you might be able to give it to us."

"What information? And who is we?"

"Information about Eiger and the lawyers he has decided to work with and what they know about the Moore case."

"Who are you?"

"Really, you don't need to know that or who I represent but you can call me Agius, that will be sufficient. I'll be direct. Your life is, shall we say, stalled. You're thirty-six, you have no real career, and your artistic talent is not supported by sufficient ambition to succeed. Johnny will leave you for a more exiting woman one day, perhaps Susan..."

Diana turned red and glared at him. He raised the palm of his hand from the table in supplication and said, "Calm down. I'm only telling you how things are, as a friend. Things can get better. We can help you in that direction, or things can get worse. It's your choice." He leaned forward further into the light. His square jaw was relaxed. His eyes were hypnotic.

She tried to control her anger and picked up her wine glass to steady her hands then asked, "What do you want?"

"We're looking for something. It's a computer memory stick, a USB device, a disk. It's difficult to speak English these days when there is no common vocabulary." He smiled, "But I'm digressing. This device, shall we say, is something we think will turn up in connection with the Moore case. If it does and we think it will, we want you to tell us and help us obtain it."

"How am I supposed to know what they have and what they don't have?"

"You can find ways I'm sure, either from Conway or Johnny. It doesn't matter to us. But time is of the essence. We can't wait too long."

"How do you know I'll do anything for you?"

Agius leaned even further forward until his face almost touched hers. "Because we know you, Miss Larsen. If you can get us the information then we can arrange for you to live in Italy comfortably for a couple of years while you paint. I think you like Florence a lot. Or so we are

132

informed."

"I'm not in anyone's pay and I won't betray Johnny, so forget it."

Agius shook his head, smiled slightly and touched her hand, "I don't think there is much point pretending to be moral. You are more flexible than you make out. Do I really need to make threats to obtain your cooperation, against you, against Eiger, against Conway? Eiger has already been threatened, by an associated interest shall we say. He's told everyone all about it so if something happens to him, no one will be surprised. We have something planned for him. But if you cooperate perhaps we can hold off on those plans. But I am sure you find this very distasteful, as do I. Threats are hardly necessary if we can agree to work together. But let me leave you with that request. We need an answer soon. Think it over, but it wouldn't be wise to think too long." He flashed a quick tense smile, then drained his wine glass as he watched her reaction, his eyes looking at her over the edge of the rim.

She sat quietly as he finished with his wine, pulled his wallet from his jacket, left some money on the table, then slowly stood up to leave. He put on his coat, bowed slightly, and gently said "Good-bye, Diana. We shall be in touch."

Diana sat up, "Wait, how am I supposed to get in touch with you I....Who's we?"

Agius turned back to her over his shoulder, "Don't worry about that. We know how to contact you. We? The Committee. You don't need to worry about that. Have a nice day, Miss Larsen and a word of advice. It wouldn't be wise to tell Johnny and his friends about our meeting today. Until we meet again." He smiled at her, then turned and walked past the bar and out onto the street leaving Diana stranded in confusion, anger and a deepening well of fear.

~

Susan woke up on Thursday with a hang over. She stretched out her body on the bed, trying to gather some energy to get up and make coffee. She slept with the window open and already, at 7am the noise of men shouting from the construction site opposite her building could be heard punctuating the noise of traffic. She moaned as she stiffly got to her feet and found a long white robe where she had dropped it on the floor.

She put it on and walked into the small corridor that led to the bathroom to the left and the living room and kitchen to the right. As she passed the entrance door she peered through the peephole, then went to make some coffee. She looked out the windows as she put the beans in the grinder. The still grey sky was scarred by scattered bands of drizzle that promised more of the same. It made her shiver and draw her robe more tightly around her.

There had been a cold rain most of the night but she hadn't heard it. She had drunk herself into an altered state of reality and when she finally slept she had dreamed of a woman's lips brushing slowly along her legs to nuzzle into her, until the lips changed into Eiger standing in front of her, naked, as she melted her mouth on the beauty and the strength of him.

She pulled a pack of cigarettes from a kitchen drawer and picked up a silver lighter. She bent her head as she put the flame to the cigarette and lit it. She blinked when the smoke came up, then inhaled deeply and closed her eyes as she let her head fall back. Her hair fell away from her, and she looked, for a second of eternity, like the Ecstasy of Sister Theresa with smoke rising gently from her mouth like an exhalation of her soul.

She stood up and slouched out to the balcony. Her apartment was on the eighteenth floor and the air was cold. She pulled her robe more tightly around her and leaned over the railing to look down. There were people in the park in front of the building and a few already walking down the path towards the subway station a block away. The main street to the left was already busy with traffic and the construction crew was taking a coffee break.

They saw her, waved and whistled. She waved back, smiled and modeled herself, just a slide of the robe up her thigh. Just a flash, that's all she gave them and then laughed. They shouted and saluted her while she dragged on her cigarette then waved to them again and turned back into the apartment to get her cup of coffee.

She was pulling down her skirt and checking herself in the bathroom mirror when the phone rang. She walked slowly over to the small side table where it sat impatiently as it continued to ring, reached down, and picked it up, cradling it with both hands.

"Hello, oh hi Johnny. Yes, good morning." She giggled like a schoolgirl, "Yes, you caught me by surprise. I was just leaving for the office."

She giggled again at something he said,

"That's funny, but what's up? You're sort of my boss, so is this business or something else? Uh-huh," she laughed again, "maybe I wouldn't mind. You have to try me. Ok, but..." she dropped her voice and became quiet, "So meet you where exactly...yes, I know it. Ok, I'll make sure I've got a notebook, yes and a pencil." Her voice dropped to a lower octave as she continued with a questioning edge, "Ok, half an hour, right. I'll be there. Tell you about a dream I had. Yep, you were in it. Maybe later." She tried to laugh again but stifled it before it could happen and hung up.

Thirty minutes later she walked into the Mad Hatter café off Queen Street and looked around at the booths and tables in the dimly lit interior, all dark wood and low lighting. She saw a hand wave in the back corner and walked along the long row of tables to the furthest booth from the door. Eiger stood up just before she got to him, embraced her, kissed her on the cheeks and stood back to look at her, smiling.

"Here, sit down. Order some breakfast if you want. We're going to be here for a while." He waited as she took off her coat and sat down opposite him. The single waitress came over, gave her a menu, said, "I'll be back," and flashed Susan a smile. As soon as the waitress left, Susan asked, "And so.....?"

Eiger leaned towards her across the table, "So the drill is this. Yesterday Rice called me and asked to meet. We agreed on 10am here. I talked to Budnick last night about it and anyway, the short of it is he and Conway thought it would be wise to have someone try to take a shot of him with a cell but not so he notices. That's your job. We hope the investigator can use it to get more of the lowdown on this guy."

She nodded. "So just act natural and I don't know you from Adam. Ok. Got it. Well then, I need some coffee and thanks, but I had breakfast at home ..."

"Which was what... a smoke, coffee and wine?"

"You must think nasty things about me, wow, ok, but you're right about the first two, the wine was last night."

He called the waitress over and ordered coffee for both of them and bacon and eggs for her against her transparent resistance. "Over easy."

"How'd you know I liked 'em over easy?"

"Cause that's how I like 'em and we're sort of in sync." He grinned and watched with satisfaction the shy aversion of her eyes and the blush of her cheeks.

The waitress brought a cup and a pot of coffee and poured some in his half-empty cup and her empty one then retreated back to the kitchen where she was heard repeating the order twice. A second later, she stuck her head back through the swinging door and called to them, "Say I forgot to ask, you want home fries with that or....?"

Susan swung her head towards her, noticed her breasts through the white blouse, and her page boy hair, "Thanks, sweetie." She fixed her eyes on her as the girl went back into the kitchen.

She turned her head back and caught Eiger looking at her curiously, his eyes questioning, his mouth indicating amusement. She felt herself blush again and looked down and then back at him, put both her hands on the table leaned forward and said, "There is something you would like to say?"

"What can I say, just not sure who the competition is."

"Does that matter so long as you win?"

Eiger laughed, "I guess not."

Susan looked at her watch, "I better move to another table, it's getting near time. What if he arrives early?"

He agreed and helped her to change to a table two booths up on the opposite side of the aisle sitting facing his booth. He returned to his seat but this time facing the wall so Rice would have to sit opposite him and in view of Susan. A few minutes later the waitress came over and brought a plate with her eggs and bacon, "Sorry, is he joining you, you didn't like that table....?"

"No, no, just he's got a meeting with someone. I thought I'd wait and leave him be."

The waitress looked over at Eiger and then back at Susan, "I'd wait for him honey, he's cute."

Susan smiled and threw out, "But so are you..." and looked up at eyes which held hers briefly and then fluttered in confusion, "Your boyfriend must be a looker too."

The waitress laughed, "Yeh, he is." She turned to go but hesitated for a moment and said quietly, "but sometimes something else is needed..." Her eyes sparkled as she looked over her shoulder. "If there's anything else you need, just let me know," and she flounced back through the swinging door into the kitchen.

Susan took a deep breath, picked up her knife and fork and began to pick at the food in front of her, occasionally glancing down the aisle to look at Eiger, who pretended to be reading a newspaper he had taken from the rack near the bar.

She was just putting a home fry in her mouth when a tall, well-built man with dark hair, and an angular face, walked purposefully past her table towards Eiger. She could only catch the side of his face as he passed her. He looked to be about forty, pleasant looking but there was something edgy about him. There was a hard tension in the jaw. He reminded her of a photo she had once seen of Samuel Becket. All cheek bones and shadows. She watched as only a woman can watch something while pretending to be looking at something else. She took her cell phone out of her pocket and made sure the flash was off. There was enough daylight coming in now the sun had broken through the clouds. The snowflakes had stopped falling and melting on the pavement. She put the phone near her plate on the table and waited.

Rice and Eiger shook hands. The waitress came over to them and left to get Rice some coffee. Eiger waited until she had disappeared down the aisle before speaking.

"I called the number in Switzerland and I spoke to someone but he didn't seem to know too much or wasn't willing to talk on the phone. I don't like to work like this. If someone wants me they have to be upfront about it. You understand me."

Rice listened, "Yes, I understand you."

"I have to tell you directly that your friend David has intelligence written all over him so what's really going on here?"

Rice took a breath and his face reddened a little, "David, intelligence, not that I know of, ..." but he evaded Eiger's eyes and looked away for a second. "Why do you think so?"

"He's worked with Italian and German government funded aid organisation's in Africa, then Tajikistan, then he was with the US forces in Afghanistan as an intelligence officer, now he's in west Africa doing I don't know what and everywhere he goes you tell me he becomes friends with these big people and wants to help them. So, is he doing this because he likes the guy or because he has orders, and why me?"

"Your research is thorough."

"It's not difficult."

"And what about me, you think I'm intelligence as well."

"I have no idea. What else can I think?"

"Well, whatever his position is, I think David is more interested in the money, same as me."

"That doesn't answer my question."

"The only answer I can give you at this point is that the important thing is Mahmoudi. The money is a side issue for my superiors. They want something done and don't care how it's done. If we can make some money on the side, why shouldn't we? And it's his money. He stole it in the first place."

Eiger picked up his cup and looked down into the remaining coffee. He couldn't decipher what it meant.

"If this is serious I want a communication from Mahmoudi directly, a letter with his signature. I never use go-betweens. I still know nothing about the real objective."

Rice looked amused but a darkness quickly overcame his eyes, "You are a suspicious man. It makes it more difficult to work this way. But I can understand your concerns if I put myself where you are. Let's say we need someone able to do a political trial and make it look like a real fight. You're a strong lawyer and you're well known. No one fights like you do. His trial has to follow a certain scenario that ...well, there is no point in talking about it because you need direct contact. We all stand to gain by this. You make a lot of money and are involved with another big case, we make some money on the side and Mahmoudi is free at the end. What could be more simple"?

"What are you suggesting?"

Rice sipped on his coffee and then sat back against the booth.

"Mahmoudi and his family can't contact you directly. He can't get messages out without everything being read and his lawyers' phones are tapped. His family is in the same situation. But David has word from him that he wants you and he wants to see you. So you need to go to Tunis as soon as possible. They'll pay your flight and expenses of course."

"I'll only go if my legal assistant comes with me."

"Why?"

"Because I trust her."

Rice pursed his lips and frowned. "We prefer it was just you and I wanted to go with you."

"Why, you have no criminal experience."

"No, but I'm tired of what I'm doing and David wants me in the case."

"To watch over me?"

Rice smiled slightly, "Let's just say he trusts me."

"She's in or I'm out, it's that simple. If you're legit you'll say yes, if not well then what you're telling me is bullshit."

Rice bit his lip then put his tongue in his cheek as he said, "All right, let me approach it from another way. We hoped not to have to do this but it is necessary. Let's just say you were given a warning in Arusha. It will be carried out unless you help us with this matter. We need things done a particular way. It's imperative that you take the case alone."

Susan, still playing with her bacon and eggs tried to hear what they were saying but only caught a mumble of sounds. She moved her phone on the table sideways between two plates and while the two men were looking at each other, engaged in conversation, quickly aimed it low on the tabletop and took a shot, then reached for her cup of coffee at the same time as she put the phone back in her purse.

Eiger stiffened his back momentarily as she put it away and she realised something had frightened him. She called the waitress over and asked for some more coffee and a toasted Danish. While she was waiting for it she watched the bodies of the two men and the subtle movements of their arms and hands, their backs. She could only guess at the emotions playing out in Eiger's face, but she saw a ripple of anger pass through the face of Rice to be replaced a single beat later by a forced smile. Then he put his hand out and touched Eiger on the arm as if to calm him. But he didn't succeed.

"So you want me to fix a trial? Look, I don't even want to be talking with you. Find some body else." He sat up and began to reach for some money to pay his bill, but Rice kept his hand on his arm and applied a calm but firm pressure. Eiger stopped what he was doing.

"The legality or illegality of it is not an issue, neither is the morality of it. We want something done. You can do it. Mahmoudi will be charged by the ICC. You will be announced as his counsel. You will express your usual outrage at false accusations. You will cross-examine prosecution witnesses who are clearly fabricated and you will expose the case as the political trial it is. The judges will be forced to acquit. Mahmoudi goes home and waits until he is useful to us again. You will become more famous, be given a lot of money, and well, we don't mind taking a piece of the action on the side. The Committee doesn't need to know everything."

Eiger just looked at him as he took in what he was saying. "You're crazy if you think I am going to do anything like that. You can do what you want. I really don't care. But I told you I'm straight, no matter how much the money. The conversation is over."

He stood up quickly and put on his topcoat. Rice put out his hand but Eiger ignored it and turned to walk away. He walked past Susan without looking as Rice said firmly to Eiger's back,

"You have one week to agree, one week," and watched Eiger walk out the door and onto the street where he turned left and disappeared past the window.

Susan watched him pass out of view. She saw Rice looking at her as she turned her head back towards him. He kept looking at her and she thought there was a distant smile in the shadows of his face but it vanished as he stood up, put some money on the table and put on his coat.

She tried to look down as he came towards her table. But, just as he went past, her head went up and her eyes locked on his. She smiled in the friendly way one does who has accidentally met the gaze of another and doesn't want to give offence and then turned back to her coffee. She felt him hesitate, or perhaps time slowed down, as she drank from the cup and she had the impression he had stopped behind her and was still watching her. But when she got the nerve to look he was nowhere to be seen.

She took out her phone and touched the screen to pull up the photo. His image appeared. She zoomed in to get a better look. She jumped a little as the picture enlarged. He was looking right through her.

*   *   *   *   *

17

Budnick and Conway were sitting in Budnick's office drinking coffee while Budnick read some documents on the Aldarizine file. "You know, this could be really interesting but there's no reaction from the press release I sent out. Nothing."

Conway put his hands behind his head, leaned back and rocked his chair, "Then there's no point in having a press conference-no one will show up. I told you. This case won't go anywhere. This isn't the States. And we still have no evidence, no experts. So what do you have to say if the press came and asked you questions?"

Budnick grinned, "Just tell 'em the evidence is confidential. Don't want to tip off the big boys. Don't worry about it. I can handle it but you're right. No point in having a conference no one comes to. And I don't know, this whole thing with Moore and the professor and the girl and Eiger and whatever he's into, it's too bizarre even for me. Moore is hiding something. This guy who was murdered, Frank, has to have a direct connection with Marina and the professor."

Conway nodded. "Right, it doesn't add up. You heard anything from the university about his case?"

"No, just a standard letter from the CEO saying he was

going to refer it to his legal staff. So, looks like a fight. Here take a look." He handed him a letter on pale grey stationary.

Conway was reading it when Eiger and Susan came through the door. They walked in abruptly and threw off their coats quickly, without looking where they put them. They went straight to the coffee machine, poured out large cups and then joined the other two.

Conway was the first to speak, "So. What happened at this meeting? You two are a little intense."

Eiger invited Susan to sit down in one of the empty chairs, sat down next to her and then began to relate what happened at the meeting, what Rice had said, what he had said, the threats that underlay everything.

Susan added, "That guy Rice got pretty angry, I could see it on his face, but he tried to hide it. I'm sure he knew I was with Johnny. But I got his picture anyway."

Budnick took the phone and looked at the screen. "Here, Jack, take a look at this guy. What do you think?"

Conway took the phone and looked intently at the image on it.

"Well-dressed, expensive jacket, Italian I think, expensive tie, nice topcoat. Hair cut just so. Likes to look cool, aware of his image. Vain. Self-important. Used to getting his way. He's been around." He stroked his chin with his hand as he continued looking, then he turned and gave it back to Susan.

"What did you feel about him?"

Susan looked out the window and considered her thoughts for the length of a breath then replied, "He frightened me. He's a cobra. He can charm you but once he has you, death is certain."

Eiger smiled grimly, "Cobra is the word, but he's just a mouthpiece for the Committee. They're behind this."

Budnick looked grimmer. "No matter what he told you,

it's all bullshit -just to get you trapped. You go to Tunisia, you won't come back."

Susan looked from one to the other and then raised her hands and shrugged her shoulders, "Ok, so who's going to tell me about this Committee cause I'd like to know."

Budnick stood and began walking around. He stopped and looked at her. "The Committee For Public Safety. It's a committee set up under the anti-terrorist laws, supposedly to coordinate emergency responses to undefined situations. But it's been expanded into a secret police network with its own structure, and personnel of the worst kind. Its finances aren't reported through the usual Parliamentary committees. It's not even known who's on the Committee or who works for it."

Conway listened quietly and quietly replied, "We're seeing how it works."

The phone rang. Susan stood up and took the handset. "Hello. Budnick and Conway. Oh yes, just a moment, professor." She held the phone in her hands, "It's the professor. He wants to talk to either of you. Sounds excited." She handed the phone to Budnick.

"How are you Professor? Yes, uh huh, right, ok." His voice became more urgent as he spoke, "Yes, yes, I understand. Is campus security there yet? Ok, don't call anyone else until we get there. Give us an hour."

He hung up the phone and put his hands in his pockets. "Some one broke into the professor's office. Tore it apart. He doesn't know what to do. Come on, you two, no point in gathering dust, let's go."

Eiger and Conway gathered their coats and headed for the door while Budnick gave instructions to Susan. "Hold the fort and let us know if any interesting phone calls come in. Try to find out if there's any disclosure ready on Moore yet, and call Pierre, we're going to need him to do some detective work on this guy Frank. We'll call in when we get there."

Susan nodded and picked up the phone, "You want Pierre to meet you out there?"

"Should have thought. Yeh. Try him." Then he turned and walked out the door, his square frame looking like a wrestler entering the ring.

They took Budnick's van. This time Eiger sat up front. Conway sat behind him, looking out the window. They passed a police patrol car on University Avenue heading in the same direction. "Hey, don't go too fast, don't need to get stopped for a ticket. These guys are all over the place. Wonder if this one is going where we're going?"

Eiger looked over at the patrol car. Two men in black uniforms looked back at them, looking grim as they always did.

"Not a lot of humour on the police force from what I can see. In Africa they would smile and wave."

Budnick laughed, "You want them to smile at you? If they do, watch out."

The police car turned off onto an intersecting road and disappeared into the traffic. They all relaxed a little.

"Going off shift travelling that fast." Budnick turned the radio on. He pulled in a music station and began singing to himself as Rodrigues sang "I wonder, how many times you've been had, and I wonder, how many plans have gone bad, and I wonder, how many times you've had sex, and I wonder, do you know who'll be next..."

Conway said, "yeh now there's a guy who gives you hope for humanity."

Eiger began moving his head with the beat, "Never heard of him, but he's good. Where's he from?"

Conway shot back, "Detroit. There's still something good in that sorry city."

Eiger looked out the window at the clouds and the trees in the distance as they entered the university zone, "Some good bands in Tanzania too, but they never make money.

No one can buy the discs."

Budnick looked over at him, "So, Johnny, talking of Africa, you still haven't told us what this trial's all about." He riveted his eyes on him for a second and waited.

Eiger took in a breath. "Ok the short version is the general was in charge of the national police. They say his men massacred civilians all over the place and he killed people himself including a baby he supposedly shot in the head while it was laying in its mother's arms. You wouldn't believe the stories they made up. Real racist stuff. It's complete bullshit. Nothing you read about that war is true. The charges are invented, the witnesses scripted and the prosecutor and the judges are corrupt cowards and hacks. Totally in the pocket of the master."

"The way the media has it, it was real bad over there. So your guy didn't do anything?"

"No. If anyone saved people he did but he's in prison while General LeMaire is a hero here. He's the one that should be in prison, along with most of the government."

Budnick swiveled his eyes from the road again, "They say LeMaire tried to save people, that he was hamstrung."

Eiger shook his head and crossed his arms, "Yeh, I know what they say and I know what he really did, what he was ordered to do. That's why they made him into a hero. That's why they threatened me. The General knows everything. They think I know too."

Conway leaned forward in his seat, "What about the Americans?"

Eiger laughed again and shook his head as he listened, "They controlled the entire war. That's why they want to keep the General on ice and keep me quiet or eliminate us completely."

Conway went quiet, then asked, "So what was the objective?"

Budnick turned his head, "Money. It's always about

money, am I right, Johnny?"

Eiger nodded, "You got it. All about money."

Budnick stared ahead at the road, "So, how'd you learn all this, Johnny?"

"The trial."

Conway and Budnick both looked ahead at the road and said nothing. Conway finally said quietly, "Man was I fooled. I believed all the shit in the papers about that war."

Budnick snorted, "I never fell for that. Whatever they tell us is bullshit. You have to figure that was bullshit too. Say Eiger, what did the President have to say about his arrest?"

"I asked him that when I first met him, why he thought he'd been arrested. He laughed and said 'Because I'm a communist and because I told the Americans to go fuck themselves ' and then all the guards around us laughed too."

Budnick chuckled, "Man, you've had the life. Now it looks like we're in it too. Ah, what the hell, things were getting boring anyway," and he pressed down hard on the accelerator to emphasise his point. The van surged forward and a half hour later turned onto a winding road that meandered lazily through the university's main campus.

The campus was in the north end of the city, on a windswept plain that had once been farmland and before that a primeval forest. The buildings were poor imitations of Le Corbusier. They succeeded in the clean lines and the concrete but never achieved anything approaching the grace or the beauty. It's a soul-chilling place but somehow manages to attract distinguished scholars and students. Conway had gone to law school there and hated it. It was still under construction then and he recalled the large parts of it that were fields of mud or snow.

They pulled into the road that snaked through the campus to a parking lot, and waited while Budnick swore at having to get a ticket from an automatic machine he had not stopped close enough to be able to push the buttons. Finally parked, they walked from the van to a long, five story building, with a blue plaque on the door announcing, Philosophy Department, and went up three floors on the elevator to a long row of offices. They found the blue name card-Professor Bloch, and knocked. The door opened as the professor stepped back and invited them in with his right hand waving at the scene around him. "This is what they've done."

The room was torn apart. All the bookshelves had been emptied, the books thrown all over the floor. A tall filing cabinet had its draws upside down near the desk and the papers scattered. The desk draw was open, some of the contents strewn on the desk, some mixed up with the books. Even the carpet had been torn up.

Budnick looked around without saying anything then his shoulder twitched, "What were they looking for?"

Bloch sat down in a chair, "I'm sorry, gentlemen, please sit down. I'm not feeling very well at the moment."

They picked up overturned chairs then Conway and Budnick sat down. Eiger remained standing, poking around at the mess on the floor.

"Well they turned my computer on so they must have been looking at what I had on it but there is nothing that could be of interest to anyone. I think they might be after a memory device I have." He hesitated, "Perhaps I should have mentioned it before."

Bloch looked at them and then down at the floor, flexed his hands, then passed one hand over his face and blinked. "You asked me about that girl, Marina. I didn't tell you everything. I'm sorry, but I wasn't sure who could be trusted. I'm still not sure. But this..." and he looked around, "convinces me that what you said, that her death and my situation are connected, must be correct."

Budnick looked over at Conway and Eiger who stood perfectly still, looking down at Bloch who struggled to speak. His mouth was moving but nothing was coming out. Finally, he bit his lip and began talking,

"I'm part of an antiwar group here at the university. Nothing very special. A few professors, some graduate students and a number of younger students. We meet regularly and talk about what's happening, government policy, how we can protest against it, what we can write in professional journals, what other anti-war or peace groups are doing, that sort of thing. Things we all did as students in the sixties, anyway everyone I knew then..." His eyes squinted as he looked at their faces one by one to make sure they were listening to him, and then he looked down, as if looking into a deep well, and they kept still, looking at him and waiting.

"Marina was a student in a course I taught to part-time students, and they are some of my best, I have to say that. Much more motivated, but, sorry. I was saying, yes, anyway, Marina was very bright and interested in philosophy and history and came up to speak to me after class, several times, in fact. We began to talk. She was full of questions about how the subject related to the world she was living in, and so I told her what could be done and what we were doing and invited her to join. She was very enthusiastic and went to all our meetings and often spoke. She was shy in a way but was not afraid to say something when she had something to say. People liked her. I liked her. I liked her very much." His eyes saddened and dimmed, and he was silent.

Eiger looked out the window for a second at the grey skies and the budding trees. He cleared his throat. "Did you ever meet her boyfriend, Tommy Moore or his friend, Frank?"

Bloch turned to Eiger, swallowed and smoothed down his jacket, "Yes, she brought Moore to a couple of demonstrations which I spoke at, he seemed to be all right, she seemed to need that kind of tough guy. Some women never make sense to me. It was clear to me he was just there because she was and he wanted to impress her. But his friend Frank, yes, I remember a man in this early thirties, very intense. He wasn't there for the women. He told me had been in the army and saw what they got up to and couldn't take it, so left. Wanted to do something to stop wars. He was a welcome addition. Moore invited him the first time. He gave the group some credibility. You know an ex-soldier...We talked differently with him than we did with Moore. Marina was attracted to him, I could see that but she was with Moore so...anyway you know how those things work..."

His jaw tightened, as he seemed to see something before him, then relaxed and he continued, "Then, one day, about a month before Frank was shot, he came to my office, with Marina. They were very afraid. I asked him why they were afraid and in answer Frank gave me a computer memory stick. They wanted me to take care of it."

Bloch hesitated, the muscles in his forehead tightened as if he was in pain and he took some slow breaths. Conway tensed with impatience, "Well, what was on it and why didn't you tell us you knew Frank when you knew we were acting for Moore on the murder charge?"

Bloch passed a hand threw his hair, as if trying to draw out his thoughts carefully. He looked straight at them again in turn and said,

"A list of names, people in government mainly but people in media, business. The names appear beside bank account numbers and lists of amounts paid into those accounts, paychecks in fact. Names of people. Assets of a foreign power. People at key positions and key levels. Why didn't I, ...I'm sorry, I didn't think my situation was connected to that and I didn't want to believe what I myself was thinking, that all this was because of this information. I didn't know if I could trust you. Now I have no choice."

Eiger narrowed his eyes as they focused on Bloch, "Names? What foreign power...?"

Professor Bloch shrugged his shoulders as he thrust his hands into the pockets of his trousers, "Who else? The great land to the south."

Budnick let out a breath and leaned forward in his chair, "Why did he give you this list?"

"He thought I could get it out to the public, that is that the other professors and our group could do it. It would be safer. He was afraid to do it himself. He didn't know how."

Conway quickly broke in, "Where did he get the information?"

Bloch, passed his hand threw his hair again. "He wasn't clear. He said he had been asked to crack the government computer systems to find a special file that contained the names. He was told one existed and where it was likely to be found. He was an expert at hacking so he was tasked with breaking the systems encryption codes and locating those files. He'd done that in the army, in a signals and intelligence unit. He said he didn't know who they were. He thought they were renegades, ex-CIA looking to blackmail the names or sell the list to a foreign government. He didn't care so long as they paid him well. He didn't know what the contents were until he found the file. They put more pressure on him. Someone must have leaked that he was searching for the file because a month before his murder two men came from the States and one man from the Committee. They told him to stop and to give them everything he had so far, that he still worked for them. He told me that he had already located the file when they came but he pretended to them that he hadn't been successful yet. But they seemed to know he had and demanded he produce it."

"Once he saw its contents, once he realised what it was he came to me. He thought the public had the right to know this information. He was a singular man. He needed the money but something in him... Well, it went against all he had come to stand for. Anyway, I agreed with him. Marina supported him. She thought the same. So he gave the disk to me. A press conference was planned for the day after he was killed. I think that was why he was killed."

Conway clenched his jaw and sat further forwards in his chair. "Where is the memory stick professor? Are there copies?"

"I think he may have kept another copy, or Marina."

Budnick sat back in his chair, "Did Marina talk about this?"

"Yes, She came to see me a day later and told me she was worried about Frank and about me, that the whole thing might be a trap for the group."

Budnick's voice hardened. "Worried about Frank. I thought she was hot for Tommy. Did she know where you kept the disk?"

"She was, but Marina wasn't one to abide by artificial rules. She only knew I had it. Not where I put it. I wanted to consult with my colleagues what to do about it. But it got around my secretary had called a press conference. Maybe that also has to do with my suspension. I never had the chance to consult with my colleagues...and Frank's murder, well..." and he began to shake his head slowly from side to side.

Eiger walked over to the bookshelves and waved his hand at the mess. As he did the door opened and Pierre Morin walked in, nodded his head to Budnick and the professor and stood quietly against a wall. His tall, square presence filled the room.

Budnick said quickly, "Professor, Johnny, Pierre Morin, investigator, my right hand man." Both of them acknowledged his presence with a nod of the head and then Eiger continued,

"Well, somebody was looking for something. Did they find it, professor?" He turned to Bloch and waited for the answer that was slow in coming.

Bloch stood up and began to pace in front of his desk,

hands still in his trouser pockets. "I'm putting my life in your hands if I tell you and once I tell you your lives will also be in jeopardy." He stood still in the middle of the room as he turned his head to look at them one by one, fixing each of them with his eyes. He said nothing and looked very grim.

Budnick broke the silence, "Look, professor, we're in this already and we need to know what's going on so we know what to do. Who are we dealing with? And we're the only ones you can trust."

Bloch began to pace again, looking at them in turn as he passed them. "This information has to get out to the public and in the hands of those in the government who are patriots, few as they are. That's our only protection. The device has caused all this trouble but it's the only thing that can get us out of it. You say I can trust you. I don't know who I can trust. But you're right. I must trust you. No, I never put it in any single place. I carried it with me all the time. Here ...." and he reached in his trouser pocket and pulled out a small black memory disk and handed it to Budnick who quickly took it and turned it over carefully in his hands.

"Doesn't look like much does it?" He tossed it over to Conway.

Conway caught it and played with opening and closing it. "We have to go to the press."

He weighed it in his hand as he spoke. "But a major paper, The Free Press."

He handed the disk to Eiger who examined it for a few seconds. "Well, I think we should take a look at what's on here first." He handed the disk back to Budnick.

Bloch shook his head, "You can't trust any of them. They only leak something when it's to their advantage. This would reveal who they are. It's not going to happen. They'll ignore us and then anything can happen. No, we have to go to someone who can protect us."

Eiger asked "Who? I can't think of anyone. I agree with the professor. You can't trust anyone."

Budnick waved his hand, "They've got all of you spooked. You're afraid of your own shadows. I know a guy at the Press we can count on. Not everyone's bought and paid for."

Budnick's cell phone buzzed and he put it to his ear. "Hello, hi Susan, what's up?" They listened and said nothing as he asked, "What is it?" His face turn a shade of grey as he pulled the phone from his ear and said,

"Moore is dead."

*   *   *   *   *

18

Bloch sat down and the three of them listened as Budnick talked to Susan. He closed his phone.

"They're saying he hanged himself in his cell while his cellmate was in the yard. Moore was too strong for that. Now they've eliminated Marina and Moore..."

"And Frank," added Eiger.

"And Frank. So of the four that knew about the device only you're left professor. And us. They'll assume we know everything. They can't afford to take chances."

Conway stood up and waved his arms around. "What are we going to do about Moore?"

Budnick stood up and faced him, "First thing to do is go to the jail and speak to the superintendent, then hold a press conference and call for an investigation."

He walked over to Professor Bloch and put his hand on his shoulder. Bloch looked up, his face grey and his eyes glistened as anger and fear grappled for control.

"What shall we do about this?" and he pointed at the mess in the room.

Budnick looked at everyone and raised his eyebrows, "Any ideas?"

"Only one," said Eiger, "The professor comes with us. We send Pierre over to watch his wife...if that's all right with you professor?"

Bloch nodded quickly, "Yes," and looked over at Pierre who smiled grimly.

Eiger continued, "When we call for the investigation on Moore we have to tie it in with this. Then we go further, ..."

Budnick anticipated him. "You think we should reveal we have the device then?"

Eiger nodded, "No choice, the only thing that can protect us is if it's public, it's out in the open. The professor's right. It solves all the problems."

Conway nodded, "I agree. But first we have to arrange a conference. Can Susan do that?"

"Yeh, I'll fill her in." and they listened as Budnick called Susan and told her what they needed.

He finished the call and put his mobile phone in his jacket pocket and addressed Bloch. "Does university security know about this?"

Bloch replied with a hushed voice as if he was afraid of being overheard, "No, I called only you. No one else knows, except them of course."

"Good. No need for them or the police to know, at least not officially. Will just give them an excuse to mess things up and keep you detained to help in the investigation. Come on professor, you're coming with us. Pierre, you follow us over to the professor's house so he can explain things to his wife. Then I want you to stay with them. We're going to the Don and see what's what with Moore."

Pierre nodded grimly, his arms crossed, "Ok, got it." He touched the side of his jacket where protection was close at hand and turned to open the door. They all followed, Bloch ahead of Budnick, Conway and Eiger close behind, quiet and tense.

They said nothing as they drove to the professor's house on Maple Street. What town doesn't have a Maple Street? It was the same as all Maple streets, shaded, quiet, splashed here and there with rusty dead leaves, and a few green buds that had begun to appear on trees everywhere in the city. The professor's house sat by itself on a half acre of manicured property.

Budnick parked the van in front of the door. Pierre parked his Lexus behind him. They left the vehicles and walked quickly to the door, Conway admiring the landscaping, the two story house with its New England shutters and gabled roof. Eiger wondered why he had become a lawyer instead of getting his Ph.D. and living the easy life. Images of a Black Mamba snake outside his door in Arusha and mould on the walls made him bite the side of his mouth. Conway saw the bitterness flash across Eiger's face and felt the same sense of bitter envy.

"Nice place you have here professor."

Bloch thanked him as they approached the door, paused, bowed with a small movement of his head and torso, opened the door, extended his arm in invitation and humbly said, "Welcome to our home gentlemen."

They followed him in to the foyer and waited while Bloch went in search of his wife. Budnick walked over to an African statuette on a side table and picked it up. "Wonder what that is?"

Eiger took it in his hand. "It's a fetish. Kongo, I would think. It's supposed to bring good health if you touch it."

Eiger put it back on the table as Budnick continued to roam around the foyer and then entered a large front room. His left shoulder hunched up a little and twitched as he looked around, his solid bulk too much like a proverbial bull in a china shop. He was about to put his large meaty hands on a Chinese vase when a woman's voice caught them in mid-air.

"That is a Korean piece. It is very delicate and very

beautiful. My husband received it as a gift when he was in Pyongyang."

Budnick turned and quickly went forward to extend his hand to hers, which she held out for him European style. He was tempted to kiss it but thought that might be a bit much. Conway and Eiger kept a respectful distance as their hands joined.

"Pyongyang?" He turned to the professor. "You're as mysterious as Johnny here."

Emma smiled and began to sit down in a small chair waiving to them to sit down opposite her on a settee. Bloch walked over to a small table and fiddled with a box out of which he drew a pipe and a pouch of tobacco. "I hope you don't mind gentlemen," and he began the ceremony of taking pinches of tobacco and putting them in the pipe held carefully in his hand.

Pierre remained standing, looking around him, at the doors, the stairs, the windows. Emma noticed he was handsome and about her age. "I'm sorry I don't know your name, do I?"

Conway stood up quickly. "Forgive me, Mrs. Bloch, this very distinguished gentleman is our investigator Pierre Morin. He's a friend and someone we trust. He used to be with the Montreal Police. Good man to have around. He's here at our request. Your husband agreed."

She looked puzzled as she turned her head to Bloch. "I don't understand, darling, what's the problem?" She looked at him with impatient eyes.

Bloch sucked on his pipe stem to make sure he had a flow of air, looked at it slowly, picked up a long match from the box which he struck on the inside and then puffed quickly as he put the match to the tobacco and clouds of pungent grey smoke rose into the air. Only when he was finished did he take the pipe from his mouth to speak.

"There was a break in at the office..." he stopped as she took in a sharp breath and flush of colour tinged her cheeks. "It seems to be connected to the Marina girl and the memory stick...."

Budnick interrupted, "Your wife knew too?"

Bloch looked a bit boyish as he looked at her warmly, "We share everything. I couldn't keep it from her. Our group met here sometimes. So, she met Marina and the others."

Emma Bloch smiled and her eyes brightened as she returned the gaze, then turned to Budnick, "Yes, I know I sometimes become controlling but I admire my husband's work and his beliefs. I share them. We have all the problems people our age do in relationships. Marina interested him, I know. But then Frank interested me." She smiled enigmatically and sweetly at all of them in turn.

Budnick focused his attention on her, a little annoyed at the professor but trying not to show it, "Did Frank talk to you about the information on the device?" His green eyes narrowed then opened as he waited for her reply. "We understand it's a list of names, evidence of foreign control of certain key people in the country, but whose list is it and who wants it?"

Emma Bloch sat forward in her chair with her elbows on her knees and her hands clasped in front of her face as she began to speak.

"Perhaps my husband has not told you everything. I understand. He has always been a very careful man. Sometimes too careful...In this case I think he was right to be so." She looked over at it him and received the confirmation in his face. "But things need to be known. The people need to know." She hesitated and lowered her head for a beat then raised it and said,

"Yes, it contains the names of people who are assets of a foreign government, and all its secret agencies. Perhaps there are others with other foreign governments. Who knows anything anymore? The list is dangerous to them, and to anyone who has it." She paused, and looked each one in the eye, raised her eyebrows, and waited for a response. There was only silence.

She smiled grimly, "You see, the person who has the list knows who controls the system and how they do it. For most people the world they live in is a fiction. But they believe in the fiction. The list will show them that the ones who have created the illusion are just cheap gangsters. Who owns it? Well, the government in the south and our own created the list, at least those involved did. Who wants it? Frank said there was a secret group in the CIA who wanted to use it for their own purposes, blackmail he supposed or to sell to other powers. The American government asked the Committee to stop Frank and to recover the information. They're also after the group that paid Frank. That's all he could tell us."

They all looked at each other. Pierre shuffled his feet and touched his pocket again.

Emma stood up, "Anything else gentlemen?"

Budnick stood up, Eiger and Conway followed. They understood the interview was over and that they were dealing with a force in Emma. They all smiled and said, "No, thanks, we'd better be going." They looked with admiration at the professor and regarded him with different eyes.

Budnick extended his hand and took hers, "Pierre will stay here. He'll be discrete. I think professor it's best if you stay here with your wife and Pierre. If Pierre needs any help he knows where to get it." Pierre nodded his head. "We're going to the jail to see what happened to Moore. Then we'll come back and decide what action to take, make plans for the press conference."

Emma looked alarmed, "Press conference?"

Conway turned from the door towards her. "Yes, we think it's the only way to protect everyone."

Eiger added, "To get the information before the public."

Budnick said, "Right," and added, "We'll keep the stick

with us for now if that's ok?"

Conway raised his eyebrows, saw the professor nod in agreement and watched as Budnick hunched his shoulders and said "Ok Emma, we'll see you soon. Take it easy professor." He said more loudly, "Pierre likes green tea." He laughed as he turned and walked, chuckling, out of the house. Conway and Eiger bade their farewells and followed Budnick out to the van. Emma and the professor watched them as they drew away and then turned back into the living room where Pierre was still standing.

"Du thé vert, Monsieur Morin?"

"Oui, merci, madame. Vous êtes gentil."

She flushed a little, and tried to hide it from her husband by turning her head, but only made him the more jealous, and Pierre, the more charmed. "C'est un plaisir, monsieur...Richard, quelque chose pour toi, aussi, mon cheri?"

"Green tea will be fine, thank you."

The return to English broke the spell Emma had briefly woven of the Pont Neuf in Paris on a misty afternoon. She seemed startled by the tear of the fabric. She tweaked the corners of her mouth weakly and walked out of the room toward the kitchen. Pierre admired her elegance and thought she was perhaps, even beautiful. Professor Bloch took the pipe from his mouth and cleared his throat, attracting Pierre's attention, "Please, Monsieur Morin, have a seat."

Pierre sat in a chair opposite the professor and settled back with his arms on the armrests. He pulled up his slacks a little. Bloch puffed on his pipe, then asked, "You were a policeman before?"

"Oui, twenty years in Montreal, Detective. Detective-Inspector when I retired. My daughter, she lives here with her husband, her mother passed away so I came here to live and so I have a detective agency here. I do a lot of work for Budnick and Conway. Other firms. You know. So, it's interesting. And you, professor, I understand you teach philosophy. I was wondering what type of philosophy. I do some reading too."

Bloch smiled, "My specialty is the history of philosophy, how it changes over time. Perhaps I chose it because it allows me to read all philosophers from all times."

Pierre nodded, "C'est exact. Nothing ever stays the same. You can't step in the same river twice, that is for sure..."

Bloch laughed, "Ah, I think we can have a pleasant time with each other while we wait."

Pierre sat up and smiled as Emma walked in from the kitchen with a tray and a tea service and watched her put the tray down on a coffee table between them and then sit down in a chair near the professor's, "I think so, professor, I think so..." and leaned forward with a smile as Emma poured him tea in a Chinese cup and handed it to him. Her fingers brushed his as he took it from her hand and he quickly looked over to the professor to see if he had noticed, but he seemed lost in thought behind a cloud of pipe smoke.

*   *   *   *   *

19

The afternoon had turned suddenly hot. A cold March morning had quickly become a sultry 32 degrees by mid-afternoon. Budnick turned on the radio while pulling down his tie and unbuttoning his shirt collar as he drove. He tuned in to a jazz station that just happened to be playing Ella Fitzgerald singing 'Summertime.'

Sometimes things are just like that, sometimes it's suddenly a hot day and suddenly your hearing '...and the living is easy...'. But it didn't feel right. It should have been cold. Conway took off his jacket. "Wow, that came out of nowhere. Nice though for a change."

Budnick snorted like a bull whose just been jabbed by a picador, "Nice, nothing, what are we gonna do if its 30 degrees above normal in July, huh? When its 120 in the shade or more? They've really fucked things up for every body. We're all gonna fry."

Eiger shook his head, "I have to say, it was cooler in Africa."

They both turned to look at him and then turned back to look at the road and shook their heads.

Eiger's mobile buzzed. He took it out of his pocket and put it to his ear. He talked while looking out the window and said 'uh-huh' a few times and then "Ok, see you at seven. Ok, you too." He closed the phone and put it back.

"Diana, misses me, wants to have dinner later."

Budnick slowed down to avoid a jam ahead, "Ask her to join us, we may have to have a meeting tonight and we need you."

Conway took in a breath and with eyes half closed said, "Sure, bring her along, but maybe we should keep this in-house. If she knows about this she could be in danger too. Security is a problem."

Eiger looked thoughtful, "You don't trust her? She's discrete, and I'll probably tell her anyway."

Conway raised his eyebrows and turned away slightly, "Ok, so long as the issue is raised," and looked out the window.

"She knows a lot already, she imagines more," said Eiger, looking out the other window. He called Diana back and told her to meet them at Flo's at 6 and hung up.

Conway reacted as Eiger put his phone in his pocket. "Never trust what a woman tells you nor count any woman constant. Their hearts are turned on a potter's wheel." He turned his face away from the window.

Eiger laughed, "And we're so faithful?"

They became quiet and said nothing more. But Eiger was in another place. He stared ahead at the shimmering mirage of a girl with the dark long hair walking along a beach under a canopy of gracefully swaying coconut palms welcoming the whispering silver waves.

~

The meeting at the jail wasn't pleasant. Conway and Budnick went in to meet the superintendent while Eiger stayed with the car. The superintendent, Brimley, was an old friend of Budnick's or at least a familiar face and they greeted each other as they always did, asking how each other's families were, how old age was coming along. Then

Budnick got down to business.

"Ok chief, what happened to Moore."

The superintendent invited them to sit down as he sat behind his desk and looked at them with sad and black-circled eyes, world weary and tired. "We're conducting an investigation. His cellmate says he was fine when he left for the yard. Moore didn't want to go, or so he says. He comes back and finds Moore hanged. Used torn bed sheets to do it. Looks like it anyway."

"Can we talk to the cellmate?"

"I've been ordered not to allow anyone to talk to him or anyone else here pending the investigation. The police are in charge of that."

"Did any cops come to see Moore in the last day or so," asked Budnick.

"Like I said, Mr. Budnick, I can't tell you. I agreed to see you out of courtesy and old time's sake but I have my instructions. I'm sorry. You'll have to go to the police for more. Det. Sgt Marko is in charge over at homicide. They're waiting for an autopsy to declare it suicide or homicide. They think it's suicide. Or so they say."

"Marko? No note?" asked Budnick

"No note," replied the superintendent.

Budnick nodded grimly, looked at Conway and stood up and shook hands with the superintendent, "Thanks, chief, if anything comes to mind, maybe you could give me a call."

Brimley nodded solemnly, as he stood up from his desk, hitching up his pants as he did so and putting his thumbs in his belt, "If I can I will, all I can say, have a good day gentlemen."

Back in the van, Conway answered Eiger's questions while Budnick drove, lost in thought.

Suddenly he spoke. "Brimley just about told us Moore

was murdered."

Conway squinted his eyes, "How so?"

"Brimley may be getting old, but he likes to talk, likes to feel he's in the world somewhere, in the action. I've had guys in there beaten up by guards, prisoners, even one guy beaten to death by the guards and they tried to pin it on a cellmate. Brimley likes to talk. This one is different. He's too scared to say anything or he's been ordered not to. I could feel it in his handshake. Let's see what the cops have to say," and he turned the van onto a side street and headed east back downtown.

Budnick went into the police station alone, thinking more than one of them showing up would make the police more hostile than needed. He decided to play it a bit more relaxed. He was gone thirty minutes. He reappeared looking sullen and angry.

"They're sticking to the suicide story but Marko's boss, Randall, asked me if I knew the professor. They've linked Moore and Frank with Marina and now us. We've got to have that press conference and go public. Call Susan, tell her we're coming back to the office and ask her about the conference."

Conway opened his phone and called.

Eiger listened to the sound of Susan's voice as Conway talked with her. She sounded matter of fact. But Conway hung up exasperated.

"She sent out a release to all the press contacts but not one reply. It's set for 9am the day after tomorrow at the office. Gives them time to react but she doubts anyone is going to show."

"What did the release say?" asked Budnick

"What you told her, simple and neutral-we are going to talk about the Moore case, nothing else, nothing about the professor or the others. But Moore's death isn't in the news."

Budnick nodded thoughtfully, "Uh-huh, ok, let's get Susan and get something to eat. Call Pierre. Tell them we'll be over later."

Susan was making coffee when they walked in. Eiger caught her eyes and smiled and she reciprocated. Conway flushed and turned to go into his office. Budnick saw the quick reactions but only smiled to himself and said, "Susan, we're going to get a bite to eat. Wanna join us? We've got to talk about the Moore case and you're involved now."

"Sure, you want some coffee before we go?" She handed him a cup which he took and began sipping on as he lumbered around the office looking at papers and files, muttering about the Aldarizine case and money.

By six o'clock they were at Flo's in a corner booth. Budnick ordered a beer and a vodka and quickly downed the vodka first, then said, "Ah, that feels better."

Conway shared a bottle of red wine with Eiger and Susan. They were quiet, after that, Budnick nursing his beer and gazing into the distance, all of them taking in the situation, trying to understand. Susan was about to say something but only managed to open her lips a little when Eiger, facing the door, raised his head quickly. Susan turned to see Diana closing the door behind her and greeting Peter standing behind the bar. They exchanged a few muffled words then Peter escorted her over to the booth.

Budnick nodded to her and half raised himself out of his seat. "Sorry I can't get up, Diana, it's not that I'm fat but this booth is very tight," and laughed. She laughed with him and tossed her hair to one side and then turned to Susan.

"Sorry, would have been here sooner but wasn't sure what to wear, it got hot so fast, now it's cold again. It's weird, really is." She took off her short jacket and sat down next to Eiger. Susan hadn't seen her wear jeans before. She looked younger and Susan found herself watching her talking and the movements of her face.

Conway leaned over to her, "Can I buy you a drink?"

She blushed, "Well, I'm not sure what I want, but, a glass of wine would be nice I think."

She smiled at them as Conway signaled to Peter who nodded and turned behind him to reach for the white wines in the cooler.

"Pinot Grigio," Diana said loudly in Peter's direction.

"Ok, got something you'll like."

Eiger, in reaction to Conway's manoeuvre shifted closer to Susan, called to Peter for another glass for her and himself and challenged Conway with a look.

Budnick raised his hands in the air and threw his head back, "Ok, I can buy myself a drink. Don't worry about it. Hey Peter, buddy, could you give me another one too?"

Peter nodded from the bar, "Be right over, my friend."

They settled down and the silence again descended on the booth as they each withdrew into their own thoughts.

Peter brought Budnick's drink and a dish of calamari. They all dipped into it quickly and then Budnick, still chewing a chewy piece of squid said,

"Well, the way I see it, we are in a difficult position. If the press conference is a zero then we are stuck with this item," and he pulled the stick from his jacket pocket and held it in the air, turning it in his hand, "that people have been killed for. So what are we going to do? That is the simple question." He continued to chew.

Diana took a sip of her drink. "I don't understand. What item?"

Eiger said, "The professor's office was ransacked today. It has to be the Committee. Or renegade CIA. Even more dangerous. They were looking for something. They didn't find it. We have it." He looked slowly at Budnick and the others as they kept their eyes fixed on Diana.

Conway lowered his voice a little, "It's information, information that is very important. We have to get it to the right people. It's why Marina was killed, Moore and Frank."

"So the professor 's involved?"

Budnick, nodded, "Uh-huh...in a round about way...I'm not sure we know everything even yet. But there are things we're told."

"So who killed Moore, who killed Marina.. who...?"

Conway raised his eyebrows, wrinkling his brow, "Frank, Moore, Marina, I bet you a thousand bucks it was those two cops that tried to fix me up. But they're working for others."

Eiger nodded and pumped his leg, "The Committee or the renegades?"

Diana looked puzzled and began to ask what they meant but Susan suddenly opened her mobile and said,

"I'll bet you the guy that met Johnny is on the same team. I'll bet you this guy is one of them."

Eiger jerked his head back, "No, that's something different. Those guys want me because of what I do in Africa. They're probably with the government but I don't see any link between that, these murders and the device."

Budnick put his hands together as if he were praying,

"You forget one thing Johnny. You joined us. You received that phone call after Jack got the call from Moore. They knew that. They seem to know everything about you. They may be trying to get you for your defence at the trial but now you've made it worse and got yourself involved in this. They'll go at each of us from different angles. They went after Frank directly and killed him when he wouldn't' tell them where the stick was and to keep him quiet about what he learned. Then they set up Moore and tried to squeeze Marina and now they're going after the professor. You're already targeted. They know Jack and I must know things. Meanwhile Pierre is out at the house all alone."

Diana tensed her forehead and lines appeared around her eyes that weren't there before. "But I don't understand. Who is this committee, these renegades? What are they after?"

Eiger turned to her, "Like we said, it's a disk, a memory stick. It contains information about foreign agents in government and society. But that's what we're told, we haven't had time to look at it yet. It's about time we did." He turned to Budnick and Conway.

Conway took the stick from Budnick who was turning it over in his hands repeatedly. "Have to wait 'til we're back in the office..."

Susan suddenly pulled her purse towards her and reached in. "No we don't. I've got my machine with me...' she pulled out a small purse size laptop and placed it in front of them on the table. 'You can use that. Just plug it in."

Conway looked at Eiger and Budnick who both looked at each other and then Budnick nodded. Susan inserted the stick in the port and waited. The icon appeared on the screen and Susan clicked on it and brought up a file named Operation Boomerang. She clicked on that and a spreadsheet opened up with lists of names and columns of data. "Here," and she pushed the laptop towards the centre of the table where the lawyers could see the screen. There were several minutes of silence and sipping of drinks as they read what was before them. Diana looked over at Susan who shrugged her shoulders and tightened her lips. Diana almost stopped breathing as she watched them.

"You ok, Diana? You look a little tense," said Susan.

"No, I'm ok, well no I'm not really. All this stuff makes me tense. I've had years of it with Johnny and what he went through with these people. You didn't answer my question about this committee. So I get the picture. They're dangerous. I'd sooner just stay out of it and wish all of you would too. It's not worth the trouble. Believe me. What can we do about anything? We have no power."

Susan kept her eyes fixed on her and answered, "Yes, I got a sense of that when I was taking the photo of the guy Johnny met this morning."

"This morning? What photo?"

Eiger looked away from the screen, "I met that fellow Rice at a café this morning and Susan was there to try to get a photo of the guy. See if we can find out anything about him. Talked about that Middle East case. They put pressure on me, know about the CIA threat against me. Basically repeated it in case I hadn't sufficiently gotten the message. I walked out, but she got the shot."

Susan rummaged in her purse and pulled her mobile out. "Take a look. Tell me what you think of this guy. Kinda cute in a way but gave me the chills, like a snake."

Diana took the phone and looked at the screen. They all heard her intake of breath and saw her mouth open and eyes widen. She regained control and gazed at it as if it was a fashion magazine. "Yeh, he's something that one."

Susan noticed a hesitation in her voice. "There something wrong? You don't know this guy do you?" and laughed.

Diana tossed her hair away from her eyes. "No. Why would I know him? Just, like what you said, even from the image this feeling comes over me of, you know..."

Susan nodded, "Yeh, that's what I said, like a cobra." And she took the mobile back and put it in her purse.

Eiger watched Diana and looked puzzled. "You sure you're ok?"

"Yeh, I'm fine, just fed up with all this shit. Makes me depressed. I'd rather talk about art. Look since you're going to talk about this secret stuff maybe I should just go and I'll meet you later." She began to put her jacket on and put her things back in her purse and laid some money on the table.

Budnick watched her but didn't say anything. Eiger put his hand on hers and pushed the money back. "Yeh, ok, maybe it's best. I'm sorry about dinner."

"No need to apologise. This is important. I understand. Call me when you're free later."

She stood up, smiled quickly at everyone, kissed Susan on the cheek, touched Conway on the arm, ignored Eiger and Budnick then turned and walked away. Peter asked her if he could he could get her a cab, but she said her car was parked in the lot across the street and she turned once again, waved at them all, said loudly, "Be careful, see you later," and left with a toss of her long dark hair and a quick twist of her heels.

They all exchanged glances and Susan asked, "What was up with her?"

Budnick turned his hands up from the table and hunched his shoulders. "She's smart that one. She doesn't want to be involved and right now I wish I wasn't. But anyway, so let's return to what we're dealing with here," and turned the computer screen back towards him and began going back over the documents that were the cause of their problem.

*   *   *   *   *

20

Diana crossed the street to the small parking lot and walked up to her car. She put the key in the lock. A quiet noise of footsteps behind her made her jump back and drop the keys. "Don't be alarmed Diana, it's just me." She turned to find Agius standing directly behind her.

"What are you trying to do? You scared me to death. How did you know I was here? Why are you following me?"

"We know where all of you are. Did you find what we're looking for?"

She picked up her keys and unlocked her car. She turned to face him as she opened the door. "They have it. I don't know what's on it. But yes, they have it." She stood still, looking at Agius steadily and wondered what came next. He nodded his head slightly, just a small move of acknowledgement of what she had said. He moved closer and put his face close to hers.

"We're happy you agreed to work with us. It won't go unrewarded."

She looked at the ground in response, appeared to almost cry but calmed herself and recovered with, "I don't want anything to happen to them. I told you because I'm afraid of what could happen."

"Of course, I understand. They are out of their depth on this. Even Johnny. What they have is very dangerous to the country and to them. My principals will do anything to get that disk, and so will a group from the States who are more ruthless than we are. We need to get it before they can do anything with it, before they make things more ugly than they already are. No one needs to get hurt. That's where you come in. If you get it for us, we'll let them go back to their lives. And we'll take care of the competition."

"And Johnny. Susan showed me a photograph. It was you, as Mr. Rice. Funny names you have. You're after him too. He told me all about that scam you're trying to run. I want him left alone or nothing else happens. You can do what you want."

"Yes, I saw that woman photograph me. She's quite attractive. I think she enjoyed the excitement. But to return to business. I will ask. Johnny did some severe damage to our interests in the African trial. The American competition is not happy. They wanted him eliminated last year. We persuaded them to hold off. After all, he's Canadian. But some of my principals think the Americans are right. So, he owes us a payback or silence. But, this is more important than him. Do what you need to but get that device. The longer this runs, the more danger he and they are in. There are people who just want to finish all of you."

He took her hand and held it for a long moment and looked in her eyes. She stared back. "You're afraid, Diana. Don't be. Just get it. We'll be in touch."

He let her hand go, kissed her on the cheek sending a charge through her spine, turned up the collar of his coat and walked away slowly down the street, not looking back. Diana followed him with her eyes until he disappeared down a side street, then collapsed onto the front seat of her car, laid back her head and began to shake uncontrollably.

~

Budnick leaned back in the booth. He looked exhausted. Eiger's face had turned very pale, as if he had malaria again. Conway and Susan took their glasses and drank deeply.

Eiger was the first to speak. "We have to get this to someone now or we won't live very long. That is for sure. They're not going to let us walk around with this. We've got to move fast."

Conway agreed. "We have to see the professor." Budnick looked at him, his arms crossed and his mouth curved down like an angry bulldog. He raised his hand and waived to Peter. "Can we have the tab, thanks we have to rush off. Business."

Peter went to the computer, punched in the charges and then brought the cheque over. Budnick took it, glanced at it and pulled a wad of cash. "Here, that should do it, the rest is yours." Peter thanked him and walked back to the bar counting the money as he went.

Budnick stood up almost knocking the booth over. "Really, gotta lose some weight. Damn. Come on, let's go," and he pushed Eiger and Conway out of their seats to get up. Susan hesitated.

"You want me to come along or....?"

Budnick paused, smoothing down his jacket while putting on his coat. His shoulders twitched a couple of times, and his mouth made small movements from side to side as he thought. "Yeh, you better come with us, until we figure out what to do. Count it as overtime." He laughed a little to take the edge off.

She laughed back, "Ok boss. Some overtime."

She picked up her purse, and pulled one of her shoes back on, as Eiger took a long look at her legs. She got up and faced Conway whose exasperation was evident. "You're cute too, honey, come on, we have things to do."

She walked past him to the front of the group and led them out of the café, her swiveling hips leading them out onto the street and across to the parking lot as they followed one by one. They walked quickly to Budnick's van and all piled in as he started the engine and pulled out of the lot. It was dusk, the street lights had just come on and traffic was heavy as they turned onto the main road and headed north towards the university and the professor's house. No one noticed the small dark car that pulled out of a lot further down and followed them into the darkening distance.

~

Diana drove back to her apartment over on Jane Street near Bloor and parked the car in the underground parking lot. She felt almost too tired to get out of the car to take the elevator up the 14 flights but before she realised it she was taking off her coat and taking a bottle of red wine from a rack in the small kitchen. She poured a large glass, turned on some Brahms on the stereo and sat down on a couch. She steadily drained the glass as she lay back against the cushions and listened to the music. She closed her eyes. She drifted off. She dreamed of a better place.

~

Eiger was first out of the van and the first to walk through the door when they arrived at the professor's house. Pierre met them at the door, his gun partly drawn, but quickly put it out of sight, when he saw it was them. Eiger asked how things were and, while Pierre was telling them that nothing had developed, the professor and his wife came out of the living room wearing nervous faces.

The professor put his left arm around his wife's waist and waived them into the house with the other, "Please, everyone, sit down and let us know what we can get for you. You all look a bit tired, if I may say so."

Budnick chuckled but quickly began to frown, "More worried, than tired, professor."

He sat in an armchair and waited while the others found their places. "Any phone calls, any...."

Pierre said, "No, nothing at all. I checked around the house a few times. Didn't spot anything obvious."

Budnick took a cup of tea from a tray carried by Emma who had left and returned with it, "Uh-huh, ok, then the situation is this. Whoever is after this stick, thinks the professor had it and now maybe we have it. They can't be sure who has it. So, they can't do anything to us until they find out. So we have a little time to plan what to do."

Conway's face was a mask of doubt, "They're capable of anything. We can't take chances. We have to assume they're going to do all they can to get it and not just that. They're going to make sure that we stay silent. So, unless we come up with something very good, like right now-I don't think we will see the sun rise."

Eiger sat in his chair staring at the floor. He lifted his head and said, "We have to go to the press."

Susan laughed. "Like you trust them? If you can find an honest one who has any guts, who's willing to expose this and face whatever comes, good luck."

Emma alerted them with a movement of her head that she wanted to speak. They fell silent and turned to her.

"Not everyone is corrupted. Not everyone is a coward. That is what they want us to believe. But there are those who cannot be bought. Mr. Budnick, you said earlier today that you knew an editor who was such a man?"

Budnick moved his head forward and back as if listening to the beat of her talk. "The editor of the Free

Press is one guy who can do it. If we can get to him in time."

Conway snorted, "What about the publisher? He can't do it on his own."

Budnick opened and closed his eyes as he thought, "This guy is ok, in my books. Once he sees this, he'll print it no matter what. Besides he'd love to be a hero for a few days."

The professor ran his hand through his hair as he entered the conversation, "Then we must try to reach him tonight. Marina was killed within days of Frank. Moore, days after her, and then, the attack on my office today. They could act at any time."

Budnick took out his cell phone and thumbed through his address book. He pressed his finger a few times on buttons and then put it to his ear. He was silent for a few seconds, then,

"Hi, Eddie, how are you? Yeh, it's Budnick, oh I'm fine, my friend. Well, let me get to the point, I've got something you should see, for the paper. Right. Important? It could set this country on fire. No, seriously, can't tell you on the phone. Yep, hush hush, is the word. No, I'm serious, very serious. We need to meet, tonight. Uh-huh, yeh."

He listened closely as he looked at the others, sometimes blinking his eyes as he listened to Eddie's voice. "Ok, but I have to bring some people. You need to know the whole story. Uh-huh, ok, your place. Ok, 2 hours. See you there. Thanks, Eddie. And Eddie, only for you, right. Ok." He closed the phone and put it back in his jacket pocket.

He looked in each of them in turn and then picked up his cup of tea and drank from it. "That's very nice Emma, thank you." He put the cup down on the table and settled back in his chair.

"Pierre, we need to get to Eddie Mackenzie's place for 9. Can you get us a couple of back-ups that quickly, we need an escort."

Pierre pulled out his mobile, "I've got two good guys. Ex military police. They can handle themselves."

He put through a call on his mobile and spoke to someone quietly for a couple of minutes, then closed his phone, and sat back in his chair.

"They will be here in one hour. Don't worry, we won't see them but they will be there. I hope others don't see them either but if they do, they will have to think twice."

Budnick nodded in blunt satisfaction then turned to the professor. "Professor, are you willing to see Eddie Mackenzie, and you Emma? You can link together all the pieces and you know the information."

Conway interjected, "There will be consequences. Serious ones. Even if nothing physical is tried, they can make sure the university shuts you out and everywhere else. It's..."

The professor looked at Conway with a commanding gaze and smiled slightly, "You too, Mr. Conway, all of you are taking that risk. I am more protected than you are. I have international recognition in my field, I am well, known, ..."

Conway quickly raised his hand and silenced him, "Yes, but look what they have done already, you're reputation won't save you. Look at Dr. Kelly in Britain."

The professor's face changed and became dark and distant, "Yes, Dr. Kelly."

Susan asked who Dr Kelly was. Emma who was sitting near her, took her hand and said, "A man who knew too much, a scientist, very famous. English. He knew people all over the world. It didn't save him. He knew too much about the war in Iraq and was willing to talk about it. He was assassinated."

Eiger nodded, "That's why they went after me about the trial. I know too much about the war in Africa."

The professor looked over at him. "I thought our role there was a good one." He saw Eiger shake his head.

"Ah, so that is all propaganda too. I have to say I never understood what happened there. The stories in the press were very confused, racist I would say-suddenly one savage African tribe is massacring another African tribe."

Eiger stood up and began to walk up and down in front of the professor as he entered into a long explanation of what he had discovered about the war and the role of the west in it. All of them listened quietly as he became more and more wrapped up in his lesson. He didn't even see them anymore. He was as mesmerized by what he was saying as they were.

Half an hour later he stopped pacing. "So, that's it in a nutshell." He looked at the professor and Emma. Susan looked at him admiringly. He looked back at her and took his teacup and put it to his lips and drank. Then he sat down.

Emma said, "Well, that was very interesting. One day you must write a book. "But," she turned to all of them, "you must be hungry all of you, let me make you some sandwiches," and stood up and walked to the kitchen. Susan stood up and followed her, "Can I help you? It would help my nerves."

Emma laughed lightly and said, "Certainly, my dear, it will calm mine too, which is why I want to do it. Come, you can tell me what they like and don't like..." and their voices faded away as they turned and walked through the open door into the kitchen.

Budnick stood up and stretched his legs. He began walking around the room. He picked up the Korean vase. "Nice work. Love this light blue-green colour." He put it down and turned to Eiger. "That is some story Eiger. If the people knew that they would be angry for being lied to."

Eiger got up and joined him and picked up the vase and turned it in his hands as he appreciated the colour and the feel of it. "Yes, beautiful craftsmanship." He handed it back. "And, yes, they would be. But, what can we do when the flow of information is totally controlled?"

The professor pulled his pipe and tobacco pouch out of his jacket pocket and began the ritual of preparing to smoke. Susan watched him as she came out of the kitchen with a tray of olives and cheese and crackers and put them on a table. With a hopeful voice she asked, "Professor, would you mind if I..." and here she took a package of cigarettes out of her purse along with her silver lighter and looked at him softly.

"Oh, no, I don't mind. Emma puts up with my pipe. Says she likes the smell. She is not so keen on cigarettes but I think she won't mind in the circumstances." He smiled at her.

Susan took out a cigarette and put it to her lips, "Sorry, I can go outside if it's going to bother anyone..." Pierre stood up,

"I wouldn't' mind one too. Come on, we can take a look around the house at the same time." He held out his arm to Susan who rose up gracefully and walked with him to the front door. Pierre stopped at the door and said to Budnick, "We'll reconnoiter. Be back in five minutes." Budnick nodded,

"Ok, Pierre."

He watched them as they went through the door together. Susan called out that she would be right back to help Emma. Emma came into the room just then with another tray. "That's all right, my dear. But I might need some help when you come back in." She turned and went back into the kitchen.

Pierre stopped on the stone path leading to the street and asked Susan if he could have one of her cigarettes. "I try to stop the smoking so I don't have any with me but the situation is a little tense. It's good for the nerves."

"You're tense? No wonder I am then." She looked at

him carefully. He was handsome for a man in his fifties, short grey hair, blue eyes, tanned complexion, someone who is usually described as fit.

"Yes." He lit his cigarette from hers and gave it back to her as he took a drag and inhaled deeply, "This is not a normal situation. I have been involved in a lot of operations and investigations that were a bit dangerous, you know, but this is not what I like to be involved in."

"What's going to happen?" she asked as she blew smoke out into the cool night air. In answer he began to walk and she went with him side by side as he went to the side of the house turning his head from right to left looking at the grounds and the surrounding streets.

He stopped by a tree and pointed at a car parked on a side street about fifty metres from the house. "You see that car. Now that car may be an ordinary car or it may be something else. We cannot be sure. So, I don't know what is going to happen but we have to get to Mackenzie's house before they can stop us. And then Mackenzie has to take the stick to the newspaper and set it up for release. But my people will be here soon. Then we can move."

He looked at Susan and thought how much she reminded him of his wife when she was younger. She noticed his eyes fixed on her and blushed and was glad he couldn't see that in the darkness. They began to walk again and completed the round of the house. They came back to the front entrance. Pierre took one last look around as they drew on their cigarettes for the last time. He smiled at her as he opened the door.

"Did I ever tell you that you are beautiful like my wife?" She blushed again, but this time he saw it as light fell on her face from the foyer as they walked into the house.

"No, Pierre but thank you for saying so. But don't you think that Emma is beautiful?"

This time he blushed quickly at the soft rejection and suggestion. "You are welcome, and yes, I agree, she is, but she has the professor while you..."

Susan laughed quietly at that, "I think we better leave that subject or I know two men in there who might have something to say."

Pierre bowed his head to her and laughed as well, "Ah yes, I noticed the tension between them when you are in the room." He was smiling as they entered the living room.

Budnick interrupted the duet. "What's the verdict?"

Pierre became professional again and serious. "Nothing has changed, but there is a car on the side street opposite that was not there an hour ago. Maybe it's nothing." But he walked over to the window, looked out and put his hand inside his jacket to make sure.

*   *   *   *   *

21

The professor was still on his feet smoking his pipe when Susan and the detective came back from their rounds. They heard him continue speaking.

"I agree, people think the internet is a wonderful tool like television but look what they have done with that. I don't know, Mr. Budnick, Mr Conway, Mr. Eiger, if this newspaper can act. But we have to try, of that I have no doubt. But we must also think about getting it to those in government who still serve the people."

Eiger shook his head, "You still think there are such people?"

The professor pulled on his pipe and blew out a swirling aura of blue smoke as he considered the question.

"I think there are. Yes, it is discouraging, the ignorance and lack of principles of many. There is an Arab saying, 'The world is a carcass and those who seek it are dogs'. It oftentimes seems that way." He puffed on his pipe again and put his head back as he savoured the taste of the tobacco and closed his eyes in a second of serenity.

Eiger poured himself a glass of scotch, a smoky Aardbeg, his favourite, which he spotted on a sideboard. He took a gulp and after a few seconds a flush of colour touched his face and his eyes seemed to be lit by deep inner fires. He took another sip and said,

"With the help of weapons and the lever man has subjugated Nature; he has made her minister to his pleasures, his needs, his very whims: he has altered the surface of the earth, and a feeble biped has become Lord of creation."

Bloch took his pipe from his lips and smiling at him said, "You are familiar with Brillart-Savarin? I commend your range of knowledge. It is rare these days. But he should have said Lord and Destroyer of creation. I'd like your opinion on Proust. I assume you have read him."

Eiger was about to say he had when Budnick, sitting in his chair, and also drinking from a glass of whisky while eating a cracker said, between chews, "Who the fuck is Proust?"

Eiger just looked at him in consternation then said to Bloch, "He got me through a very bad period."

Bloch nodded. "Yes I know what you mean. He can do that." He turned to Budnick, "French writer, early twentieth century, first world war, stream of consciousness, brilliant observer of humanity. A great writer, a philosopher in fact."

Emma came from the kitchen again with a tray of sandwiches that Susan had helped her to prepare. They came in together, chatting as women do, about the paintings displayed on the wall, one a real Kandinsky, an inheritance from her family she was quick to assure Susan, a large Riopelle on the long wall in the dining room that gave the impression of a moving vibration of light, about the furniture, about the colour of Susan's nail polish.

Susan put the tray on a coffee table, took one of the sandwiches herself and sat down in a chair between Eiger and Conway.

Emma smoothed her skirt, smiling as she invited everyone to take a sample of her originality and asking,

"How long gentlemen do we have to wait?"

Budnick screwed up his face as he bit into a crustless sandwich and tried to talk at the same time.

"Pierre's team will be here soon, then we leave."

He continued chewing and brushing the spilt crumbs from his trousers. "And remind me to call the wife, she doesn't care but she'll bitch if I don't check in," and he laughed, more to himself than them, then blushed as he noticed that Emma was watching him as some of his crumbs fell onto a very expensive Persian carpet. He quickly took a plate and held it under his chin as he ate and said, "My wife is always complaining I have no manners and she's right," and chuckled in that way that disarms everyone. Emma smiled back,

"I'm sure you have many other qualities, Mr. Budnick."

Pierre's cell phone buzzed. He answered it, listened, and said simply, "OK, you know the drill." He clicked his cell shut and put it in his pocket. He lifted his head slightly along with his eyebrows. Budnick, still chewing on a piece of bread nodded. He stuffed it into his mouth and stood up.

"Ok, everybody, get your coats. It's a little chilly out there now. The temperature is dropping fast. We need to leave."

As they prepared to go they heard Eiger's cell phone. He looked at the screen before putting it to his ear. "It's Diana,...Hi. What's up? Look I can't meet you now. What do you mean? Tell me what? Look I don't understand you, I'll call you back." He snapped the phone shut. His irritation was palpable.

Susan decided to explore the situation, "Troubles?"

"I'm not sure. Says she knows something about the stick, says we're in danger, wants to meet me."

"Yeh right, we all know we're in danger. So what's new? Seems to me she likes to control things and she's feeling left out. Ignore her. Just a head game."

Eiger looked at her pleading, dazzling eyes. "Maybe, but she sounded serious."

Pierre was waiting by the open front door. "What are we doing boss?"

Budnick put one foot in front of the other and approached the night air putting on his coat as he went. "We're leaving." He looked at Eiger.

"Send her a text. We'll visit her later."

Budnick walked past Pierre, followed by the professor and Emma, Conway, Eiger and Susan trailing behind them. They were herded by the guiding hand of Pierre. Once they were out of the house he opened his phone, and said one word, "Avance," closed it, and took a last look around before disappearing into the darkness.

The three lawyers and Susan got into the van. The Blochs got into Pierre's Lexus. Two lights flashed, one fifty meters ahead and one the same distance behind them. Pierre talked on his mobile again. The Blochs could not hear what he was saying, but he turned the ignition on and flashed his lights at Budnick and then followed the van as it pulled out onto the road.

Pierre saw the black Chevy approach from behind and keep a distance. He also saw the dark car on the opposite side of the street, the car he had pointed out to Susan, come to life and begin to pull away from the sidewalk. Pierre put his phone up to his mouth again, "Drop back, vehicle on your left. Let him in...yeh ok," and looked in his mirrors. Break lights flashed twice ahead of him, He flashed is hi-beams once. He looked back in the mirror. "Everyone all right?"

The professor answered with a question, "Are we? You tell me."

Pierre responded by calling Budnick on his mobile "Yes, ok, my men are in front and behind us. No, everything is ok, no problem, but just to let you know, we have company."

As Budnick put his phone down on the console next to him, Eiger took his phone out of his pocket and examined the screen. It lit his face and cast deep shadows across his eyes. "It's Diana, again. Says we have to meet. No delay."

Susan focused on him and tried to project her thoughts into his. The evidence for thought transfer is doubted by most but still, Eiger appeared confused, and spoke slowly when he reacted. "Yes, she can be very neurotic sometimes. She is capable of playing games. This is not a game."

Susan rolled her eyes and looked out the window in dramatic disbelief. Budnick twitched his shoulders and hugged the wheel intent on getting to Eddie Mackenzie's place. Conway, sitting next to Budnick, continued staring at the side mirror watching the road behind them, aware of a black car a few lengths distant. Then he twisted his neck so his face almost touched Susan's who was seated behind him and was now leaning forward looking into the road ahead through the windscreen.

"What do you think?"

Susan's perfume drifted in the air as he remembered how she took him inside her and how she smelled then. His lips began to form the beginning of a smile when Eiger answered him,

"She may be in trouble. They must have seen her with us. She may be involved. We have to see her tonight."

Budnick, turning his head slightly from time to time to listen, said, "We can't afford a diversion now. When we get to Eddies, you three can go and talk to her. Me and Pierre and the boys will stay there with the Blochs and set things up. Maybe one of Pierre's boys goes with you. Ok?" He turned his head to look at them. They didn't answer but just looked at each other. Budnick put his attention back on the road. "Ok, that's the way it is."

~

Detective Sgt. Marko put a two-way radio to his ear. "They know I'm here. They have help. Not sure. One car. Maybe two. Hmm, hmmm, right. You tap into their phones yet? What? Still waiting for the Company? You're fucking me. Unbelievable. I say we take them all down. The Company boys don't want-yeh, right, like they know what they're doing. Ok, got ya. Yeh, right, headed south back into the city. Gotta be important. What's made them back off? The Committee? Hey, I'll deal with who ever so long as I get my money. Later." He put the radio on the seat beside him, rubbed the stubble on his face, and tried to guess where the cars ahead were going.

~

The notes of Brahms' violin concertos were still drifting through the air in her apartment but Diana was no longer drifting in dreams. She was agitated and walking around her living room, wringing her hands and pouring glasses of wine which were drained too quickly to savour. She lit one cigarette after another and inhaled deeply. She only just managed to calm her nerves enough to stay this side of shattering into a thousand jagged pieces.

The bottle of red wine on the coffee table was empty. She strode over to the wine rack in the kitchen to get another. She inserted the corkscrew and began to turn it while holding a cigarette in her mouth. She was angry and twisted it with force and her face was almost red with the effort. The cork wouldn't come out.

"Fuck." She said loudly, just once and then, startled by the ringing of the phone in her bedroom, slammed the bottle and corkscrew down on the countertop so violently that she nicked her forefinger with the tip of the corkscrew.

It began to ooze blood. She swore again, almost cried, took a towel and covered the cut and went to pick up the phone. "Hello, who is this?" she challenged, her teeth clenched, her eyes blazing.

"Agius?" She felt faint when she heard the voice but managed to take hold of her self. "All right. Give me a minute." She drew in her breath and pulled the phone from her ear, then put it back by the bedside table.

She looked at the cloth around her finger. She felt faint from the sight of blood, but gathered herself and went to the bathroom to find a proper bandage. She had just finished cleaning the wound, and putting a band-aid on it when there was a sharp knock on the door. It was repeated once a second later. Then nothing.

She turned off the tap, made sure the bandage was in place, dried herself, smoothed her hair and went hesitatingly toward the door. She paused for two heartbeats as she put her hand on the handle. She didn't look through the peephole. She couldn't. She closed her eyes for strength and a second later she was standing in front of Agius, who's face was shadowed by the upturned collar of his coat.

"What do you want? I don't know anything else yet. You're frightening me. I don't like it."

Agius responded by walking past her into the apartment. She closed the door and looked at this man in the long dark coat. He stood still as if he were listening then slowly turned to face her. She didn't move.

"You have hurt your hand?"

"It's just a cut. I'll be fine, careless with a corkscrew. What do you care?"

"Ah, Diana, that's too harsh. I am not the monster you think I am. I care. The Committee cares. In fact they care so much that to make sure you are ok, they have asked me to check in with you and see how things are, whether you need any encouragement, that sort of thing."

"How do you do what you do, threatening people who've done nothing to you?"

Agius smiled and laughed softly, and rubbed his chin. "You're a naïve one. I'm doing what every body else does. I have a job. I do it. I don't do it. I have no job. One has to survive. Besides, my mother always said I had a sadistic streak. Didn't like me pulling the heads off my sister's dolls."

He smiled tightly as she jerked her head back in response.

"I'm joking. I'm sorry I frightened you again. Forgive me. How do I do it? Well, ask my shrink. The real question is what are you going to do about it. May I sit down?" and he waited for her to respond.

She didn't. She stared at him like she was trying to understand a cubist painting, trying to rearrange the misplaced humanity to make up a real face, cocking her head to one side. She couldn't fit the images together. She closed her eyes, opened them and, pointing to the sofa offered him a seat. He took off his coat, threw it over a side chair, and sat down.

Now he was in the light she got a better look at him. She heard Susan's voice remark about a cobra. "Susan thinks your attractive but like one of those Indian snakes." As she let her words take effect she said, "I was trying to open a bottle when I did this," and raised her bandaged finger. "Mind if I have some wine?"

Agius crossed his legs and relaxed back on the sofa. "Why not? A snake. Not very flattering but I suppose I can be deadly."

Diana took a bottle of wine from the rack. She winced as she made the mistake of trying to use her bandaged hand. Suddenly, Agius was behind her, very close. She turned into him. He took the bottle from her. She felt his breath on her face. He casually turned away, picked up the corkscrew and pulled out the cork. He offered it to her to check but she stepped away and went into the living room and lit a cigarette and stared out the window.

The wind had picked up and the naked trees whipped and tossed their branches at each other as if they were playing a game. Clouds scudded by from the west, side lit by a half moon low in the sky. There were people on the street hurrying along in the cold. Cars made their endless procession up and down the street. It was a normal evening.

Agius approached her with a glass of wine in his right hand. He offered it to her. She took it, with barely a glance, and said, still staring through the window, 'Your fake charm is wearing a bit thin.'

*   *   *   *   *

22

The moon retreated behind a line of clouds as Diana withdrew from the window, and walked past Agius to sit in a chair. He continued standing, looking at her then went to the kitchen and poured himself a glass. "I hope you don't mind," he said when he returned. "One shouldn't drink alone."

She crossed her legs so he could see her knees and the shadows above and looked him up and down, examining him. "Be my guest." She lit another cigarette from the pack on the table next to her. "So, are you going to tell me why you're here or am I supposed to guess?"

Agius stepped towards the sofa across from her and sat down, but stayed leaning forward. He drank from his glass, then leaned back and put it down on a side table. He said nothing as he leaned forward again and put his head in the palm of one hand that rested on his knee, the thinker, thinking. He regarded her with suspicion and desire.

"My instructions are to act with more dispatch. They are very impatient. They want results. So, I want results or it comes down on my head. You have to get that stick."

"I can't." She pulled on the cigarette with her lips and inhaled then blew the smoke into the air above her head. "I tried to meet them but they've ignored me."

"They went to the professor's house and now they are on their way downtown. Do you know what they are going to do?"

"No, but I think Johnny will come here."

"I hope you haven't warned them. That would not be very wise." He stopped and arched his eyebrows slightly as he watched her turn to the window to avoid his gaze.

She put the cigarette to her lips again and focused her eyes on his. "I told you. I don't want anything to happen to them. And how can I help you? You know more than I do. Why don't you get what you're after yourself?"

"We can. Things are moving very quickly. But if I have to act myself then it could be unpleasant. If you can get it or tell us how to get it then, well, it would be easier for you, for Johnny, for everyone. And we need to know if they made copies. The information has to disappear forever."

Something beeped in his coat pocket and he reached in and pulled out a phone. "Agius. Yes. Yes, I'm listening. All right. Keep me informed." He put it on the sofa next to him.

"Well, if Johnny is coming, I think I have to wait here with you to greet him. He and I are almost old friends. I am sure he won't mind."

"I mind." She retorted and her eyes narrowed as she glared at him through a cloud of smoke.

"You have no choice. Perhaps you can show me some of your artwork while I'm waiting. I have an interest."

"Everything is in another room and I'm not interested."

"Very well, as you please." He reached for his glass and held it while watching her. "It would be more pleasant to pass the time in conversation. But, have it your way." He brought the glass to his lips and looked at her steadily as he sipped.

~

Budnik picked up his phone. "Pierre, can we lose the tail?"

Pierre saw Budnick looking back at him in his rear view mirror. "Let's see what we can do." He put his phone down and picked up the walkie-talkie and talked quietly into it. The Blochs could only hear a murmur of words, spoken in French. Then Pierre put the radio down and looked back at them in the mirror.

"Something is going to happen. Budnick wants us to lose the car that is following us. So that is what we are going to do. Make sure your seatbelts are tight. Just in case."

Emma's heart began to race and she quickly tightened the belt around her waist and reached for her husband's hand. He took it and felt the heat as her blood raced through her. He looked over at her and smiled reassuringly. She squeezed his hand that she was all right.

Her eyes shone in the reflection of passing streetlights and traffic. He saw her in Berlin walking towards him one evening across the Alexanderplatz, when they had first met. He had stopped in mid stride as he noticed her walk confidently towards him with her hands in her raincoat pockets, a purse slung over her shoulder, a hat slouched over one side of her face, hiding it and framing it, a mystery until she turned to look at him as she passed.

He remembered the sudden light of her smile and still wondered that he had the courage to follow her to a violin recital and talk his way into a seat next to her without having a ticket. When he sat next to her she had simply turned to him and smiled then turned back to the stage and said to him quietly, "I hope you enjoy it."

"Remember Alexanderplatz?"

He saw her smile and her eyes shone more brightly, "Of course. I saw you from a long way off, you know. I wanted you to follow me and you did. I have my magic." She looked at him with uplifted head, teasing and daring him to challenge her.

"Well, my Emma, I think we need a little of that magic now." He looked around the car and behind them to see what was happening.

Marko picked up his radio. "They've picked up speed. We're near Crawford and Yonge. Yeh, I think I've got a tail. Right. OK."

He put the radio down and took a gun out of a shoulder holster, placed it next to him and looked in the mirror. Suddenly the two vehicles ahead turned right onto a side street. Marko accelerated. He veered to the right to make the turn. A horn screamed on his left, right next to his ear. It startled him for an instant. A black car sped past him as the horn sounded and pulled to the right, into his path. He braked and swerved to avoid it. It drew ahead fast. He put his foot down on the pedal. His car shot forward and streetlights flashed past like streamers. His blood pounded in his head. He was flying high. The world had stopped being dull. It got less dull fast.

There was a sudden red flash of lights as the car ahead squealed its brakes and turned sideways across his path, and stopped, blocking the road. Passing cars blared their horns, lights flashing in protest, as Marko stepped on his brakes, pulled the wheel hard to the right, fishtailed to the left and slid to a stop five feet from the other car, both engines still purring hot.

Marko shook his head to recover himself and his position and quickly looked around. A tall man in a black leather jacket and black jeans wearing a baseball cap slowly got out of the other car and walked towards him. He was carrying something in his right hand. Marko lunged for his gun. But he couldn't find it. A shiver of panic passed through his body as he dropped to his right to search for it on the floor. His fingers touched the hard grip of the Glock, curled around it and pulled it up level with the seat as he raised his body and turned to the door. But he was too late. His door was opened and his head came up to feel the barrel of a Browning 9mm pistol pressed firmly against it while his ears heard the words, "Any move will be fatal. Place your gun on the seat." He did as he was told.

"Put your hands over your head and get out."

He raised his hands. The man in the cap stepped clear of the door and signaled to him to come out. "Now, start walking down the road, no, the direction you came from. Don't look back. I will wait two minutes. Walk fast."

Marko looked at the man in the cap but his face was blackened with camouflage stick. His hand was steady and his voice was determined. Marko obeyed without question, turned and started to walk. He didn't look back. There was no point. The target was long gone. Besides, the walk was refreshing. The wind had picked up and it was cold. He thought himself lucky. Cars passed him but none stopped to offer help. His lone figure gradually got smaller and smaller as the man in the cap watched him shrink into a dot in the distance and then walked back to his car, put his gun in his jacket, got behind the wheel, signaled left, entered the flow of traffic and casually drove away.

Seconds later Pierre's radio squealed and hissed and a phantom voice said, "It's done."

"Merci, David, Any problems?"

The radio hissed again, "Only for him, his pride is hurt...and it's a long walk."

The radio crackled again and Pierre put it down. He picked up his mobile. "The problem is dealt with. Looks like he was alone but it won't stay that way."

He put his phone down as Budnick's van turned left into a boulevard of expensive homes bordering a treed ravine and began to weave through beautiful streets of fine old homes and grand and ancient, naked trees. He followed him through the maze of streets to a cul de sac backing onto the ravine. The van turned into a long driveway, flanked by an iron gate that was already open. Beyond, lit by small floodlights, appeared a two story stone house draped with ivy.

Pierre picked up his radio, "Entrons, ici. Prenez garde dehors." His radio crackled in response as he drove into the grounds and stopped his car next to the van. He waited in silence with the Blochs as Budnick climbed out of the van, followed by Susan, Eiger and Conway, and walked over to his car. He rolled the window down.

Budnick leaned his head in. "Ok, Pierre. Keep an eye on the grounds while we go in. It's a little hairy."

"Yes, don't worry, boss, everything will be covered. My men will alert us if there is anything. But they will track us here soon if they have not already. Time is short." Budnick nodded grimly.

"OK. Professor, Emma. Come and meet my friend Eddie Mackenzie." He opened the rear door and waited for them to make their way out of the car, then walked with them to where the other three were standing. Then the group approached the house.

The door opened before they could ring the bell. A man of middle height, and stocky build, wearing reading glasses on top of his balding head stood in the doorway, dressed in corduroy jeans and a blue sweatshirt. He came towards them and took Budnick's hand.

"Come on in Walter, I'm all fired up about this mystery of yours. Please," he stepped aside as he waived them in. "You are welcome."

He turned and walked into the house. They followed him in single file and took up positions in a large room off the foyer. It was twenty feet long and as wide. The walls were lined with hundreds of books and scrolled documents lying scattered on tables and shelves. A large oak desk occupied the far end of the room. Eddie Mackenzie invited them to sit in leather chairs that faced the desk and he went over to a side cabinet and took out a bottle of liquid amber. "Scotch?" He cocked his head to one side as he waited for an answer. Eiger asked, "Single malt?" Eddie said, "Of course, Arbelour, but I have Johnny Walker if you wish."

"Black?"

"Yes. But try the Arbelour. I think you will like it."

Budnick and Conway also accepted the offer and were soon sitting in their chairs holding a glass while Eddie poured a glass for the professor as well. He offered red wine to Emma and Susan. They accepted with gracious smiles.

Susan sat down in a chair near Budnick. Emma followed her husband to a love seat set to one side of the room and they both waited with anticipation for Eddie Mackenzie to sit down. They followed him with their eyes as he gently lowered his body onto his high back chair, put the whisky bottle on the desk in front of him, picked up his glass, lifted it to them and proclaimed, "To Burns and all that is right."

They raised their glasses in reply and all the men took a strong shot and savoured the sensations that warmed their courage. Emma and Susan raised their glasses and tasted the wine. Eddie Mackenzie turned his attention to the solid figure of Budnick sitting in the chair in front of him, trying to control the twitch in his shoulder.

"OK, Budnick, what've you got. It better be good." He put his glass down, leaned back in his chair and crossed his arms waiting to be convinced their visit was worth the scotch they were drinking.

Twenty minutes later Budnick's account of events, repeatedly punctuated by spontaneous comments and asides by Conway and Eiger, came to a conclusion and Eddie Mackenzie leaned forward and began asking the professor questions, questions about Moore and Frank, about Marina and questions pointedly about himself and Emma. The relaxation induced by the whisky evaporated into tension as Mackenzie probed and tested like a lawyer cross-examining a hostile witness. Eiger listened and watched in admiration. He had rarely seen it done better.

"You got the stick with you?"

Mackenzie stood up and walked over and poured himself another glass of whisky and took a gulp. He turned to scan them as he waited for the answer. Budnick took it out of his pocket and put it down on the desk in front of him. Eddie walked back and sat down in his chair and picked the stick up and held it between the fingers of both hands as he examined it.

"I still can't get over these things. Always amazes me. Anyway, you're right Budnick this is dynamite if what you say is on here is really there. But I gotta take some time to look at it. My publisher has to see it. The lawyers have to consider it. How do you know this isn't fake?"

The professor began to become agitated and dropped Emma's hand. "I can assure you it is authentic. Frank wasn't killed because he created a fake document. He secured access to the most secret files. I trusted him and…"

Mackenzie rocked back in his chair, raised his hands and rested them on top of his head. "No hard feelings professor, I don't doubt your sincerity but sometimes people can be taken in and….." He was suddenly interrupted by the sharp but commandingly soft voice of Emma,

"Mr. Mackenzie, I am a very good judge of character and of people and I know when someone is lying to me. Frank was telling the truth. His friends trusted him and died for it. Now we are under threat. You trust Mr. Budnick. He trusts us. We trusted them. It is very simple. The question is whether your newspaper will publish these documents or not. That is what we wish to know. Otherwise there is no point in wasting each other's time." She fixed her eyes on him and watched as he reacted to her words.

Mackenzie's solid frame appeared to wither as the energy of her voice allowed no retreat. He lowered his hands from his head and put them on the desk, his hands clasped and leaned forward towards her. "I meant no disrespect to you or your husband or those who have died already. Forgive me."

He turned to the professor and asked, "Are you prepared to appear in print, to repeat what Budnick told me, what the rest have told me?"

The professor sat bolt upright in his chair, defiant of the world, "I will be proud to do so, Mr. Mackenzie, if you will have the courage to publish it."

He took hold of Emma's hand again. Emma continued to transfix Mackenzie's eyes with hers. He returned the gaze and it seemed for a second that their eyes were linked by a single beam of light that echoed back and forth between them. He blinked and quickly disengaged. "What do you think, Budnick?"

Budnick got up, walked over to stand behind the professor and his wife and placed his hands on their shoulders. "I don't know these people, Eddie. Never met them before a few days ago. But you know me. We go way back. I know people and like Emma said we all trust each other. Conway and Eiger, Susan too..." and he looked over at her as she held her wine glass in her lap and watched him. "We've seen the documents. Looks real to us. Help us, Eddie."

* * * * *

23

Eddie sat back in his chair and rubbed his jaw with his hand. "I can't do it alone Budnick. I gotta get the ok from the publisher on something like this. This will have to wait 'til tomorrow. I can't call him at this hour. I think you better hang on to this until we can arrange a meeting with him." He handed the device back to Budnick.

Budnick took it without smiling and nodded grimly. "We're in a bind Eddie. This needs action. I thought I could count on you."

Just then Budnick's cell buzzed. "Hang on, Eddie," and he put it to his ear. There was silence as he listened, then closed it. "You invite anyone? Looks like you have visitors."

He got up and walked to the front door. Eddie got up with him and followed. Conway and Eiger stood up to look out the windows.

As they got to the door, Pierre walked in, gun in hand. "A couple of cars cruised by, two men each. Likely just surveillance, but what you want me to do?"

Eddie Mackenzie stepped back from the open door. "Who is this Budnick? What's going on?"

Budnick made the introductions and said, "I told you we were in a bind Eddie."

Mackenzie had turned pale and beads of sweat formed on his brow. Pierre stood with gun in hand, waiting for instructions. Budnick put his hand on his shoulder and spoke softly, almost in a whisper. "Can you dissuade them?"

Pierre looked at him. "Flies can be difficult to deal with. The grounds are large. I don't like the ravine. We can't cover all the angles."

Mackenzie broke in, "How did they track you here?"

Pierre shrugged and said, "Maybe there was another spotter, maybe our cell phones. It does not matter. They are here. We are here."

Pierre received a call on his phone. "Yes, where? All right. Oui, let them know you are there. We don't want them going to ground."

The radio crackled and hissed, as they listened to the two men outside respond to Pierre's instructions. Then there was silence. Pierre turned to Budnick and Mackenzie and spoke in earnest, "It is better if some of us leave. Maybe they will make no move if they do not know who has the stick."

Budnick nodded quickly, "Maybe you're right." He turned to Conway, Eiger and Susan, "You three go to Diana's and find out what she's nervous about. Take Pierre's car ..." Pierre nodded in agreement, and gave Conway his keys. "The disk stays here."

Susan picked up her purse and took a last sip of wine. She pulled her lipstick out and nervously applied it, looking in a small hand mirror. They all watched her as she touched the stick along her lips and rolled her lips together. She looked back at them.

"What? Hey, if something exciting is gonna happen I wanna look good. OK?" and pretended to pout like a defiant schoolgirl.

Pierre smiled at her, "It's no problem for me, it makes everything more romantic I think." Conway shook his head at her as Eiger said, "Sorry Pierre but that goes for me too," and held out his arm for her to take.

Budnick stopped them just as they were about to pass through the door. "Call me." The men nodded, while Susan kissed him on the cheek. They walked over to Pierre's car. Conway took the driver's seat. Susan got in the back and sat behind Eiger.

A man in black jeans, leather jacket and baseball cap appeared from the shadows of the trees on the edge of the driveway and said something to Conway who nodded and started the engine. The man put a radio to his mouth and spoke, then lowered it and waived his hand. The car spun its tires briefly as too much torque was applied, then, under control it disappeared into the tunnel of trees that led to the road.

~

Agius watched Diana as she sat smoking cigarette after cigarette, drinking too much wine. She acted as if he was not there for the first hour, but that became tedious and impossible to carry off so she slowly accepted his presence as a prisoner finally accepts the cell, as one of the conditions of life.

The wind was rushing through the trees below her apartment with the loud whispering sound of breakers rushing up a pebble beach and she remembered the waves breaking on the shore of Cape Cod one late September day when the tourists had left and she had wandered the dunes alone, feeling the Atlantic breeze running its hands through her hair, when she was still young and lived on bright hopes.

She drew on her cigarette, leaned her head back, closed her eyes and walked through the dunes to the beach where shells glittered in the sand. She could smell the ozone in the air and began to dream. But the buzzing of a fly annoyed her and she tried to knock it away and almost knocked her glass over. She sat up to catch it, opened her eyes and found the buzz was him – on his phone-murmuring and listening. She kept still. He continued to listen, then said, "Good. They will come here. Let me know when they arrive. No, give them room."

He put his phone down on the table and relaxed back into his chair. "Your friends are on the way. It seems they went to the house of a newspaperman. That was a stupid thing to do. There are others in the area. They are dangerous." He suddenly stood up and went to the window to look out at the street below.

He turned back to her. His voice more tense, "They will be here in twenty minutes. I expect your cooperation."

Diana remained silent and sat with her long thumbnail touching her lips, a cigarette held between two fingers curling smoke past her half closed eyes.

"What are you going to do?"

He pulled the sides of his mouth wide in an attempt to smile, "So, she speaks." The smile vanished into a mask of stone. "That depends on them."

~

The Lexus sped through the dark streets with Conway at the wheel. Eiger was on his cell phone. 'She's not answering.' He sent a text. "Be there in 20." Then looked around at Susan who was snuggled back in one corner of the back seat, hidden in the shadows. "You, ok?"

"Yeh, sure, but I don't exactly get paid for this. Can't you guys take me home and deal with it yourselves?"

Conway talked to her in the mirror, "Sorry, honey, but you're as involved as us now. Shouldn't have got you involved but it's too late. Don't worry. We'll take care of it. Besides we'd miss you too much, right Eiger?"

Eiger attempted a smile, "He's right. And anyway I thought you got a kick out of taking the photo this morning."

Susan sank deeper into the shadows, "Well, yeah, I did. But there was a cute chick in the scene then and I was hungry."

Conway and Eiger looked at her and then each other. She looked back and asked, "What?"

Eiger, like Conway, just looked ahead at the road and replied, "Aren't we good enough?" then, "You don't need to answer."

Conway turned on the radio and tuned it to a jazz station as the dj said softly, "And now the golden voice of Frank Sinatra backed up by the great Tommy Dorsey, a big hit way back when, here is...'Imagination', sit back, listen, and enjoy the sounds they make no more...." as the trumpets came in slow and sexy, the clarinets kicked in behind them and, gently, in sympathy with the sweet siren horns, Sinatra began to sing of love lost and Eiger, Conway and Susan could only mourn with him.

~

Eddie walked back to his desk, poured himself another scotch and offered the same to the professor. A nod to the wine bottle drew a mouthed "No thank you." from Emma who stood up and walked over to the bookshelves along the wall to the left of the desk.

She hesitated and pulled out a volume. "You like Ovid, Mr. Mackenzie?"

Mackenzie picked up his glass and walked over to where Emma was standing, "Yeh, if only I could write like that I'd be a happy man. But we each do what we can. You're familiar with Metamorphoses?"

Emma turned her face from his as she put the volume back and pulled out a slim volume. "Yes, of course. Nothing is forever. Everything changes. That's what gives us hope. But this is also very interesting." And she opened the book to the first page. "Have you read 'Is This A Man?' Mr. Mackenzie?"

"Yes, but a long time ago."

Emma smiled briefly and presented it to him with open and direct eyes.

"Then perhaps it is time to read it again to remember what the fascists did and what must be done to stop them. These types of people, people without morals, without pity, charity, any love of mankind, without honour, are always with us, Mr. Mackenzie. They can only be kept in check by lifting the rocks to expose them to the light. You are the person to do that. You must do that before we end up in camps like Primo Levi in Auschwitz, with no one to save us."

She smiled at him again, put the book back on the shelf and walked back over to her husband who remained in his chair, once again preparing his pipe, simply out of habit, while reflecting on the grace and the beauty of the woman he had first me that night in Berlin. But like his wife, he also waited for Eddie to answer Budnick's question.

Budnick was still by the door with Pierre who was listening on his walkie-talkie. Pierre looked tense and did not say much, just a few one-syllable responses while staying in eye contact with Budnick. He suddenly put the radio down and said something they could not hear. Budnick walked over to Eddies desk, arms down by his sides, thick neck twisting as he tried to calm his tic.

"So, what can you do for me Eddie? I know you have the authority to publish what you want. The publisher be damned."

Eddie turned to the professor and Emma, who kept her challenging gaze, fixed on his. He bit his lip, then said. "OK, tell me again, and tell me slowly while I write this up. I'm not the best writer for this but to hell with it, I can run two sentences together. But I want this in affidavit form, Budnick. You can set it up and swear it?"

Budnick grinned broadly. His eyes beamed with new energy and his shoulder twitched again. Then, while nodding slightly, said, "So, let's do it. Pierre says the wolf pack is ready to attack," and sat down at the desk.

Eddie turned to his laptop, opened it up, turned it on and then, as his glasses dropped from his head to his nose, faced the professor. "OK, professor, give it to me again. I work for the Free Press if I rightly remember. I'll get this out somehow." He began typing quickly as the professor sat forward, and began to speak.

~

The apartment was quiet, except for the mournful howl of the wind as the gusts rushed between the buildings and down the streets, rattling windowpanes and already rattled nerves. Agius sat without moving or even seeming to breathe. He seemed to be in another world. He sat with his head back and eyes closed, his mouth relaxed, as if he were an innocent. Diana wondered how angels fell and sat nervously, fidgeting, flicking more ashes on the mound in the tray next to her, biting her nails. Time tricked her and twenty minutes felt like twenty hours until, near the limit of angry patience her apartment phone rang. It startled her. She put her cigarette down into the tray forcefully and spilled some on the floor. She winced with the pain in her hand.

"You must be careful. Do not hurt yourself." He stood up, suddenly stepped towards her and stroked her hair. Then he walked to the front door and stood to one side of it. He removed a pistol from under his jacket. He waived it at her and ordered, "Answer the door. Invite them in. Invite them as you normally would."

Diana went to the phone, "Hi, Johnny, Yes, come on up." She put the phone down. She waited at the door looking at Agius as he looked at her and pointed his gun at her. They waited in silence, in expectation.

There was a sharp double knock on the door. Agius nodded his head and pointed his gun at the door. Diana walked to it and turned the knob. She opened the door and stepped back as three figures walked in one by one and one by one were ordered at gunpoint to sit down and make no moves.

Eiger was the first to speak, "What is this? Who the hell do you...."

Agius pointed his gun with more directness at Eiger,

"I don't give many warnings. Calm down. You know me. I know you. Our beautiful friend over there knows me too, isn't that so, Susan?" and he forced a grin at her. She sat open mouthed, unable to say anything.

"Mr. Conway, I presume?" he lowered his head in salutation. "I've heard of you. A pleasure. But we have no time for this chatter. I will get to the point," and he looked at each of them in turn. "I want that disk. We know you have it. It must disappear. The Committee will not permit that information to be released. Your newspaperman is making a mistake helping you."

Conway drew in his breath sharply.

"Yes, we know what you are trying to do. He will be dealt with."

Diana stood apart, still near the door. Agius turned to her. "Diana has hurt her hand. No, it was not me. An accident. Perhaps you would like to join Eiger over there?" She obeyed and slowly walked across the room to sit next to him at a dining table. Conway and Susan were on the couch.

Eiger spoke again, slowly, with deliberate emphasis. "I told you I would not cooperate with you. What's all this for? You going to shoot us if we don't cooperate?"

Agius laughed out loud at the joke, "I hope that is not necessary but I will if it is. Or some body else will. The Committee is not the only hunter of the device you have."

He abruptly stopped laughing and spoke in earnest. "The Committee gives me the power. I can let you get on with your lives of monotonous worries or I can terminate them. The method is not important. But we are not barbarians. There is no need for violence for its own sake. It must have a purpose."

Susan laughed cynically and shot back, "Very big of you I'm sure."

Agius smiled at her, "It's not charity. It is just a fact. The Committee wants order, their order of course, but order nonetheless and unnecessary violence threatens order. Too much of it makes the people nervous. But they can tolerate a little and even demand it if it appears in their interest. But believe me, we can do it without violence. I can arrange prison as your solution, for terrorism of course. None of you will ever come out." He shrugged his shoulders and twisted his face and continued, "So, it's a matter of logic that you cooperate. Diana sees what I mean," and he smiled and watched their reaction as they turned to look at her. She avoided their eyes, put her cigarette to her lips and deeply inhaled, "Thanks, Agius, for nothing."

* * * * *

24

Eddie listened and he typed as he listened. The professor paused in his narrative from time to time to fiddle with his pipe and collect his thoughts and when he did Eddie poured himself more scotch and drank a dram to keep him going. Budnick paced the room like a gladiator waiting to enter the arena of death, nervous and tense. Sometimes he stopped and pulled out a book and read a passage, rocking his head back and forth like he was at the Wailing Wall, his lips moving but without any prayer. Then he would pace again or go to the windows and look out into the darkness beyond the trees lit by the floodlights. He saw nothing, not even Pierre.

His mobile buzzed. He opened it while still looking out the window. "Hi, sweetie, yeh, yeh I'm fine, you? Uh-huh, uh huh, yeh I can make it. I promise, the school charging for tickets? Uh-huh, look, let me go, I'm in a meeting, tell your mother I'll be late. Oh, she'll be late too. Uh-huh, ok, and take the dogs out." He chuckled as he listened and then closed the phone and walked over to Emma, waiting for her turn to speak while watching Budnick with amusement.

"Mr. Budnick, I am glad you have joined me. You were making me a little edgy. Here," and she took his hand and pulled him down next to her, "A woman?"

Budnick's eyes twinkled, "No, just my daughter, fifteen and starting to learn things."

"You don't approve of your daughter learning things? This is very strange."

Budnick touched her hand and chuckled again, "Not the things I'm worried about. Hangs around with hoods, intellectual punks. Don't believe in anything, don't care about anything, and don't want to know anything."

Emma nodded and became sad, "Yes, I see it as well and Richard, at the university. There are some very interesting students but most of them —well, what can we say Mr. Budnick, we now live in a world where people boast about their ignorance. What can we expect?"

"We can expect more...and," he hesitated and looked up as the sound of quick steps foretold the sudden opening of the door revealing Pierre standing in silhouette as he stepped from the cold night air into the vibrating tension of the room. Eddie stopped typing. The professor stopped talking. They looked in his direction. Emma stood up, alarmed but calm. She stood with her hands held together in front of her.

Pierre stepped into the foyer like a leopard about to spring.

"There are maybe six of them now. Three cars. I think they will try something. One of them is the man we stopped. He's a cop. That one you know Jack, Marko."

Budnick got up and went towards him. "The others?"

"I don't know. Could be police, could be freelancers. They all look the same, baseball caps, bulletproof vests. But they are not here on legitimate business, boss. I think we must leave this place and we must leave now."

He put the walkie-talkie to his ear. It hissed and crackled as his men made situation reports. "D'accord, prenez garde, reste en contact."

"They say they can stop them but there will be trouble and people will be hurt. They suggest we leave. But we need another route out."

He looked over at Eddie who quickly rose to his feet, and breathing quickly said,

"There's a back driveway —it exits onto the ravine road, then into the city. I have two vehicles parked at the back. But what's happening? Shouldn't we call somebody?"

Budnick shook his head at him, "Nobody to call, Eddie. You're our only hope right now. You gotta come with us so you can finish this up and get it out tomorrow or I don't know what's gonna happen. Publish-then you'll know who your friends are, who you can call."

Eddie shook his head. "Look you guys. Take the cars. Here are the keys." He reached in his desk drawer and pulled them out onto the desk. "I'm not going. This is my house. They can't touch me. I'm too well known. They want you. I'm gonna call the police —you get out of here. I'll be fine."

Budnick started to protest but Eddie cut him off with a wave of his hand as he picked up the phone to call 911.

The sudden rapid pop of firecrackers startled them all. There was stunned silence. Eddie looked pleadingly at Budnick. Pierre shoved the front door shut and went low to the floor and like a crab went sideways to a window.

"Kill the lights!"

Eddie, frozen in place, didn't react. Budnick grabbed him and pulled him down to the floor next to him as three more sharp pops punctuated the silence followed by what sounded like the tapping of old typewriter keys. Emma stood frozen in place until her husband dropped from his seat to the floor, pulled her down with him and covered her body with his.

"Pierre, can you see anything?" Budnick half raised himself from the floor.

"Just some flashes in the dark."

His radio crackled loudly but the transmission was too broken to make out what the excited voice was saying. There was a second burst of tapping as the front door flew open and one of Pierre's men fell through it and onto the floor in front of them. Blood flowed from his right leg staining the floor red.

He squirmed away from the door, holding a pistol pointed at the darkness. "Sorry, too many, David is still out there. They are coming."

He turned white and sagged against Pierre who caught him as he went down and held him cradled in his arms. He repeated, "Budnick, we have to kill the lights. Now!"

Budnick leaped from the floor like a lion leaping a tree and pounced on the light switches just by the door that still lay open to the night. He felt a faint brush of air pass his head as he touched the switches and the whine of an angry mosquito, followed instantly by a loud crack as a wood panel on the opposite wall splintered into pieces. "Jesus!" he dropped to the floor again and kicked the front door shut. The lights were still on.

The radio came alive once more. "David, what's your status?" A distorted voice replied, "OK,... Marcel?"

Pierre tried to look into the darkness outside to see if he could see David, but could see nothing. He saw the flash of a pistol to his right near the driveway, then heard the quick retort of tapping from the left.

"With us, hit, we're going out the back-driveway, two cars. Cover us...best you can, then follow."

The radio hissed as he put it down. "Budnick give me your tie." Budnick understood at once and ripped it from his neck. A few seconds later, the blood stopped flowing from Marcel's leg.

Pierre looked over to Eddie who lay on the floor white as a sheet. Emma and the professor were still down too but now they both looked serenely calm as they lay there.

Pierre examined Marcel's wound. "My friend needs whisky."

Eddie was paralyzed. His whole body trembled but he couldn't move. Budnick was flat to the floor expecting the next whine and slap of a bullet on bone. An exasperated professor saw what was needed. He left Emma and crawled along the floor to get the bottle of scotch left on the desk, then over to Pierre who thanked him and tilted the bottle to the man's mouth and Marcel drank and began to regain some of his lost colour.

Budnick was ashen but calm. He raised up and asked quietly, "What do we do now, mon ami?"

Pierre rested Marcel's head on the floor and while looking out the window said, "We need to move now. We must get to the cars now. Marcel needs assistance. Help him to get there."

Budnick suddenly stood up. "Come on, Eddie, let's move, you want me to get shot standing here?" He reached down and pulled Eddie to his feet. Eddie recovered some colour and began to mutter, "I'm sorry, I don't know what happened ...to me..."

Budnick cut him off, "It's fine. Don't worry about it. It happened too fast, I don't feel so hot myself. But we've gotta get outa here. You believe me now?"

"Yeh, I believe you now."

He picked his glasses up from the floor, looked quickly around at Emma and the professor, and said, "The keys." He picked them up from the desk. "Let's go" and he picked up his laptop.

Budnick went over to Emma, "I'm sorry about this Emma. I..."

Emma raised herself to a sitting position and leaned back against a chair.

"It is not you who should apologise Mr. Budnick. It is my husband and I. We created this problem for you, for everyone. We should apologise to you. This is terrible, terrible. Who are these madmen shooting at us? I didn't expect... Richard, are you all right?" Before he could answer a powerful flash of light and a crack like a lightning strike lit the night outside and for a second moving figures were silhouetted against the darkness.

Pierre lifted Marcel to his feet, "Flash grenade! The escape. Mr. Mackenzie, Show us the escape. Budnick, the radio."

Budnick picked it up then Eddie signaled them to follow and led the way quickly through a hallway to a large room near the kitchen that led to another passage leading to an outer door at the back of the house. The professor and Emma followed behind him while Budnick helped half carry half walk the wounded man along with them. There was another loud bang and a flash of light through a side window and the reply of three quick pistol shots in the distance. Pierre answered Budnick's silent question with "David, they are trying to flush him out."

They carried Marcel through a final door out into a graveled circular driveway at the back of the house. It seemed to go nowhere but into a void surrounded by menacing trees. A BMW F10 and a Range Rover sat side by side, waiting for action. Eddie ran to the sedan, opened the door, put the laptop on the floor behind him and climbed into the seat and started the engine. He threw the keys for the Range Rover over to Pierre who grabbed them, quickly jumped in the front seat and started it up as Budnick kept Marcel from falling. Budnick helped push Marcel into the back seat and barked at the Blochs,

"Go with Eddie, I'll go with Pierre and Marcel." He watched them rush over to the sedan. More shots were heard near the house. Someone was shouting commands. Budnick ran over to Eddie. "You gotta follow us once we get down the ravine road but you know the way so take the lead then wait for us to pass. OK?"

"Yeh, I got it, but where we going?"

Budnick looked him in the eyes. His dilated pupils were like a cat's. He slapped him on the shoulder and said, "Figure that out as we go, Eddie. Figure that out as we go. See you later professor. Hang on Emma. And Eddie, don't lose us, we don't know the way. Keep your cell on." Then as the F10 purred to life, he turned and ran to the Range Rover and took the seat next to Pierre.

"David?" Budnick asked.

Pierre took the radio from his coat pocket. He revved the engine as he spoke rapidly. "Give us five." A voiced acknowledged. "You got two, gotta leave. Go. Later."

Pierre said, "D'accord mon ami, prenez garde monsieur," put the radio down, engaged the gears, and took off into the darkness of the ravine road. As they followed the red taillights of Eddie's car down the winding decent of the ravine, Pierre handed his gun to Budnick, "You know how to use this, boss? I think Marcel is not able to help us now."

Budnick looked at Marcel, lying across the rear two seats, his eyes tensed with pain, but not complaining. "No, but I learn quick." Pierre looked at him warmly. "OK, then start learning. They are determined I think." He stepped on the gas pedal hard and the vehicle shot forward into the naked night, as a cold rain began to drum and beat on the windshield and the rapid taps and dull syncopation of automatic pistols faded into the night.

The rain began to come down in sheets. It was difficult to see more than a few feet ahead of them. They slowed down just in time to avoid hitting the F10 stopped in front of them at the bottom of the ravine road. Pierre muttered "Idiot." and then drove around the black car and pulled up next to the driver's side. He rolled down the window as Budnick leaned his head out into the solid rain and shouted,

"OK, follow us, I'll get us some place safe." He waited with his head cascading rain down his face until Eddie waived his hand, nodded and said, "OK, sorry, Walter. If I pulled off you might've missed me in this." Budnick laughed, "OK, Eddie, but you gave Pierre a scare." He pulled in his head and wiped his hand over his short hair to squeeze out the worst of it.

Pierre looked over at him as he edged the Rover forward past the F10 and out onto the main road. "Where to boss?"

Budnick looked straight ahead as if looking at a map in the air, "You remember where Billy Stark's place is?"

Pierre looked quickly over in surprise and then back at the road. "The Choice?"

Budnick looked at him and then at Marcel and back. "Angels now I hear. Where else? Tell me. He owes me. We need time and we need to get Marcel treated. They've got a safe house and they have a doctor on the payroll. It's getting late. Not my idea of home but we don't have a choice that I can see, except Starkey's place." Pierre stared ahead at the road grimly, "OK, Boss. OK, Marcel?" and he looked in the rear view mirror. Marcel turned his head and lifted it, "Ça va, I have no other suggestions, mon ami," and lay his head back and closed his eyes.

*   *   *   *   *

25

Agius opened the door on the first knock and two men walked in wearing long raincoats. One of them whispered something in his ear. He didn't reply but turned to the group still sitting and waiting.

"Things are a bit out of control. Your friends were approached at Mr. Mackenzie's house. People have been shot." He raised his hand as Eiger began to stand and Susan rose to join him. "Your friends have left. It appears they were not the ones who were shot. But they have disappeared like thieves into the night."

Conway ignored Agius warning hand and launched himself out of his seat to confront him, "Who the hell are you? Who are you calling thieves, you goddam....What the fuck is go...." Agius stepped back and made a nod to the tall man standing next to him who suddenly pulled a pistol from his coat pocket and pointed it at Conway and said, "He told you to sit down."

Conway stood his ground and dared him but he felt Susan's hand tug on his hand and when he looked at her she shook her head no, her eyes wide, harassed. He relented and very slowly sat back down but continued to glare at Agius and the man with the pistol.

"Very wise. We do not want to repeat what has

happened. We hoped to obtain the stick without any problem but now we have a problem."

Conway stood up again and shouted, "You're the mother fuckers who have the problem. You're crazy. You've killed how many people now and you tell me we have a problem?"

He couldn't say anymore. The second man shoved him hard in the chest with his open hand and he collapsed back, stunned by the blow.

Agius sat down on a chair opposite them. "We did not kill those people. The ones who paid Frank to obtain the information are responsible for that."

Eiger laughed. "What are you giving me? Local cops killed them. They couldn't do it without you."

Agius remained calm and pursed his lips in acknowledgement that Eiger had a point but replied, "Nevertheless it was not the action of the Committee. We have our Special Operations Unit. I am part of it. If we wanted to take such action we would have done it by now. We prefer to be more discrete. The Americans though, well they are in love with violence. One can say it is even a sexual phenomenon with them. The symptom of a society without love. But we digress into national psychology." He paused. "We will find that team in the next few hours. They will be dealt with. Our associates there have already picked up their confederates in the south. The people here in their pay have exposed themselves. They are not many but they are ruthless. We were only informed they were active just before Frank was murdered. But don't blame us. The Americans should not have let it get this far."

Eiger laughed again, "You make me laugh. These days everyone's out for themselves. You guys break the law everyday, the entire structure of the country is infected with a poison that rots everything good we ever had. Why wouldn't some of your guys go off on their own thing? You really have to be kidding me. You're the Committee we're all supposed to be scared of. Give me a break."

Agius bristled and his face flushed as his eyes narrowed. "The poison is disorder and chaos. The Committee cannot permit that. The Principals here or in Washington cannot permit that. You talk about democracy and truth in your trial, in your tiresome lectures. You talk about justice. There is no such a thing. A crisis exists. You can see it all around you. In a crisis you must have order. The people are told a myth. It makes them feel good about themselves. It panders to their egos. You want to take that myth from them and tell them there is no god. They don't want to be told that, Eiger. They are children."

Diana stood up and walked over to the kitchen. The man who had shoved Conway moved to stop her but Agius waved him off. She looked over at them unconcerned, weary. "The lecture bores me. Need a cigarette. Susan?" and looked over at her.

"Yeh, sure, thanks."

Diana walked over and offered her the pack. Susan took one and put it to her lips. Diana bent towards her and lit it as Susan looked in her eyes. Diana stood up and went back to her seat and as she sat she pulled her skirt up high, and leaned back to smoke. She stared at Agius and saw that he was looking at her legs. She smirked. "So, like I asked you when you got here. What do you want from us?"

Eiger answered, "It's clear what they want. We're hostages."

Agius smiled at him, "Of course. Until we get the disk you will not be released. If we get it in the next hours we shall leave you alone. If not, well, we will take you to a more secure place."

Eiger fired back, face reddened with anger,"You mean a secret place."

"Yes. If you want to be dramatic, yes, a secret place. You have always had a flair for the dramatic, Eiger. It is one of the things that make you a danger to us in the trial.

People tend to believe you. You are sincere. But sometimes, really, you are a bit over the top. The danger is clear. We cannot allow you to continue. You must bend or you will be broken. We can make you rich or you can spend the rest of your life on the street without any friends. It is not difficult to arrange."

"And that is exactly why the information must be released; to stop this madness. Your type will disappear from the world one day."

"You are very old fashioned, my friend. You are out of touch. Liberty is gone, and only a minority ever enjoyed it anyway. We all have to play our part. You will have to play yours one way or another."

"In a farce, staged by hypocrites."

"As you will, Eiger. It does not matter to me what you think. Everything now depends on Budnick and the Blochs. Where will they go?"

Conway said contemptuously, "I thought you guys knew everything. Johnny's right. This is a farce. Thought your guys were on top of everything. And how should I know where they are?"

Agius tried to stay calm but he was becoming a little irritated with all the chitchat and the insults and attitude. He said slowly and firmly,

"We shall track them. If their phones are on, their radios, we'll know. But so far they've been silent. So where will they go?"

Conway laughed again, "I told you, no clue." He turned his head away and looked behind him out the window.

Agius went over to the kitchen while the other two men kept watch by the door, one with his gun still drawn but pointing at the floor.

"Very well, then we shall wait for them to make contact. More wine anyone?"

~

The two vehicles sped down the highway headed north. The broken white lines flashed by like blasts from a ray gun. The headlights of cars approaching them and cars following, cast changing shadows on the faces of Budnick and Pierre. Pierre stared ahead at the road, his face hard, only softened by the shadow of a beard beginning to appear. Budnick sat quietly, his hands in his lap, thinking of the next step, his face the expression of a bulldog. Marcel lay motionless in the back, only breaking the silence with a quiet moan when the pain escaped his control.

Behind them, in the F10, Eddie Mackenzie wondered how a quiet night at home had become a desperate flight into the night and occasionally glanced at the mirror to make sure that Emma and the professor were really there. Nothing was said for several miles as they left the city behind them. The professor broke the long silence with a simple question.

"Where are we going Mr. Mackenzie?"

"No idea, Professor. No idea, my friend. We just have to trust Budnick. And I trust him."

The professor looked back at him in the mirror, "Yes, we trust him too, but none of us can control events. We are swept up in them like debris in a flood and carried through life on a raging torrent. What can we do?"

Eddie looked back at the professor and his lips formed a half smile as he nodded and replied, "I don't know professor, but right now we need time. The information you have will change the entire country once the people know what's going on. The people don't like to be lied to and played for fools. If we can get a day, a few hours, I can get it into the paper."

Emma's eyes flashed from the dark of the back seat into the mirror, "Then they will come after you and your paper will they not?"

"Let 'em try, this is a free country still, or so I thought. Sure, they'll be pissed, but they'll be pushed out before they can organise."

"I hope so Mr. Mackenzie but they are very powerful, how do you know the people at your paper will help you?"

"They will, or I've wasted my life."

Just then Mackenzie's mobile beeped. He put it to his lips.

"Yes, Budnick, what's happening? Uh-huh, right, you're kidding me, wait a minute. I did a bad piece on them a couple of years ago, I...yeh, ok, ok, understand. Ok, whatever you say. We'll keep close."

Budnick closed the phone and chuckled, "Eddie's worried. Did a piece on the Angels once. Not exactly flattering." He chuckled again. Pierre smiled and half laughed, then put his mobile to his mouth. "David, what's your status? OK, no, Marcel, he will live, OK, here Budnick, tell him where we are going." He handed the mobile over. Budnick talked for a couple of minutes and then broke the call.

"He'll join us there. At least he's OK, but Conway and company are quiet."

"I don't like that boss. We been driving for an hour and nothing from them."

Budnick nodded and typed a text, "Out of the house, OK, what's your situation?" then held the phone in his lap waiting for the answer.

Eddie Mackenzie was shaking his head and muttering to himself as he stared at the lights of the Range Rover ahead of him. Emma leaned forward and touched him on the shoulder gently.

"Mr. Mackenzie, you are agitated I think and we would like to know what Mr. Budnick said to you."

Eddie's body tensed, then relaxed. He answered the mirror, "I'm sorry Emma, professor. Budnick told me

230

where we're going and I'm not exactly happy about it but he says he can't think of any place else."

"And where is that, Eddie," the professor asked insistently, as if he were faced with a slow child.

"Budnick, has a client, one of the biker gangs. They owe him. They trust him. They have a place up north a ways. Trouble is I did a hatchet job on them a couple of years ago saying they should be expunged from the earth. You see what I mean?"

Emma asked, "Which biker gang, Mr. Mackenzie?"

"You know them?"

"I try to keep up with current events on many levels. I know many things you may think I should not." She looked in the mirror and expected an answer.

"OK, Emma, you got me. The Angels."

She looked startled as she retreated into the shadows of the back seat. "I see." She tightened her grip on her husband's arm and tried to hide deeper in the seat.

Eddie pressed on the gas pedal to keep up with the vehicle ahead. He gazed ahead as he spoke, and checked the side mirrors back and forth, "You ever heard of the Hell's Angels, professor?"

"Ah, yes, of course, I remember they were involved in that Rolling Stones concert back at... but I didn't think they were up here."

"Altamont, yeh, that's them, professor, same guys. Bad guys. Real bad, if you cross them. So, these guys are like the Canadian version, some say they're linked. I said so anyway."

Now it was the professor's turn to say "I see." Eddie nodded, resigned to his fate, "I see, is right professor, I see is right." He gripped the steering wheel tighter like he was hanging on to a life ring thrown to him as he drowned in the deep end.

26

Conway jerked when his phone beeped to tell him he had a message. Agius stood up from the kitchen chair he was sitting in and extended his hand. "Give me the phone."

Conway sullenly gave it over and waited to see what would happen. Susan touched his arm as she stared at Agius and then looked over at the other two men. She half smiled, partly out of fear, partly in an attempt to seduce them and put them off guard. Neither of the men answered her look. But Agius did. He began tapping on the phone. Eiger and Conway half rose to challenge him but again the man with the gun waved them down. The third man moved closer to the door to block it and also pulled out a pistol.

Agius looked at them and shook his head. "Not wise to try things. There," he said, as he stopped tapping, "Here you are Conway, you can read it to the others." He smiled like a barracuda in the sea.

Conway took the phone and read to himself, his lips moving almost imperceptibly. He stopped, then started again, this time out loud.

"At Diana's. Need to meet. Have a problem. Where are you? Everything OK?"

Eiger bit his thumbnail as he listened. Diana lit another cigarette. The ashtray next to her was running over with ashes. Susan stood up suddenly.

"I have to go to the bathroom. Or is there a rule about that?"

Agius smiled at her, then nodded at the man by the door. He walked towards the bathroom door, opened it and nodded his head for her to go in.

She walked over slowly, eased past him and went into the bathroom, flipped on the light and began to close the door. The man put his foot forward to block it. She pulled the door back and walked out to confront him and Agius, hands on her hips, "You better think twice about that."

Agius raised his eyebrows slightly, "Let her, she's not armed. We're not barbarians. Ladies have privileges."

The man stepped back and let Susan go back in. He smiled at her as she passed. She turned her head away, went in, and slammed the door shut.

"Anybody else?" asked Agius. "Might as well all do it at the same time. I don't want to be bothered with a lot of commotion. It makes me nervous and I don't need to get nervous."

Diana stood up.

"OK, Conway, Eiger, you?"

Eiger stopped biting his thumbnail and stood up, "Yeh, sure, this sitting all the time is getting to me. You don't want to make me nervous either." He looked at each of the men in turn. But they said nothing to his challenge.

~

Budnick saw the message light blink on his phone and read Conway's message. He glanced back at the car behind, then said, "Twenty minutes til we get there, you think?" Pierre flicked his eyes off the road, "Yes. About."

Budnick dialled Conway and put the phone close to his face. He waited. On the other end Agius looked at the screen and saw Budnick's name. He pressed the green icon, and said "Good evening Mr. Budnick. We have not met but I think we will soon. My name is Agius. I speak for your partner."

There was a brief silence as Budnick took in the situation. Agius had a half smile on his face as he looked at Conway and Eiger. He whispered, "I would say he is surprised."

Pierre looked quickly over again, and then at the man lying in the back, eyes closed, breathing steadily. "Something's up." He said it with certainty as if he had heard the voice on the phone. Budnick turned his head to him and nodded, then began to speak. "Who are you?"

Susan came out of the bathroom as Agius began to speak again. She stopped near the door, close to the man standing there. He looked her up and down but didn't smile, just waved her to her place. He watched her return. Diana began to return where she came from but stopped to listen with the others.

"Let us just say that I'm with the Special Operations Unit of the Committee. You have something we want and we are not prepared to wait. My principals are pressing to have the information returned. So long as you are in possession of the device that contains that information, so long are you in danger."

Budnick spoke quietly and calmly but from determination not fear. "Where are my people?"

Agius surveyed the room as he spoke, fixing his eyes on each of his captives in turn. "You must understand that we found it necessary to take measures to force your hand. Simply put Mr. Budnick, your friends are hostages to guarantee the result. They will not be released until that device is in our hands and if it is released to the public or if it falls into the hands of the renegade formation then a price will have to be paid. Your friends will be detained indefinitely and secretly. In other words, Mr. Budnick, they will disappear, as they like to say. And, in the end so will you and those with you. Everyone connected with that device and that information have no future unless we have complete cooperation."

"You have no authority. The Committee has no legal existence. Once we expose this information all of you will be brought down. It's you who will end up in a prison. You won't dare do anything. You're bluffing. The rats are panicking and they've sent in weasels like you to do the dirty work."

Agius began to walk around the apartment, more and more agitated but trying to stay in control. "You amaze me. Really, you do. That is never going to happen. The illusion will never be broken. The whole society depends it. Give me your answer." He waited but he heard nothing. "Budnick? You have to give me an answer."

Budnick sat still in the seat, staring at the road ahead, the dark sky, the trees bowing and dancing to the beat of the wind and the drumming of the rain. He said nothing, just listening to the voice demanding an answer and sound of the Rover humming down the road. He made a decision. He spoke. "All right. But I don't trust you. You take delivery on my terms."

Agius stopped pacing and looked up to the ceiling and then down again, "The delivery cannot be used against our interests. That would be very stupid."

"My terms. Wait one hour. I will call you back and tell you where and when."

"No longer, my friend. No longer. And thanks for keeping your phone on. I expect to know where you are very soon." He gave the phone back to Conway who fired out, "Budnick, yeh, we're fine, yeh, OK. Understand. We'll wait. Good luck." He closed the phone.

Agius took it from him. "All right. Pray you friends do the right thing. Diana, you were on your way to the bathroom. We have one hour. Make good use of it. The rest of you, Relax."

He walked over to a chair near the kitchen, put one leg up on it, rested his arm on his thigh, pointed his pistol at them and gave them an amused but threatening tight-lipped smile while the two men by the door relaxed against the wall on either side of it.

~

Pierre turned the wheel sharply right. They turned down an off-ramp north of Newmarket, onto Highway 9 and then headed west towards Orangeville. Just past the Holland Marsh, Pierre turned the wheel to left and entered a long dirt road that led up to an old farmhouse surrounded by trees.

The rain turned to a light mist as they drove toward the house. The darkness made it difficult to see but the thin shapes of pine trees could be made out lining the road. There were lights in the windows of the house and several vehicles were scattered in the front. The road petered out into an old garage and a fenced in yard full of junked cars.

Two Doberman's on long chains lay on either side of the front door to the house. They sprang up together to face the bright headlights coming towards them, their mouths open, their fangs revealed, their breath quickened. Their ears went forward as the vehicles drew up and stopped in front of them and low growls began in their throats, controlled but prepared.

For a second there was silence except for the wind and the deep growls. Then in tandem Pierre and Budnick descended from the Range Rover and walked towards the door and the dogs. One of them barked a warning. It stood still. Budnick walked right up to it and put out his closed fist for it to smell and said,

"Hi, Queenie, trying to frighten people again, huh?" The dog sniffed his hand, then licked it and looked over at her companion. Her tongue and mouth relaxed. She turned her head back to Budnick and seemed to smile at him, then lazily sank down on the ground. The other dog followed her lead and soon he was resting on his long legs and large paws content, once again to relax and think of other things. Queenie, lay on her belly, paws extended, accepted a pat on the head from Pierre, and watched with interest as they both approached the door.

Budnick kicked it. He had to. It was a heavy steel door with several locks. There was a slot in the middle that a person inside could open to look out. Nothing happened. Budnick kicked harder and shouted, "Starkey, its your pal Budnick, come on, open up."

The slot opened and closed. After what seemed like a long time spent listening to locks being unlocked and chains pulled aside, the door opened and a tall, thin but muscular man with long dark hair and a greying beard stepped into the light of the doorway. He was dressed in black jeans, black shirt and motorcycle boots. His face was tanned, but deeply lined. His long bony face made him look cadaverous but suddenly he lit up with a smile and threw his arms in the air towards Budnick and shouted, "Budnick, what the hell are you doing up this way, where's Conway, say, better, where's Susan. Good to see you man."

He looked past Budnick and saw the two cars. "What's up? Who's this you got with you?" He looked at Pierre, "Hey man, long time," and he clapped him on the arm as well, "Long time, come on in, got a few old timers here, and ...." He stopped suddenly and took a second look at the BMW and Range Rover. "Nice machines, what's that about, man?"

Budnick stood solid in front of him. Starkey removed his smile and replaced it with questioning eyes and a firm jaw. He waited and got, "Need a safe place. Need it now and we have a guy with a gunshot wound. Can't take him to hospital. Cops can't know."

"Fuck, man, what you got yourself into?"

He looked at them again then put his arm around Budnick's shoulder and in a quiet voice said, "OK, bring 'em in. I'll call the sawbones. He's down the road. He'll come. Come on, welcome to what's left of the Choice. It's all Hell's Angels now."

Budnick thanked him and said, "Let me get my people. They're real VIPs."

Starkey nodded and waited as Budnick and Pierre walked over and said something to the people in the BMW. Pierre then went over to the Range Rover and helped Marcel off his back, out of the vehicle and hobble towards the house. Budnick went over to help Emma out of the car followed by the professor, then went to the driver's side and said, "Come on, Eddie. They won't bite," and laughed, trying to kid Mackenzie into action.

Just then Starkey was joined by another man, dressed the same except he had a black t-shirt under a leather jacket and a fat gut from too much beer. His face was in the shadows. They watched Pierre and the wounded man with the same interest the Dobermans had first displayed and paid equal attention as Mackenzie got out of the driver's seat and stood staring at the house, mesmerized.

Starkey spoke under his breath to the fat man while indicating with his chin and lifted eyebrow, "Wonder what his problem is? Looks like he's about to take off running." The fat man grinned and laughed quietly in return, "Yeh, he might yet. So, what's up, exactly?"

"Don't know but it can't be good. Not with a man shot and Budnick running from the cops. He's been in some serious shit before but this ain't usual for him. Anyway, stay cool. We owe the brother."

They fell silent as Pierre, with Marcel leaning on one

shoulder, and the Blochs, Budnick and Eddie Mackenzie walked tiredly past them into the foyer that opened onto a large room, where four other men sat. They were dressed in the same dark uniform of jeans and shirts as the others, looked rough, but welcomed them with friendly smiles and,

"Hi. How's it going?"

They didn't' seem to care about the answer and took swigs from beer bottles, or dragged on joints. A girl with long dark hair in black leotards and a tight-black t-shirt, cast her eyes at them, a flash of green light. She quickly crushed out a cigarette. Pierre was quick to appreciate the curve of her breasts as she leaned forward from the couch she was sitting on and noticed the tattoo on her left arm of a naked man. She saw his appreciation and smiled but stood up and walked down a hallway, into another room and closed the door behind her without looking back.

Starkey directed Pierre to take Marcel into a second room and set him down on a bed. He left them there and returned to the main room. Budnick walked up to him. The fat man stood nearby.

"How you doing Billie?" The fat man smiled but only to be polite. There was some reluctance in it as he replied, "I'm cool, Budnick, I'm cool," and stood there looking cool.

Budnick spoke to them both. "OK, this is the thing. The Committee has a marker on us. The why is-we have something they want and, well, it's like this...." And he proceeded to tell Starkey the events of the past days and hours. At the end he took a long breath and finished with, "So, that's it."

Starkey looked at the fat man then back to Budnick. He put his hand to his face and began rubbing his chin and jaw with it as he looked down at his shoes and then over at the rest of the group. Starkey stopped considering and put his hands on his hips.

"Fuck the Committee and the cops. You're welcome."

Pierre entered the room and joined them and Starkey asked, "Your other man, is he comin'? Just wanna know what force we have, you know what I mean?"

Pierre said laconically, "Yes, half an hour. A good man."

"OK, Budnick, friends, make yourselves at home. These guys are my close protection, if you know what I mean."

Budnick guided the Blochs to a couch at the far end of the room and sat next to them where they sat nervously near the other four men who offered Emma a joint, which she politely declined. Budnick made some jokes to relax the scene. Pierre went over to a window and looked out. "You have a security system, spotters, anything?"

The fat man met his question with a terse, "We're always expecting trouble. We can put out security. What do you want?"

"Two men out back and two out front."

Starkey nodded and the fat man caught the attention of the other men and said, "Ok, you heard it. Keep alert. Bad guys may try a raid. Report anything."

They all stood up, put down their bottles, and walked over to another door and into another room. A couple of minutes later, they walked out and through the main room to the front door each of them with submachine guns, radios slung over their shoulders and night vision goggles around their necks. Pierre watched in satisfaction as they went outside.

*   *   *   *   *

27

Budnick stood up and with Starkey went over to a dining table. They pulled out two chairs and sat down facing the others. Budnick began, "We need to free our people, otherwise we're finished."

Eddie Mackenzie saw an open whisky bottle on the coffee table in front of him along with half filled glasses. He looked over at Starkey, who smiled, "Go ahead, I think you need it. But I'd like to know the name of the man who drinks my whisky."

The words 'Eddie Mackenzie' began as a plea but ended as a challenge.

Starkey leaned back in his chair and looked him over. "Can't say it rings any bell with me, mister. So who's he with Budnick?"

Budnick picked up one of the glasses of whisky but asked. "You got any coffee? He's with the Free Press. It's ok. I smell coffee," and walked into the kitchen.

As he did, Starkey laughed at Eddie, "OK, I got it. Yeh, I saw that piece you did on us." He laughed again and then rocked forward and picked up a beer bottle from the same table and took a swig. "Don't worry about it, Mr. Mackenzie. You got it all wrong anyway. We just pissed ourselves reading it. Man who feeds you this stuff?"

Mackenzie began to defend the paper, but Pierre at the window called out tersely, "Boss, we don't have time for this-they gave us one hour. There is a quarter of that left."

Budnick walked back into the room with a cup of black coffee. "I hear yah." he sat down and began sipping at the cup.

Starkey leaned forward again with his elbows resting on his thighs, his hands clasped in front of his mouth. He examined Emma and the professor and then inspected Mackenzie again.

"So, you wanna change the world, huh?" He shook his head. "I'll let you figure out how to do that, all I can do is keep them off your backs for awhile. What's the plan?"

Mackenzie jumped in, "The plan is to print it in the paper. Get it out. Then they can't touch us. I need time to set it up, send it in, get it in the computers so we can run it."

Starkey chuckled again, "Look you guys, you tell me they already know what you're trying to do so your computers won't function. They're not gonna let you. It ain't gonna happen. Send it in Eddie. Try. But it won't happen. You got once choice, hand it over and hope they leave it at that."

Emma began to bristle and her face flushed, "I thought your gang was afraid of nothing. We are not afraid. If you are not willing to help then I am prepared to leave this place now." Budnick tensed up but remained quiet.

Starkey replied, "Hell no, I'm with you all the way. Just being realistic, is all."

She held the professor's arm and retreated into the couch. Starkey just looked at her, amused but angry at the insult. He said nothing and pulled on his bottle of beer. Pierre turned from the window. "First thing is Marcel."

Billie answered, "Called the man. Be here in half an

hour." Pierre nodded thanks and turned back to the window.

"OK, second thing," Budnick broke in, "We have to free Conway and...."

Budnick stopped himself, looked at Starkey and Pierre then over at Eddie and the Blochs. "But how are going to do that. We don't know how many there are, whether the building is covered. Starkey may be right, Emma. If we go ahead we risk their lives. We don't have the right to do that. We have to hand it over, make the exchange and hope for the best."

He fell silent and the only sound that could be heard was Starkey rocking back and forth on his chair and the sudden chatter of a radio in another room. Billie left and came back talking into it, telling the men outside to keep in touch. Pierre turned from the window again,

"It's time my friend. The hour has passed. They will expect an answer."

Budnick looked around the room as if the walls would speak and give him one. But he heard nothing except the blood pounding through his head.

~

Agius looked at his watch, "Your friend should be calling me soon."

He stood up and took Conway's mobile and waited for it to ring.

Traffic on the streets below continued in fits and starts. The wind calmed then rattled the windows then calmed again. The apartment was now too warm for comfort and every one was tired from boredom, tobacco smoke, and fear. The call came at midnight.

Agius put the phone to his ear. "Yes, Budnick, I am glad

you called on time. It shows a commitment to cooperate. I hope we can clear this tonight." He listened as Budnick said,

"Alright, we will meet you in Newmarket. We'll tell you where at different points. You come with our friends. You get the stick. And no repercussions."

Agius laughed gently, "No, That isn't going to work. You must come here. You will come alone, with the stick to Diana's apartment. We get the stick, we leave, everything is fine."

Budnick went quiet as he thought about it. He held his hands over the phone and whispered, "Wants me to come alone, Diana's place, exchange the stick and its over."

Pierre shrugged his shoulders. "Don't know boss. May be a trap."

Mackenzie and the Blochs kept silent. None of their options looked good. But Emma and professor were looking downcast and just a little betrayed. Starkey leaned back in his chair, took another swig of beer and said, "I wouldn't ever trust the pigs, man."

Budnick took his hand from the microphone, "I want something in writing from the Committee that this is the end, no repercussions, the Americans are dealt with and our lives go on as before. You guys don't exactly follow the law, so how can we trust you."

"Law? The law is for the weak. You have no choice but to trust our word. I can assure you the Committee wants this handled as discretely as possible. We understand, in your naïve enthusiasm for the truth, shall we say, you all got carried away. Cooperation with us is the only way forward. I can answer for the Committee. I can write you such a document if that will satisfy you. You can keep it in your desk draw and feel safer. And you will be safe so long as you keep your mouths shut." He waited. Could hear Budnick breathing, and occasionally whispering to someone near him.

Beneath The Clouds

"OK. Let me speak with Conway. Give me two hours to get there. But I bring my investigator, and no interceptions on the way, from anyone."

"All right. One man. We will wait. The Americans, I cannot guarantee. We lost track of them after they ransacked Mackenzie's house. We've identified the local police working with them but where they are is not known. If you tell me where you are I could send a team to escort you here."

Budnick said, "I don't think so. We'll take our chances."

Agius handed the phone over to Conway.

Conway looked at the floor as he listened. "Yeh, yeh, I understand. No, I'm with you. OK, no. We're OK, so far. OK. See you soon." He looked up at Agius and gave him back the phone.

Conway turned to the others. "Budnick's coming with Pierre and the stick. We just have to wait."

Eiger was very quiet, almost brooding and looked pale even in the dim light of the room. He sat next to Diana when he returned from the bathroom. He could feel her thighs pressing against his. The heat from her body seemed like a flame in the cold tension of the room. She looked over at him when she felt their guard was wandering.

Just a fraction of a second passed, a shift of the eyes, an imperceptible turn of the head. Eiger shifted his eyes to meet hers then locked them onto Conway who was leaned back against his chair his head resting on the back. Conway made no sign of recognition but as soon as Eiger broke contact he leaned forward and stood up without warning and said, "I've got to take a leak."

He began to move towards the bathroom. The man at the door reacted before Agius and moved forward to stop him. Just as Agius asked, "What now?" Eiger launched himself at Agius like a cat springing at a dog. He almost growled as he flew at him with closed fist and took a shot

247

at his face.

Agius reacted instinctively, surprised by the sudden attack and threw his arms in front of his face. He would have knocked him down with his gun but before he could make another move Diana jumped up beside him, seized his arm, and grabbed for it.

There was a yellow flash and a sharp, loud bang. Diana cried out. The other men yelled and moved to help Agius but, as they did, Susan put her foot out tripping the first one who fell to the floor. The second man tripped over him but tried to stay standing and regain his balance. In the same instant, Conway saw Diana standing stock-still, looking stunned.

He froze as he looked at her and her eyes connected with his, pleading. Agius' men tried to get up. Conway suddenly moved and jumped for the light switch and shut it off. The only light now was from the streetlights as the men attacked him and Eiger. The struggle continued in the shadows as the streetlights cast grotesque shapes on the apartment walls. The rigid shadow that was Diana's slowly became fluid as it melted into the floor.

There was another flash as the second man quickly recovered himself and fired at Conway. He missed but never got a chance to fire a second time. Susan ripped an ashtray from the table and smashed it into his hand knocking the gun to the floor. He cried out in pain, and Conway dove to the floor, grabbed it and as quickly stood up and called out sharply, "Tell your men to stay down Agius or I'll kill them both."

Agius was still on the floor, rubbing his jaw and trying to remember what just happened. All he did was laugh for a few seconds then became quiet. No one knew what had happened. Later on they would never agree on the details. It was a few seconds of chaos. A few deep breaths of time. The only sound as Conway waited for Agius to answer was the sound of their hard breathing, like runners after a fast race who have nothing left inside them. Eiger held the gun

Diana had dislodged from Agius' hand. But he wasn't looking at Agius. He was staring down at Diana.

Agius slowly rose up to a sitting position and ordered his two men, "OK, stay down." Conway turned the lights back on. Then Agius added, "I think you better take a look at Diana. She doesn't look too good." He pointed his finger to where she lay on the floor between the couch and table, her long black hair splayed out behind her, on her side, her eyes slowly opening and closing as she sank into shock and her skin turned ashen white.

There was a stain of red on her hand where she held it to her stomach. She whispered. "I'm shot. Help me. Hold me. It's cold," and then closed her eyes and lay her head back into the floor. Still she breathed.

*   *   *   *   *

28

Agius shared glances with his men who were still on the floor, one holding his hand, the other his shin but they didn't make any moves. Eiger took the first man's gun, gave it to Susan then ordered the three men to get into the middle of the room and sit on their hands. Agius looked resigned as he took in the changed circumstances. He watched Susan as she went to the bedroom and came back with a blanket.

She placed it around Diana's shoulders, caressed her face with her free hand, looked at her wound and whispered into her ear, trying to comfort her. She held the blanket tight against her but Diana didn't seem to hear and shivered uncontrollably. Susan looked up at Conway and Eiger, "We have to get her to a hospital. You guys know any first aid."

One man looked over. Agius nodded again. The man with the bruised shin said, "Let me take a look."

Susan moved away as he examined the small hole in her side. "Get me some gauze or bandage and a belt. Have to stop the bleeding." Susan gave Conway her gun and rushed to the bathroom. They could her hear frantically searching for bandages.

She returned, knelt down and assisted the man tending

to Diana. The wound had stained Susan's skirt as she knelt beside her. Susan slowly stood away as the man began to tend the wound in Diana's side, first applying the gauze then fixing it in place tight with a belt round her waist. Then he sat back, "That should stop the bleeding, or most of it, but she needs a hospital."

Eiger kneeled down and put his face close to Diana's and whispered something to her. She turned her head to his and tried to open her eyes and smile, only to close them and sink below consciousness and pain.

Agius sat himself upright and moved back to lean against the wall behind him. He smiled grimly, shook his head as he looked at the three of them and asked,

"What was the point of that? You're no further ahead. Now Diana is in danger. That was very stupid."

Eiger grew red with anger and bent down to smash his face with the gun in his hand, but stopped in mid-air. "You goddam smug bastard, I swear I'll kill you I will, I swear I'll...."

Conway broke in. "Eiger. Calm down. We're not them. Remember. It doesn't help."

Eiger turned and his face was contorted, but he caught Susan looking at him in surprise and he let it go. His face softened. He dropped his hand and stood up. He ran his hand through his hair and walked over to a chair and sat down. "Sorry, but I've had enough of these guys pushing me around. They don't obey rules why should we?" He looked exhausted and slumped down into the chair, the gun resting in his lap.

Conway took charge. He walked to the center of the room and stood over Agius. "You're going to help us out of this."

Agius took a deep breath, twisted his head from side to side as if getting rid of a knot in his neck, "I'm not doing a thing. If I don't make contact soon, another team will be here. You can't escape. You've just made things worse."

Conway looked at him coldly. "Johnny is right, just shut up. We'll figure it out."

He looked for his mobile, dialled and then began talking, "Budnick, you left yet? Why? 'Cause everything's changed. Everything." He related what had happened.

~

Budnick put down his phone and turned to Billy. "That doctor be here soon?"

"Anytime. Let me check." He sent a text message out and received the laconic reply, "Five minutes."

Budnick explained the situation to the others. Eddie Mackenzie pressed his lips together and then took a slug of whisky from the glass next to him. "So, we have time to publish."

Budnick said simply, "Yes, we have time to publish but we have to get the doctor downtown. I think I have to go with him while you and the professor finish the piece and get it sent in. Starkey, can your guys cover things here. The American gang is still out there."

Starkey thought about it and drawled, "That depends on what shows up."

"Pierre, what do you think?"

Pierre stood away from the window where he was on constant watch and walked into the bedroom to check on Marcel then walked back out and said, "Marcel can still function if he has to. I'll go with you. David should be here soon too."

Just then the radio next to Billie came alive and a voice said, "Cars coming, the doc and someone else."

Billie looked at Pierre, "Your man?"

Pierre nodded, "Yes, has to be."

Billy spoke into the radio, "Let 'em both come up."

They heard their engines approaching. Headlights swept the house as two vehicles drew up in front. A man got out of one carrying a bag. He walked with a limp and carried a cane in his other hand. A tall man got out of the second vehicle. He walked like a soldier and wore a black leather jacket and a baseball cap.

Starkey went to the door and opened it before the man with the limp could knock. "How ya doing, doc?"

There was a short muffled answer and a middle-aged man in an old black suit entered the room. His spectacles covered dark circles under his eyes and his head drooped as if he was as tired as he looked. His thick hair was curly and tangled strands hung over his forehead, like loose ropes on a derelict ship. He cast his gaze around the room and nodded his head to Budnick.

"Long time, Budnick."

"Yep, long time, doc." Budnick walked over and took the man's hand. "Got two patients for you, one here and one downtown, gunshot wounds."

The second man walked in. Pierre gathered him in his arms and hugged him. "David. I was worried." He pointed with his arm, "Marcel is in the bedroom there." David looked tense. "They are serious people. Who are they? They know what they are doing. Sure hope this is for a good cause."

Without waiting for an answer he pulled away from Pierre and entered the bedroom and began talking in French.

The doctor shrugged his shoulders in resignation, "OK, show me to the first one."

Starkey walked ahead of him and showed him into the room where David sat on the bed talking to Marcel. Pierre followed as Marcel rose up to a sitting position on the bed. Starkey made the introduction, "This here is Doc Wainwright. Good man. He'll take care of you."

254

Marcel, said nothing but lay back as the doctor examined the wound in his leg. David stepped away from the bed and stood next to Pierre. The doctor looked at the wound, closely.

"You're lucky. Clean in and out. No bone broken. I can stitch it up. You'll have to stay off it for a few weeks if you want it to heal right." Marcel looked up at his friends and smiled, "Ça va doc. No problem."

"OK, I'm going inject a local anaesthetic first. You won't feel a thing. Then I'll clean it, and do the needle work."

"How long?" Budnick asked.

The doctor, still looking at the leg, and taking things out of his bag, sighed and twitched his eyebrows in exasperation about being pressed. "Maybe twenty minutes. Not long."

Budnick appeared edgy, but tried to speak calmly. "OK, just the one downtown is a wound in the side. Dangerous."

"One at a time, my friend. Only way to do it." He went back to preparing a hypodermic and needle and thread.

Emma and the professor came into the room to watch. Emma looked apprehensively at the man tending to Marcel. "Are you a real doctor?"

He didn't respond but his shoulders tensed a little as he injected the area near the wound and then began to clean it and set it up for the stitches.

Budnick went over to the Blochs and put his arm around Emma and reassured her. "He's a real doctor all right. Or was. He was kicked off the register a few years ago for prescribing extra food allowances for people on welfare. They would have starved without it. The mayor complained. Medical board got all fired up about the good doctor helping the poor. Said he was profiteering. The doc here had a lot of support in the community. But they wanted his head. Wouldn't play ball with the establishment so they destroyed him. One of the best doctors this city ever had."

Wainwright looked up and over at Budnick and smiled bitterly, "You're very kind Budnick."

Emma said, "Pleased to meet you doctor. I didn't know such things went on in this country. I am learning a lot the past few days."

Budnick squeezed her shoulder and then released her and walked over to watch the doctor sew up the wound.

"Yeh, I was his lawyer on that. They were real dirty. It dragged on for two years. Now he does whatever it takes to make a living."

Wainwright said, "Don't remind me," as he carefully inserted the needle and drew it through the flesh. He asked for the lampshade to be removed so he could see better and Emma and the professor got a better look at his face. Its once handsome profile was slack with premature age and etched with care. She felt sad inside and reached for her husband's hand. He looked over at her. She saw the question in his eyes and he saw it in hers. She smiled to reassure him and he stroked her hand with his.

Budnick saw the reaction. "The doc knew the risks. He did it anyway because that's what a person has to do. Right doc?"

Wainwright laughed gently, as he continued to close Marcel's wound. "I'm no saint. It's just if you're brought up right, then you're brought up on the golden rule. That's the only rule to follow. No matter what they do to you. 'Cause if you don't, you're just one of them, a nothing." Marcel winced a bit and the doc, spoke softly to him, "Sorry my friend, it'll be over soon," and continued what he was doing.

Budnick watched Wainwright stitch the wound for a minute then returned to the main room and sat down across from Eddie Mackenzie. Emma and the professor soon followed him and sat next to Eddie on the couch. Starkey hung close by but Budnick gave him a look and he backed away and joined Pierre who had returned to the window.

Eddie spoke first, "I really don't know what we should do. If we publish this it's a sure thing bad things are going to happen to all of us. These people don't care a goddam about any rules or laws or morality, or..."

The professor interrupted him firmly, "Mr. Mackenzie, you are a journalist, more than that you are an editor. You decide what gets printed, what the people get to know. Frankly, your newspaper has been as bad as the rest, always getting people fired up about going to war, never telling them the real facts. I have little respect for people who make a living lying to the people. Such people are lower than scum in my opinion."

Emma cast him a sharp glance, and he caught himself. "I am sorry to use such language but that is what I see. So, I had little confidence in going to you. But I respect Mr. Budnick. If he trusts you then I will, but I am telling you, you must publish this information. The people have the right to know who rules them and how it is done. The country must be returned to the people and it is your duty, Mr. Mackenzie to inform them. That is supposed to be your job." His rising voice fell silent and he sat back next to Emma and took a deep breath.

Eddie Mackenzie didn't move a muscle in his face. He sat still as he listened. When the professor stopped speaking, Eddie, in a low voice, slowly said,

"You make me ashamed professor. I could tell you how it is, how that all works. But, there's no point in talking about corruption, even mine. We gotta end it, right? Ok, let's finish writing this up. Finish where we left off just before the attack on the house tonight. Then I'll send it in. But I need my computer." He turned his head to look around, "Where'd I leave that?'" He looked up and saw Starkey carrying it to him. "You left it in your car when you came in, man." Eddie thanked him and set it on the table in front of him, opened it up and began to type and, once again Emma and the professor were reliving the events and explaining the explosive information on the stick.

A few minutes later the doctor came out of the bedroom looking still tired but pleased with himself. "Marcel will be alright. Now, you taking me to the other one?"

Budnick stood up, patted Mackenzie on the shoulder, and smiled at the Blochs. He walked up to the doctor and shook his hand. "This could be a little dangerous doctor, you still sure you want to help?"

Budnick saw the doctor's eyes twinkle in the light and energy flush through his face. "Well, it 's very intriguing. Tell me what it's about on the way. We must get going if we are to help your friend. That wound you described can be dangerous."

"Yeh, sure, doc, let's go. Eddie, you stay with the Blochs. Keep working. Pierre, let's move."

Budnick went towards the door followed by Pierre. But the doctor didn't follow. Instead he disappeared into the bedroom and then as quickly reappeared carrying his medical bag and walking with a big stride.

"OK, I am armed. Come on." He walked past Budnick and Pierre through the door into the cold night air.

Budnick went to the BMW. "We'll take this one. It's faster."

Pierre took the driver's seat. Budnick helped the doctor into the rear, then took the seat next to Pierre. Starkey and David came out of the house and walked over to Budnick's window. Starkey asked, "So, what's the score boss?"

Budnick looked him in the eye, and said softly, "Take care of my people. Maybe nothing will happen but if it does David, here and Marcel, they're ex military, work together on this one, we need it and take care of Eddie and the lady and the professor. They're what it's all about."

Starkey exchanged glances with David and then said, "OK, we'll take care of it," and turned and walked back into the house side by side with David who drew his gun from a side holster and checked it as he went through the door and out of sight.

*   *   *   *   *

29

As the F10 sped through the night, Agius kept his eyes fixed on Conway who kept pacing up and down the living room, the gun in his right hand resting against his leg, cold, grey and threatening.

Susan sat on a stool in the kitchen, smoking a cigarette with one hand while she aimed a pistol in the other at Agius and his men. Diana had been moved to the couch and was covered with a blanket. She was conscious but her face was paler than the moon that sailed behind the clouds, and Eiger sat beside her, one hand holding a gun on his knee, the other caressing her forehead.

Conway's mobile buzzed. He stopped in front of Agius, listened and grunted a couple of times, then said "OK, we're not going anywhere."

He looked over at Susan, then Eiger, "Budnick and Pierre are on the way with the doctor. Be here in an hour."

He looked at his watch. "Gonna be daylight soon. Man, I'm tired."

He caught Agius watching him, "What are you looking at?"

"A dead man. That's what I'm looking at, unless we get that device."

"I told you before to shut up. The only way you're gonna see what's on the stick is to read it in the newspaper."

Just then Diana's telephone rang. Conway picked it up. He listened. "Who's this?" He held the receiver a second longer then slammed it down.

Susan and Eiger looked at him, waiting. Agius looked at him and his face was grim. "No one there?"

Conway didn't answer him but went to the window and looked down onto the street below.

Agius tried to sit up straighter, "You'd better let me handle this. Some one is coming and it's not my people. Not yet. That door won't stop them. But we can. Don't wait too long. Death waits for no one."

Conway weighed the gun in his hand as he turned his head from the window, "I was in the army once. I can shoot. You're staying put."

Susan stood up, "The ones that killed Marina and the others?"

Agius turned his head to her, "I would say. They think you have it or think you know where it is and if they take you, they will find out where it is I can assure you of that. Give it up Conway. You're not made to play the hero. They come through that door, they'll be quicker than you. You don't have a chance. Then we're all gone. They kill you, they will have to kill me. Let me up. Let my men up. Give us the guns."

Conway hesitated. He flicked his eyes to Eiger who looked down at Diana before answering. "No, we keep the guns. Could be a false alarm. Wrong number. We give you back the guns we're fools. Nice try, Rice or Agius whatever your real name is. We'll take our chances."

Agius' face became clouded and he clenched his teeth to steel himself. "If I'm right, these other guys are gangsters. Mercenaries. You don't know what you're dealing with. Let us handle it."

Eiger stood up over him. "So you want the chickens to trust the fox."

Agius looked him in the eye. "Trusting me is the only thing to do, Conway. I'm sure you can handle that gun but not what's coming. Move quick and take Diana into the bedroom and the rest of you get in there and stay there. Well?"

Conway waved his gun at Agius and the men on the floor. "Keep quiet. You're starting to bug me."

Susan was trembling. She moved over to Conway and asked, "What next?"

Eiger said, "We wait for Budnick like we said. One step at a time. But one small change. Agius, I don't want to see your face right now so you and these other two, lie face down, hands behind your back."

One of the men said, "Make me," but Susan replied without a pause, "Don't make me," and put her gun close to his head, her hand shaking. They slowly turned over.

Agius lay flat on his stomach smiling at her, "Good with a gun as a camera. Fascinating lady."

"Shut up. Just shut up. Always have something to say."

Conway looked out the window again. "Maybe one of us better go down and check it out."

Eiger stood up, "Yeh, we're blind up here. But nothing we can do with those three here. It's 5:30. No traffic yet. Budnick should make good time. We wait."

Outside, underneath the windows, in the shadows, where Conway's eyes could not see, Marko and two men sat in their car, the engine running against the cold air. Two other cars sat a few metres away, deeper in the shadows. Marko was drinking out of a plastic coffee cup and eating a donut. A tall thin man was getting into the rear seat.

"Anybody answer up there?"

The man settling into his seat nodded, "Yeh, they'll be wondering who it was. Should freak them out a little."

Marko sucked more coffee past the donut in his mouth and spat out a garbled,

"For fuck's sake, how long we gotta sit here? The people at Mackenzie's house have the stick. This is just wasting our time."

The fat man sitting next to him dragged on a cigarette then looked up at Diana's apartment through binoculars. "You do what I tell you to do."

Marko shrunk down in his seat, not daring to respond. The fat man continued,

"Agius is smart. He expects it to arrive, or he wouldn't be up there. We just have to intercept it before he gets it."

Marko grabbed the binoculars to look, "Yeh, well they ain't paying enough for all this. You told me it would be simple. Now we're competing with the Committee. You can leave the country. I'm stuck here. Whose gonna protect me when you've got what you want?"

"Your childish griping is too late and very irritating. We pay you well enough."

Marko grunted and took another bite out of his donut. "Not for what I've done."

The thin man with the long hair next to him laughed, "You sure seemed to get a kick out of holding that girl when I put a bullet in her head. You're paid well enough. Pay attention."

Marko sneered but the thin man couldn't see it. Marko took another bite of his donut and was about to swig his coffee when he suddenly jerked up in his seat and focused his eyes on the driveway leading into the apartment grounds.

"That's the Beamer from the house." He pointed to the F10 as it came down the road and turned into the driveway, and drove into the guest parking lot in front of the building.

The fat man said, "Yes, it's them all right. I say three." The voice in the back said, "Right three men."

The fat man reached into his coat and pulled an automatic pistol from a holster, flicked the safety off and then said, "Marko, get in the lobby, quick. We'll follow them in. Don't move against them 'til we do."

Marko nodded, quickly opened the door and jogged from the shadows over to the door, entered the lobby and sat down in a chair next to a potted fig tree that was losing its leaves. The other two stayed in the car.

They watched as Budnick, Pierre and the doctor slowly got out of the F10, paused to look around and then even more slowly approached the door to the lobby. Pierre was carrying his gun down by his side looking around. He saw the two men sitting in the car thirty metres away, hesitated and gripped his gun more firmly. Budnick noticed the hesitation.

"Something?"

"Maybe, boss, I don't like it."

Budnick looked over at the idling car and then at the building and said, "Let's keep going. We haven't got a choice."

They walked through the door, Pierre in front. He was halfway to the elevators when he saw Marko. He stopped in mid stride.

"It's a trap. That's Marko."

Budnick looked over just in time to hear a voice behind them say, "Yes, that's Detective Marko, a very good man when he obeys orders," and felt something hard pushed into his back. "You gave us a bad time at the house, Mr. Budnick. Your men are good. Take his gun."

The thin man took Pierre's gun and put it in his coat pocket. Marko stood up and walked over to Budnick.

"How ya doing Budnick? You know I owe you for going after me in that case awhile back. You cost me a promotion."

Budnick said, "Uh-huh. That's too bad Marko. Guess you shouldn't have been such a lousy liar."

Marko raised his hand to hit him but the fat man said, "I don't care about personal business. The stick. That's my only concern."

Budnick turned to face the fat man behind him and saw a round, bald skull with a roman nose and a full-lipped mouth and black eyes separated by high cheek bones.

"We don't have it and our friends upstairs don't have it. But soon the public will have it."

The fat man walked up to close to Budnick and pressed his face to Budnick's almost swallowing him with menace.

"I don't give a damn who's got it. You're going to produce it. We're not like you or the Committee. We don't give a damn about the public, or power, just money. That little piece of computer jazz is going to make us rich. Now that can't happen if the public knows now, can it. Hand it over. We'll send you some money for your trouble."

Budnick stepped back from the fat man's face. "That's what Agius said. You're as bad a liar as he is. And I told you. I don't have it."

"Liar? I have some sense of fair play Budnick. Frank would be alive today if he had fulfilled his contract. But, he got religion and feeling all self-righteous and fell for a girl. We tried to persuade him but, well, Marko got carried away." He looked over at Marko whose gun was now drawn and who shrugged at Frank's name.

"Yeh, and Moore, and his girl. Too bad about her, she was pretty hot. She felt nice when I put her down."

He smirked as Budnick and Pierre both tensed and began to go for him. He laughed and stepped back. The fat man gave Marko a cold look and he lost the grin.

The fat man looked at Budnick and then at the doctor's black bag.

"This man is a doctor? Why is he here?"

"Our friend has been shot. Yes, he's a doctor."

"Shot? Well, well, well, that is too bad. We had no idea. Been a lot of action tonight. Let's not keep the doctor waiting. So, who has the guns up there?"

Budnick didn't answer but the fat man caught his reaction with Pierre.

"So, your friends do. It's too bad for Agius. Bad mark on his record to lose control like that. Excellent man I hear. OK, move. People are going to start coming down on their way to work soon. We don't want to alarm them now do we?"

He shoved Budnick hard towards the elevators as the thin man and Marko forced the doctor and Pierre to follow. Budnick went in to the back with Wainwright, Pierre next to him. The fat man held a gun on them while Marko and the tall man entered and secured control. Then the fat man went in and pressed the button to ascend. The few seconds up to the 14th floor seemed like an eternity to Budnick as he saw Marko's fingers twitching on the trigger of his gun and his eyes gleaming. Budnick wondered if he was drugged up.

They left the elevator in reverse order and walked down the long hallway to Apartment 1414. A door to their left began to open but then closed as a hand reached down to pick up a flyer left on the floor. In another few seconds they were at the door. The fat man made a motion with his head to one side telling Budnick to knock. Marko had a smirk on his face Budnick wanted to wipe off but he gripped himself and hit the door with his knuckles.

He tapped three times then stepped back and waited. The door swung wide open and Budnick walked in. Conway, who held the doorknob with one hand and a gun with the other found another aimed at his face before he could say a word. Marko kept the gun near his forehead as the tall man quickly disarmed him. Budnick walked over to the couch where Eiger had risen to stand next to Diana and said, "Sorry, they were downstairs.'

The tall man then took Eiger's gun and Susan's and shoved them together on the floor with Conway and Agius and his men, all huddled together like seals on a rock. Budnick looked down at Diana, "How is she? Got the doc here. Doc, our patient is over here."

The fat man stepped aside and politely waived Doctor Wainwright into the apartment, closed the door and stood looking down at Agius and his men on the floor.

"An embarrassing position to be in, I would say Agius. Not good for your career."

Agius turned his head to the side so he could see. He groaned when he saw the fat man standing calmly in his long coat with one hand in his coat pocket and another pointing a gun.

"Go to hell," he said in a quiet drawl. "You think you're getting out of this in one piece?"

The fat man chuckled, "Oh, I think so. Don't you? Never mind. It doesn't matter. Let's get down to it shall we. Time is wasting. Where is the stick?"

Budnick turned away from the couch. Diana moaned a little as Wainwright checked her wound.

"I told you. It's not here. How is it doc?"

The doctor gently probed the wound. "She needs to be in a hospital. I can stabilise her but she's lost some blood. Her pulse is weak." He rummaged around in his bag and took out a syringe and a bottle. "This will help with the pain."

Diana barely opened her eyes and then closed them again as he injected her arm. Eiger sat tense on the floor as Susan held his onto him eyes alert but wide with fear. Budnick and Pierre were waved down onto the floor to join the rest.

The fat man suddenly became animated and began raising his voice.

"OK, people are going to start to die if someone doesn't tell me where it is. I've got no time for this." He gestured with his head to the tall man who reached into his inside coat pocket and pulled out a cylinder and attached it to his gun. "No one will hear a thing."

Eiger suddenly sprang up and went for him but didn't get to his knees before Marko clubbed him on the neck with his gun. He went down like a sack of stones and lay there stunned. He began to rise but Marko hit him again, in the face, opening up his cheek. Blood oozed down his face as he collapsed to the floor.

"Do we need to do this people? Marko enjoys this work. I don't understand his pathology but he is useful."

Budnick shouted, "Stop. I'll take you to where it is. But everyone else goes free."

Agius tried to get up but was pushed down by the thin man as he said, "The Committee can't let you have that stick anymore than we can allow them to have it. It's a matter of national security, of public order. It's...."

The fat man said, "Come now. You mean it's protecting the powerful. That's not my concern. In fact I have a powerful customer for the information who wants to be more powerful. It's very logical when you think about it. But that is their affair. I need money. They are willing to pay for it."

"Who, Russia, China, the Israeli's?"

"What's the difference? It's all the same to you in the end. But enough of politics. So, Mr. Budnick, are you going to talk to me or do I have to kill someone here?"

"I told you, free the others and I'll take you to where it is."

Agius laughed, "You promised to bring it, remember,

you lied to me."

In response the fat man made a small movement of his head and the tall man walked over to the two men sitting next to Agius, put his gun to the back of the head of one of them and fired. The man's head bounced once and then he lay still, a pool of blood gathering under his startled face.

Agius started to get up but was knocked down by a blow from Marko and kept down by the thin man's gun. Susan turned white. The others recoiled from the sight in front of them. The doctor looked up at the fat man in disbelief. "How could you do such a thing? How could anyone...."

The fat man answered, "Shut up. It's easy, and this man is next," and he directed the thin man to the second of Agius men, "unless I get the answer. If that doesn't do it then I'll start on your group Budnick."

Conway quietly said, "You're going to kill us all anyway."

*   *   *   *   *

30

"Kill him." There was another shot and the man next to Agius spasmed for a few seconds then lay still.

Agius steeled himself and forced himself to his knees. "You people are always killing. You're in love with it. You're sick with it. Ok, you have to kill me now. So, I'm waiting..." and he raised his head in defiance. The fat man made a slight move of his chin, his eyes and the assassin pointed his silencer at Agius' head.

Agius ignored the gun, "The Committee will have you. You're as dead as I am."

The fat man smiled, "I salute you. You are cool under fire. As for your Committee, it will be under new direction very soon. I'm not worried. And you have no time to be. Until we meet again."

He flicked his finger and the tall man fired a single shot between Agius' wide-open eyes. They stared blankly ahead as black blood oozed from the hole between them. His jaw fell open and he slumped slowly to the floor, rolled his head to one side and met the blank gaze of the man lying next to him.

Susan began to shake and Eiger, still holding his face where it was bloodied drew closer to her while Conway put his head between his knees and drew deep breaths to calm himself. The doctor sat paralyzed next to Diana, looking from the fat man to Budnick to the dead men on the floor, his mouth open in utter astonishment.

"There, that's cleared the field, or have we cluttered it?" the fat man mocked. "Well, things are simpler now. Now you only have to deal with us. So unless I get your instant cooperation my friends here will continue their work but this time Mr. Marko will use a knife and you do not want to see what he can do to a woman's face with a knife."

Eiger began to laugh hysterically, manically, frightening Susan even more,

"Marko the knife, that's funny, that's very funny." He continued to laugh until his face began to bleed again and he shouted, "Fuck you. Why don't you go back to that madhouse you came from!" and jumped up and tried to take the gun from the thin man but was again clubbed to the ground and lay groaning on the floor.

"Enough of these dramatics. Daylight has come. The sun is rising. The buds are on the trees. Spring is in the air. There is hope, people. Just cooperate."

Pierre exchanged glances with Budnick and Conway and then returned his focus to the men that stood over them searching for a weakness, but found none. Marko noticed the attempt and walked over to Pierre and slapped him in the face with the back of his free hand.

"Let me do this one too. He's their muscle and I don't like him."

Pierre shot back, "You Toronto cops are cowards. In Montreal I would have shot you by now," and snorted at him and spat in his face. Marko turned purple with rage and raised his gun hand to hit again, but the fat man grabbed his arm, "Calm down, besides he's right."

Marko pulled his arm free and twisted back from the fat man, "I don't have to take this from you...we got a contract. I do my thing, you do yours, I don't take insults from anyone. He's right about you Americans, goddam think your superior to everyone. How about we just get rid of you and run things ourselves, you fat fuck. I oughta...."

The fat man remained perfectly calm through this tirade like he was listening to the yaps of a hyena waiting to steal a lion's kill. "Except you have no customer. Calm yourself. And nationality has nothing to do with it. Money has no country. I'm sure you'll be able to kill someone else. Does that make you happier?"

Susan grew paler, "I have to use the bathroom, I feel sick, I..."

The fat man looked at her and narrowed his eyes. "Alright, but don't be long."

She slowly and unsteadily rose to her feet. Her hair was disheveled and her skirt was soiled with Eiger's blood. She let go of Eiger's hand, touched Conway on the back of the neck then made her way past the three men and into the bathroom and closed the door. The violent sounds of her throwing up quickly followed.

The fat man turned again to Budnick, "Diana also does not look very well. She must be treated soon or she will die I think. And you look tired, sir. You need a shave. Your family must be wondering where you are."

"Stop this slaughter for God's sake," Budnick pleaded. "The stick is at my farm. I'll take you there."

"Where is that?"

"North of the city. Orangeville," the thin man said, "Not far from the farm where we killed that girl. A half hour to the west."

The fat man acknowledged him with a small movement of his head and eyes like a lizard regarding a fly. He flicked his tongue out to wet his lips. "So, we will go there."

He retracted his tongue and squeezed his lips into a smile. "But we, that is, I, have a small security problem. I only need you Budnick to get there and a hostage to

273

guarantee your cooperation but there are too many, don't you think. Marko and my friend here can resolve that quickly but even I am a bit tired of the smell of blood. So, what do you suggest?"

Budnick trembled with rage but controlled himself enough to answer, "I'm tired fat man. Play your games if you want."

"Who is babysitting the disk? There must be some one."

"Just the professor and his wife...."

"Ah yes. Fine people. Too honest for this world. Anyone else? What about the newspaperman you fled with?"

Budnick drew a deep breath and looked over at Conway who looked back at him blankly. "Yes, him too."

"Any security?" Budnick shook his head no and looked down at the floor.

"Call them. Call them now and tell this newspaper man to do nothing. We take the stick. We disappear. You live. I shall be rich. Everybody is happy."

Conway stood up, "You're insane."

The fat man laughed, "That's as may be. But, as they say, what is a madman in a mad world?"

The door to the bathroom opened and Susan came out and leaned against the wall. "I feel very faint. I'm so tired. I want to sleep now," and she slowly slid to the floor.

Doc Wainwright eased away from Diana, went over to Susan and picked her head and shoulders up. He took a vial from his pockets and put it under her nose. Immediately she began to struggle, to push him away and opened her eyes. "I'm sorry, I was..."

Wainwright, hugged her, "Never mind. It's all just a very bad dream. I know because I'm having the same dream. But it will pass like everything else."

"Yes, yes, it must be a bad dream it must be...." Then she sat up and saw Diana still lying there and the horror of the pool of blood under the torn faces, lit by the rising sun, and she screamed and screamed and screamed until the doctor hugged her close to his chest and she burst into deep, heaving, steady sobs.

The fat man looked on placidly, as if watching a passion play in a church. He walked over to Susan and the doctor. Looked down at her. Then he turned back to Budnick.

"This one and Budnick will go. The others, handcuff them."

He turned to Marko. "You stay here and make sure they behave themselves."

The thin man drew several pair of thin plastic handcuffs from his inside coat pocket. While the fat man and Marko stood guard, the tall man forced Conway, Pierre and Eiger to the ground. They were soon handcuffed with their arms behind them.

"Good, I don't think that is necessary for you doctor." He waived his gun at Budnick and Susan, "Both of you, on your feet."

Susan wiped her eyes with her hands and slowly, with the help of the doctor, stood up. Budnick rose with her, stepped over the bodies of Agius, his men, and the blood, and walked over to stand next to her. Conway mumbled something into the floor. Eiger responded but couldn't make himself understood. Pierre turned his head and said, "They're going to kill us all in the end, boss. They have to."

The fat man chuckled, "A pessimist, or a realist? Well, Mr. Budnick, what do you think? Going to trust me or try something desperate?"

"Let's go. Just take me. Let Susan go. She shouldn't be in on this."

"Oh, I can't do that, sir. She is my guarantee you won't try anything on the way or once we get there." He seized her arm and pulled her to his side.

"Marko, you stay here. Keep your phone open. If they give you any trouble, deal with it."

Marko grinned from ear to ear, his eyes shining with death lust. "It will be a pleasure, a real pleasure." He sat on a chair overlooking them and aimed his automatic pistol at Pierre's face. "He'll be the first."

The fat man shook his head, "To kill for pleasure Marko, like you, that really is the Devil's work."

Marko widened his grin, "You Americans and your religion, never made any of you follow the golden rule. Hypocrites everyone. I just like some kicks. You kill for money. Whatever. Don't worry. Just don't leave me high and dry when you get the stick." His grin narrowed into a menace.

The fat man threw back the menace with his own with a violent twist of his lips then he signaled to the tall man, "The door. Don't worry Marko. You'll get your share. I keep my promises. Even to madmen."

He turned and walked out of the door, without a look back, dragging Susan with him. The thin man shoved his gun into Budnick's back, "Move."

Budnick threw a glance at the others, said, "It'll be fine," and disappeared out of view as the tall man and the slam of the closing door followed him.

Doc Wainwright turned back to Diana who lay with her eyes closed, breathing deeply. Eiger raised his face from the floor to ask, "How is she, doc?"

Wainwright pursed his lips, and wrinkled his brow, "She's stable. She's weak from losing blood, but the problem is infection and shock. She's got to get to a hospital. What about it Marko, you just going to let this woman suffer?"

Marko laughed a little, "Why should I care? I didn't shoot her."

Eiger struggled to sit up, cursing him but Marko leaned

forward and slapped him down with his left hand. "But I will shoot you. So shut up."

He pulled himself back into the chair looking satisfied and contented. Eiger rubbed his face on the carpet to ease the pain from the blow. "You're going to wish you hadn't done that."

"I told you to shut up."

Conway called out, "Marko, what's in it for you anyway? Trying to set me up when I did Baxter's case was one thing but treason is another. The fat man isn't even going to tell you if he gets the stick. He'll be gone across the border while you're still sitting here like a dummy."

"Yeh, well you shouldn't have been working for Baxter. We warned you. Baxter was looking for trouble, him and all those other blacks. The fat man will pay. He's paid so far. I agreed to do a job. I'll do it."

"Loyalty from you, that's a laugh."

"I got my own sense of honour. None of your business. Just keep quiet. I'm tired of the conversation."

Conway allowed his head to sink into the carpet and lay still. Eiger kept trying to wriggle his hands out of the plastic cuffs. Pierre lay on his side, quiet, unmoved by the words around him. He looked like he was sleeping except his eyes were open, looking at the bloodied face of Agius shattered like a bloodied marble bust.

The fat man pressed the button on the elevator for the basement. "We don't need to see people," he said in answer to Budnick, who was standing with his arm around Susan. "And I don't think we will call the professor after all. No need for them to try to escape. A little surprise is always more fun."

Budnick turned away from the leering smile that split the fat man's face in two and stared at the elevator doors.

The elevator came to rest and the doors opened onto a long narrow corridor lit by florescent lights and painted a dull yellow. The four left the elevator, then hesitated as the thin man nodded towards a grey door at one end with the word 'Exit' stenciled across it. "There."

He led the way. In ten seconds they were out of the building and in the back parking lot. A man walked past them his face cocked to one side as he talked into a cell phone. He approached a car and fumbled in his coat pocket. He didn't notice the three men and woman walking towards the back of the lot.

Budnick stopped when he saw two more cars standing in the far corner. There were two men in each car, the men who attacked the house and shot Marcel. His stomach tightened and he gripped Susan harder as one of them got out of the first car and called out, "You get it?"

The fat man didn't answer. He kept walking until he was face to face with the man from the car and then replied, "Budnick is taking us to it. Says it's at his farm, a place called Orangeville. You know it?"

"Yeh, it's north, maybe an hour from here. Maybe more. Why the girl?"

"Insurance."

"OK. What about the Committee men?"

"That unit isn't functional any longer. But there will be others. Time is pressing. Life is short."

Another man armed with a gun got out of the second car and opened the back door. The thin man pushed Budnick and Susan into it so hard they almost fell. The door was thrown shut. The man got back into the passenger seat and turned towards them as the driver put a radio to his ear and waited. The man with the gun asked, "What's taking so long?"

"The fat man's going for the car in front. Hold on." Then the radio exploded with chatter as the three cars came alive with humming engines and the quick movement of wheels turning on the grey cold asphalt, as they pulled out onto the side street, then onto Jane, headed for the 401.

Susan sat still, her colour coming back with the cold morning air and the freedom of movement. She leaned into Budnick and put her face close to his as if seeking warmth. "You have a plan?" she whispered.

He whispered back, "It's developing. It's developing," and hugged her closer to him like a protective bear.

*   *   *   *   *

31

Eddie Mackenzie looked haggard and old as the night died and the day dawned. He woke up slowly and didn't recognise where he was at first. His eyes were bleary, his breath was bad and the ache in his back from falling asleep in the chair felt like a rib was broken. He slowly lifted his head and looked around him. The lights in the room were still on, his computer screen was still flashing, and the whisky bottle, next to his left hand, was empty. He almost knocked it over as he stretched his arms out and took a breath. Then he realised where he was.

Two men were sitting in chairs by the main window. Starkey and David. Starkey was asleep but David kept watch and only turned when Eddie rubbed his eyes and cleared his throat.

"A long night, mon ami."

"You got that right. Any word from Budnick?"

"Nothing. Nor Pierre. It's been hours. Something is wrong. Trouble is coming. I can feel it."

The sound of their voices stirred others in the room. Professor Bloch lay with Emma on a couch and lifted his head carefully so as not to disturb her and nodded to Eddie and David.

"What time is it?"

David stood up and shook Starkey on the shoulder, "Just after 7. Sun just came up."

"Where is Budnick?"

"Don't know. His mobile is off. No word from him or Pierre. Or the others."

Eddie stretched and stood up. "Man I'm hungry. Any coffee around?"

At the word coffee Starkey roused himself and sat up in his chair, shaking his head and running his hand through his hair. "Hey, Angie, make some coffee will ya. Angie, where the hell are you?"

A muffled response came from a door down the hallway and a few seconds later the girl with the nice breasts and tattoo stumbled out of her room dressed in a black and yellow kimono, and walked the walk of a zombie into the kitchen, muttering under her breath all the way.

Eddie watched the girl until she disappeared from view then stretched some more and looked at the computer screen once again.

"Professor this could change a lot of things if it gets out..."

"We must get it out," replied Bloch adjusting his body as Emma slowly opened her eyes and moved against him. He looked down at her with great tenderness in his eyes. Even Starkey was affected and cleared his throat and called, "How's the coffee coming, Angie?" which was answered with a head and torso suddenly appearing round the kitchen door and a surprising smile from Angie, whose breasts filled her kimono to everyone's satisfaction, who chirped, "It's as ready as I am," then disappeared back into the kitchen.

Starkey smiled, shook his head at her and drawled, "She's something, I mean, isn't she." He got up and walked into the kitchen. There was silence there except for the steady drip of the coffee maker and a suppressed moan.

Eddie stared toward the kitchen for a second longer then turned back to the professor, "Yes, we must." He sat back and read again what was on the screen.

Budnick sat silently as the three cars drove north out of the city and into the no-man's land of abandoned farms and the endless banality that was replacing them.

The rosy finger of dawn warmed even that desolation and, sometimes, the low sun lit a remaining stand of trees with a golden ray, or fired the diamond flecks sparkling in the lingering snow. But most of the trees were gone. For mile after mile the beauty that had once existed was buried deep beneath acres of dull housing tracts that looked like camps in a prison archipelago. It made Susan more depressed.

Budnick said nothing for a few minutes as they drove in silence and then said, urgently, in a quiet whisper, "When we pull into the farm, lay very low, keep down." He squeezed her arm in emphasis.

Susan didn't understand, but saw the command in his eyes and whispered, "OK, but what's...?"

"I'm not sure. Just react quickly."

A head turned in the front seat. "What are you two up to? Budnick, where do we turn off 9?"

Budnick looked at the road, "Next right, you'll see a long road lined with trees."

The head turned back to the front. The car sped up and Budnick looked behind them to see the two cars that followed were keeping pace. He tried to shrink down into his seat and pulled Susan closer to him.

The side road came up fast as trees and poles flashed by and the tires quickened their rhythm and song. His throat got dry. He felt short of breath. Susan felt it and squeezed his hand. She looked at him for comfort but could see the fear he tried to control. She turned and looked ahead at the road coming up and wondered what fate had in mind for her.

The fat man looked to his right and said, "OK, Budnick, I hope for your sake the stick is here." He turned his head back towards them and looked at Budnick and Susan with twisted eyes. "It is here isn't it?"

Budnick looked at him, blinking a couple of times, before saying, "You'll get it. Don't worry."

The fat man fixed his eyes on Budnick for some seconds, searching, then once again faced the front as the car began to pull off the highway and turn onto the long gravel road that led up to the house.

Starkey's radio chattered to life on the table and he jumped from the kitchen and Angie's hot lips to pick it up and listen. David tensed by the window and put his hand up to his eyes to reduce the glare of the morning sun so he could see better down the road.

He said in rapid staccato, "Cars are coming, three", and called out,

"Marcel, we will need you my friend."

A quick, "Je viens," came from the room where Marcel struggled to keep his balance as he stood up on one leg while holding a gun. Billie came from a side room and stood next to David, flicking off the safety of the automatic pistol he carried as they both looked out the window. Angie went up to them with two cups of black coffee and gave one to Starkey and one to David. As they all stared down the road, Angie turned to Eddie and Emma and the professor, and with a look begging forgiveness, said, "I just thought they would need it first, I'll bring yours now." A shy smile appeared and vanished as she moved silently out of sight.

Starkey's radio squealed again. An urgent voice said, "Not friendly, we can take them. Coming straight at us, ...Starkey?"

284

Billie said, "Stop 'em. Stop 'em now." Starkey echoed the command into the radio.

There was silence for a few seconds except for the faint sounds of the engines of the cars as they came fast down the long road, watched by the tall, thin trees. Then suddenly Budnick and Susan heard rapid cracks in threes and glass exploded through the air. There were more cracks, again in threes. They heard the driver shout in surprise as he put his hands to his face. Susan looked up and saw blood spurt through his fingers.

The car swung to the right hard and fast, and hit a tree, as more slugs hit the metal, the hood collapsed and the fat man's head punched through the windshield, cutting his throat from ear to ear. Budnick pulled Susan back down to the floor. As he did she saw the fat man's head collapse onto the broken glass.

Susan pulled her eyes away and dropped down as close as she could get as Budnick fell over her, hoping life was still a possibility, shouted, "Oh, my god!" and contracted her body as tight as she could.

The chatter of guns ahead of them continued as the other two cars stopped in front of theirs. The men in them got out on the side away from the house and took up positions and fired back with machine pistols. But they were facing the sun low in the sky. The rain had stopped. The clouds had cleared. They were perfect targets. They could see nothing. They could do nothing. They finally stopped firing blindly. There was a long silence. The morning air stirred the branches in the trees. The grass swirled with its caress. The men in the trees who had sprung the trap and the men trapped both drew in the cold clean air and felt invigorated, as they waited for movement, for action, for a decision. But everything was still.

In the house Starkey talked into the radio, "What's the situation?" An excited voice replied, "Two down, looks like four more guys. Thought I saw movement in the first car.

Should we finish them off?"

"What do you think, my friend?" David turned and looked at Marcel who had managed to get to the window beside the door and was half-laying, half sitting on the floor with his automatic resting on his good leg. Marcel looked out the window, studying the field of battle. He replied, "We need information. The two men in the car by the tree are finished. But you are right, someone else is in there, but not armed, not trying to resist. ...David, you have to find out."

Starkey spoke into the radio, "Stay still. One of us is coming out. Cover him."

The radio screeched and hissed and a broken, "OK, stay still, cover, got it, over."

Starkey put the radio down and pointed to a clump of trees just ahead of the cars and the men who hid behind them.

"Two of our boys are there. Two on the other side of the road. They'll keep their heads down."

David nodded silently, checked his gun, looked around at everyone, smiled at Emma and the professor, said, "Make me front page, Eddie," and walked out of the front door.

He ran low to the ground, zigzagging to the clump of trees as the two men positioned there helped him by pulling the triggers on their guns. They sprayed the cars and trees behind them with fragments of metal and shards of wood. The men behind the cars responded with two short bursts as David reached the trees, a little out of breath. He crouched behind the two bikers who stood, one on each side of the tree, aiming their submachine guns at the men a few metres away. It was quiet again.

"We can take 'em now, if you want, no problem," said the man on the left. He chewed gum as he spoke and lined up his sights with the target. "They got no ammo left, looks like. Weren't expecting us, I don't think." And he chuckled,

"Ah man, they are so fucked."

David moved in for a closer look. "Cover me, I'm going to that car."

The man chewing gum looked sideways at David, squinted, and as he turned back to his sights said, "Do our best, but I hope you move fast." He flashed a smile as David dropped to the ground and crept towards the car where the fat man's head lay impaled on shards of broken glass.

A burp of firing came from one of the cars. Mud and stones kicked up just behind his feet. Emma, watching from the house, sucked in her breath in fear as he reacted and suddenly jumped up and ran with desperation to the car and threw himself to the ground.

The man chewing gum threw a few rounds into the car where the shots had come from. But there was no further response. David breathed in deeply and wet his lips with his tongue, then called out, "Who's in there? Come out, now."

He thought he heard a familiar voice say "David, is that your voice? It's Budnick," and dared to raise himself to look through the side window. Staring back at him was the grinning face of Budnick while Susan, lying under him, slowly uncovered her hands from her eyes and smiled as David winked at her and said, "Cheri, a pleasant surprise. This way, keep low," and he helped Budnick out first followed by Susan crawling carefully over broken glass and dripping blood until she was sheltered by his arms.

The three of them crept low through the long grass to a stand of trees a few metres away. Then David pulled Budnick on the arm and took hold of Susan and ran with them along a low ditch next to the row of trees until they reached the house. David looked back before they went through the back door and saw two of the men who had fired at him stand up and throw down their weapons then walk slowly out where they could be seen.

The man chewing gum shouted, "Tell your friends to come out, or we'll kill you where you stand." The two men stopped in their tracks and looked at each other, then back at the cars, "Give it up, there's no point," one of them shouted. "They're not joking."

A third man stood up and walked into view with his hands in the air. He stopped when he saw the gun aimed at him, raised in caution. In a monotone he said, "The other guy's dead," then walked over to join the two standing exposed to the threat of the men in the trees.

Two other men appeared from the trees on the side of the road nearest them and said something. No one in the house could hear, but they next saw the three men lower their raised hands and lay on the ground with their hands resting on the back of their heads. One of the men from the trees stood over them with his submachine gun aimed at the backs of their heads.

The radio hissed and crackled, "OK, what next?"

Budnick twitched his shoulder nervously while looking out the window.

"You got a place you can lock 'em up for awhile, Starkey?"

Starkey kept his gaze fixed on the scene outside. His face was taut and he chewed his teeth as he thought.

"Yeh, we can put 'em in the cellar."

He moved closer to Budnick who was still breathing hard and said to Susan, standing close with David, "We haven't met. Name's Starkey. I own the place."

He smiled at her and called to Angie, "Hey, Angie, can you help our young friend here. Think she needs a drink. Am I right?"

Susan released David's hand and swept her left hand through her hair and replied,

"You know too much already," and tried to look uninterested.

Angie, who had come from the kitchen, was looking curiously at Susan, sizing her up. She clenched her teeth and narrowed her eyes before turning sharply away to fetch a whisky bottle.

Starkey switched his gaze to her retreating slowly swaying buttocks, then turned back to Susan and while staring, said to David, "Good work, my friend. She is beautiful."

David smiled, put his arms around Susan from behind and gently said, "Oui, elle est tres belle. From hell came heaven." Susan blushed deeply.

Starkey knew enough to switch back to Budnick before he crossed the line and said,

"Man you sure you know who you're dealing with? 'Cause I don't."

Budnick's shoulder twitched and he walked away from Starkey saying, "The Man, Starkey, always the Man."

Starkey stepped back and picked up the radio, "Take 'em to the cellar," and then watched through the window as his men shoved the prisoners towards the back of the house.

Budnick sighed deeply and sat down opposite Emma and the professor and said, "Eddie, you gotta get this story out this morning. People have to know. It's our only chance."

The professor asked, "What happened?" Budnick proceeded to tell him.

*   *   *   *   *

32

Budnick regained his colour as he related the chain of events. Everyone scattered around the room observed in rapt silence. Susan sat smoking a cigarette, her head down, listening, only raising her head to describe what she saw when Budnick couldn't find the words. They both looked exhausted, tired, dirty, eyes dark-circled, hungry. Eddie was leaning back in his chair taking it all in, slowly turning his head side to side, trying to understand what he was hearing. He sat forward as Budnick finished and rested deeper in his chair, and watched as Susan blew smoke into the air above her head. Then he quietly spoke,

"OK, I've got it set up. Front page. Bold type. Biggest font we can use- 'Country Betrayed' – Important members of the government, business and media receiving payments from American secret services. Revelations go to the highest levels of government and business. The people are betrayed."

"Then there'll be a side title, smaller print, 'Committee of Public Safety tried to prevent release of this information. Dramatic Events - several people murdered."

"Hope you like it. So there it is. The rest is details. I can get it out for the afternoon edition."

Emma smiled and took the professor's hand, "Thank

you very much Mr. Mackenzie. I will never forget this day."

Eddie looked grim, nodded and replied, "You and me both, but there is going to be a reaction and there's going to be trouble, they're not going to take this lying down."

Susan took the cigarette from her lips, "They can throw out all the bullshit they want. I'm tired of being shoved around by these jerks. Let them react. We'll react back." She lifted her chin in defiance.

Budnick harrumphed and twitching his shoulder looked at Eddie squarely, "OK, Eddie, anyway we have no choice. Do it."

Eddie just said "OK," opened his mobile phone and after a minute waiting said, "Yeh, hi, look something urgent's coming – my encrypted email. Yeh. Story and instructions. Just follow it to the letter. Right. No don't tell anyone who doesn't need to know. Right. Not even the publisher. You'll see why when you get it." He snapped the mobile shut, turned to his computer and pressed some keys then raised his hands for the whiskey bottle on the desk. "OK, it's done. This is going to be interesting."

Susan stood up suddenly, "I need a shower. Angie, can I?" Angie, standing in the doorway of the kitchen responded by closing her eyes softly, like a young doe, "Come on, I'll show you. You can borrow something of mine to wear." Then she looked over at Emma, embarrassed that she hadn't thought of her. Emma smiled graciously, and shook her head no, "It's OK. Susan needs to stand under hot running water for as long as she can after what she's seen. Don't worry about me."

Angie looked perplexed but took Susan with her tattooed arm and led her down the hallway. Susan hesitated midway, and turned back to Budnick, "What are we going to do about the others, that guy Marko is crazy." She fixed her eyes on Budnick who twitched his shoulder again, and said in a low voice,

"We'll take care of it." She nodded and turned and

walked towards the bathroom with Angie. Budnick turned his body to the others and said "Starkey, David, give me a plan. We have to go back to the apartment. We can't wait. She's right. Marko is unpredictable."

David sat down at the dining table. Starkey pulled up a chair there too. Marcel stayed where he was on the floor. It was easier on his leg. He spoke first.

"I say we just call the police. Tell them there's been a mass shooting. The building will swarm with them in two minutes. They'll kick the door in if he doesn't answer it. They won't know Marko's a cop until they get there and he'll be on the ground before he can talk. The other cops can't be with that renegade. He was freelancing. Him and the others in the cellar."

Starkey sat with his hand to his chin. "Sounds good to me. He's right. The pigs will be over that apartment in minutes. If we go, it's rush hour into the city now. Every one's going to their crummy jobs. It'll take two hours to get there. Sounds like anything can happen in that time especially when he doesn't hear from the fat man soon."

Budnick twisted his neck a little to relieve the tension. "Hmmm-hmmm. OK, I'll make the call, I can't see another way either."

He reached into his pocket, but withdrew an empty hand, "Forgot they took mine back at Diana's. Give me your phone would yah, David? Thanks," and punched in the emergency number then hesitated, "But Marko has them hostage. They'll be in worse danger if he's cornered. I don't know," and he put the phone down on the table.

David shook his head. "Tell the police it's a hostage situation; that lives are in danger. Their sniper team will take him out, I guarantee you. He won't know what hit him."

Budnick looked down at the floor and his shoes, then over at Eddie. "What do you think Eddie?"

"He's right. The Toronto cops will shoot first. They

always do. Marko won't have a chance to connect with anyone on his page. Yeh it's risky. But if he doesn't hear from the his boss soon he's gonna start adding things up and he's going to react."

Budnick clenched his jaw tight and said, "OK," picked up the mobile, clicked on the numbers and waited a second for a woman's voice to ask, "Are you reporting a traffic accident or an emergency?" In a firm and slow voice Budnick replied, "There's been a shooting, yes, a multiple shooting, there are hostages, very dangerous man, name, that's not important, the address..." and he stood up as he continued to talk to the woman on the other end and told her where and then hung up and said, "They're on the way."

~

Marko was restless. Conway could sense it. Marko was tired, like the rest of them. His eyes half closed from time to time and he had to jerk himself to keep awake.

Eiger watched his head drop again and his fingers began to uncurl from the gun. But Marko caught himself and startled, opened his eyes to see Eiger staring at him, "What are you looking at?"

Eiger was about to say something sarcastic when Conway nudged against him with his body and said, "Don't push him. He's edgy."

Doc. Wainwright pulled himself up from the couch near Diana and pointed at Marko and his gun.

"You're tired, that gun could go off. You should..." At that Marko jumped up and clipped the doctor with his free hand, "If I want your advice, but I don't so shut up. What the fuck is taking them so long? Things better be cool or its gonna get hot in here I can tell you that."

He began to pace up and down in front of the window. He began swearing and waving the gun around, agitated, pacing and turning, pacing and turning like a caged panther. Suddenly he stopped in front of Conway. His face was contorted with rage. He shoved the barrel of the gun in Conway's face and screamed, "I swear I'm going to kill you, man. I'm going to blow your goddamed head off right now." He suddenly looked very surprised and took a step back as the window shattered, blood shot from a small hole in his forehead and the back of his skull shattered against the wall behind him.

He stood completely still as the doctor said, "My god," and Pierre shouted, "Keep down, keep down!"

The doctor lunged for the floor. Conway and Eiger looked on with open mouths. Marko's legs folded under him as he went down, with a very surprised look on his face and collapsed next to Agius. A single electric spasm passed through his body, as life fled the scene. Then he lay still.

Seconds later, before they could react, the door to the apartment was blasted open with the loud bang of a battering ram and a swarm of shouting cops in black combat gear surged into the room, guns thrust out, screaming commands not to move, threatening death with every move.

~

As the door burst in Eddie received a call on his mobile. He listened closely, said, "Got ya. Print it. Get it out. No matter what happens get it out," and closed the phone.

"It's gone to print. Be out in the afternoon edition. Online in five minutes."

The professor stood up. He walked over to Eddie and put out his hand. Emma went over and bowed her head slightly and said "Thank you, Mr. Mackenzie. It is rare to meet people who do right these days. Sometimes I think things could really change."

"You proved that to me," he replied his head down, his eyes looking up to hers, and then, turning to Budnick, then David, Starkey and the rest, "But this has just begun. They're going to try to bury the story, control it, spin it, to bury us. It's just beginning." He picked up the bottle of whiskey and poured himself a full glass.

Budnick said, "We had to save ourselves first, we had to release it." He raised his head as Susan walked towards them down the hallway her hair damp, her body languid in Angie's white shirt and black jeans, barefoot. Just as she came into the room, Budnick's mobile rang. He smiled,

"It's Jack. They're fine. Marko's dead. They're at central division being questioned....uh huh, and Diana?....uh uhuh. The others, Pierre, Johnny? Thanks Jack. It's a big relief. Yes, we'll come in. I'll phone the division. Ok Jack, thanks, my friend. See you as quick as we can get there."

He put the phone down, Susan looked at him and waited, her hands in mid air, open palmed, "And so, well, Diana? Budnick, talk to me..."

"She's fine. Took her to emergency, stable, should be ok. Doc Wainwright's gone with her." Susan sank down into a chair and began to cry. "

Budnick's face turned cloudy, "But we've got to go in. They want to question us."

Starkey asked, "You gonna trust them?"

"We have no choice. Our protection is the paper and hoping there are some honest cops. They don't control everybody."

Emma walked up to Budnick and, looking at him directly said,

"We can't keep running. Just one night has been enough I think. We are doing what is right. We will go in."

The professor smiled, winked at her and put his pipe to his mouth and repeated, "Yes, we will go in. There is nothing else we can do."

Starkey said, "Fine, man, it's your gig, but we've got dead men here and what are we going to do with the three in the cellar. This ain't coming down on my head. I'm with you but..."

Budnick nodded grimly, "It'll be cool. Shouldn't have brought you all this trouble ..."

Starkey looked angry and his face flushed briefly but he was aware Angie was watching him. He softened and said, "I owe you man. Always will. Whatever you say man, it's cool with us. But what do we do with those guys?"

Budnick thought for a moment then asked David what he thought.

"We can't risk transporting them. They stay here. Police can pick them up later. Or Starkey can deliver them. I'll stay here but Marcel needs to see a doctor about his leg. I'll stay here. Marcel goes with you."

Budnick nodded, then faced Emma, the professor and Eddie who sat calmly around the desk. "We should go now. The sooner this is over the sooner we can sleep. I'm getting too old for this."

Eddie stood up, grabbed his laptop, gave the stick to the professor, grabbed a last swig of whisky and said, "Let's go."

Emma and the professor stood up and walked toward the door. They both turned, blocking Budnick behind them to say, "Thank you Mr. Starkey, if there's anything the Hell's Angels need sometime, well, Mr. Budnick can put us in touch." She smiled gently and warmly at him. Starkey moved up close to her and kissed her on the cheek and then stepped back,

"Wouldn't do that for most broads," to which Angie responded, "That is for sure. Where'd you pick up the charm?"

"Hey, I can watch movies too. Good luck professor, Mr newspaperman. Try to get the story straight this time and spell my name right." Eddie said calmly, "I'll make sure of it Starkey," and shook his hand.

Budnick looked impatient, "We gotta go. Later Starkey, I'll call you about the cops and those guys in the cellar. Keep your phone on. Come on Marcel. Susan." She took a last drag on her cigarette and said, "Thought you'd never ask."

Budnick walked out of the door, helping Marcel limp over to the F10 where he, Susan and Marcel got in. The Blochs and Eddie Mackenzie got into the Range Rover with Eddie at the wheel. Budnick looked briefly back at the house, waved at Eddie in the mirror and rapidly drove away followed by the sound of grinding of gears as Eddie put the Range Rover in motion, accelerated and disappeared into the now bright morning sky.

Starkey and David watched them fade from view, then Starkey turned to him and touching his arm asked, "Bacon and eggs, my friend?"

David smiled, "That would be wonderful. Are you cooking?"

Starkey laughed, "Believe it or not, I am. But Angie will help." He laughed again as they closed the door behind them and walked back into the room where Angie was waiting in the kitchen and Billie was talking on the radio to the men guarding the cellar.

David asked, "They secure?" Billie nodded, "Yep, for now." Then he sighed and said, "Ah man, I need a joint. This is stressing me out," and walked over to a bag of pot on the coffee table and began to roll one.

Budnick and Mackenzie parked their vehicles on the street across from the central station. Budnick turned to

Susan and Marcel. "We'll go in now. Let me do all the talking. Say nothing to anyone. And try to stay calm."

They looked nervous, exchanged grim glances then followed Budnick out of the car, Susan helping Marcel. The Blochs and Eddie Mackenzie joined them on the sidewalk. They grouped themselves together, exchanged looks and then Budnick, his mouth grim, expanded his stocky body as large as he could make, rotated one shoulder and led the way into the police station.

The area in front of the reception desk was alive with police officers standing around talking. They looked at Budnick and the others with hostile curiosity as they walked past. Budnick asked the desk sergeant for the Commanding Officer. The sergeant asked his name, then told him to wait and picked up his phone and mumbled some words, put it down and pointed at a meeting room down a corridor to the right of the front desk.

"They're in there. What's wrong with him?" he asked nodding towards Marcel.

"Needs a doctor, gunshot wound. Should go to hospital."

"Talk to the CO. But I'll call an ambulance now. Be here in 5 minutes."

Budnick nodded and, helping Marcel, and followed by Emma and the professor, walked towards the meeting room and opened the door.

*   *   *   *   *

33

Shouts of relief shook their ears as Conway stood up from his chair opposite them and pushed past several detectives standing between him and the door. Budnick took him in his arms. They hugged until Budnick noticed Eiger, still sitting between two policemen, grim faced, drinking coffee from a plastic cup.

Budnick nodded. Eiger raised the cup in salute. "Had my doubts I'd see any of you again. Hello, professor, Emma. Come on in and join the circus."

He appeared drunk, but was intoxicated with life. When he saw Susan his face lit up at the same time as Conway's, who shook his head at seeing her, grinned and asked "How ya doing darling? Boy have we missed you." She walked over and took a chair in between the two of them and cadged a cigarette from one of the cops.

Pierre was standing in one corner smoking a cigarette next to a No Smoking sign and talking to a cop. He stopped both when he saw Budnick walk into the room. "Ah, mon ami. C'est bon." He smiled broadly and walked over and also embraced Budnick, and then stepped back holding his hand, "I was pretty worried, my friend, pretty worried."

Budnick asked, "Marko?"

Pierre didn't get a chance to answer. A senior detective in a dark grey suit, and greying cropped hair to match his deeply lined face and grey eyes walked up to Budnick and extended his hand. Budnick shook it,

"Hi, Smitty. What happened to Marko? And while you're at it what happened to Tommy Moore?"

"Our sniper team got Marko. He never even heard the shot. Moore? Looks like Marko, and friends on the inside. We'll deal with them. I promise you. I've never lied to you before, Budnick. I won't start now. So, you want to tell me what's going on."

Budnick's answer was interrupted by Marcel, standing next to the door, leaning on the wall, keeping off his leg, who called to Pierre, who asked, "What about David?"

Pierre spread his arms and embraced and kissed Marcel, and replied, "David is OK. Still up at the farm taking care of business. Here, take this." He guided him to a chair and helped him sit down then turned to the commander, "This man needs to go to a hospital right now."

The detective looked at Marcel, then his leg, "He'll be there in a few minutes, ambulance on its way, I'm told." He turned and beckoned to the Blochs and Eddie Mackenzie, still standing by the door, to enter.

"Please, all of you, come in. I'm Chief Inspector Smith. Budnick calls me Smitty. You are?" and he bowed his torso and head slightly to Emma and patiently took in their names and their place in events.

He showed them to chairs as three of the policemen left the room. He asked if they wanted coffee and food, and asked his men to attend to their needs. He turned back to Budnick, who was sipping on a plastic coffee cup a cop had just handed him.

"I have orders directly from the Chief that I have full authority to do as I see fit. So let's sit down, and you are going to tell me everything and I am going to listen."

Budnick sat down at the head of the table. Smith was adjusting his chair when the door was thrown open and three men in dark suits walked in, one holding a badge in front of him like an icon, who declared, "Committee of Public Safety. We're taking over this investigation. All civilians here are detained under our authority. Which one is Mr. Mackenzie?"

Smith expanded his chest and remained standing,

"No one is interfering in my inquiries. I don't recognise the Committee. You can go fuck yourselves." He pointed at two uniformed men and said, "Escort these people out of here and out of the station. If they resist, arrest them."

The man with the badge stood his ground but the other two hesitated and began to retreat. The leader said, "Stay where you are. Sir, the Committee's authority overrides yours, you can contact the Minister of Public Safety if you..."

"All right, arrest them. I'm not listening to this crap. Put them in the cells."

The two uniforms hesitated as much as the Committee men, unsure what to do. But their commander's voice rose to new heights and he thundered,

"I gave you an order, obey it." They quickly moved forward as did other officers and grabbed the three men and hustled them out of the room. The Committeemen's protests and threats of serious consequences faded gradually into the distance as they were hauled away. Smith yelled after them, "And lock 'em up. I don't want those kind of people loose in my city." He gathered himself, took a breath, hitched up his trousers and said,

"Mr. Mackenzie, perhaps you can tell me what the hell is happening."

"I can only tell you what has happened since last night when Budnick called me. But I can also tell you to read the latest edition of the paper."

"Well, why don't you tell me what's in the paper? Don't

play games with me."

Eddie looked over at Budnick and Budnick in turn looked at Emma and the professor. Budnick began to speak,

"I can put it together for you, Smitty. It's gonna take awhile," and he leaned forward in his chair, put his hands together and related the events of the past two weeks and that last night, slowly, earnestly and methodically.

An hour later, after Budnick had finished what he had to say and Eddie Mackenzie had told the detective the contents of the article, and Conway, Eiger, Pierre and Susan had added to the mix, the detective turned to the Blochs,

"This information, you think it's legitimate, Professor?"

"Yes, I have the device here. Frank convinced us it is. His death is proof of that. The device is in my custody. People have died for it and I, and Emma, were entrusted with it. We will not give it up. People have died for it because it contains the key to the people's freedom, at least a real chance at it. I can only hope that you are not associated with anyone on that list, because it is clear that some of your men are."

"My job right now is to explain these shootings and all these bodies, not subvert democracy. You're going to need protection. I'll assign some men I trust. But now that device and the evidence on it is part of a murder investigation. I have to demand that you give it to me."

The professor looked over to Budnick. Budnick said, "I think you're going to have get an order to do that. We've told you all we know. That stick's no use to you, Smitty."

"Sorry, Budnick, but it's also evidence of crimes against national security if the information on it is legit and I'm taking it as evidence in that investigation that starts right now."

Budnick paused and exchanged concerned looks with the Blochs and the others. Smith stood waiting, with his hands on his hips also looking from one to the other. "Look, it will be in our custody. It will be recorded, registered. It can't be tampered with. Don't worry. The information won't disappear. I promise you." He looked at them intently again.

Finally Emma said, "We have no choice. We have done all we can. Now it is up to others to do their part. Give it to him."

The professor took it slowly from his pocket and handed it to Smith who looked at it curiously and weighed it in his palm. "Thank you. You did the right thing."

"Mr. Eiger." He turned to Johnny. "You're free to go to the hospital to see your lady friend. The rest of you are free to leave. But wait for me to arrange things. Mr. Mackenzie, I'm giving you a man for protection. You can rely on them. I'd like a real democracy for a change, so would they. I'll look forward to reading the paper. I'll contact the Minister of Public Safety or maybe the Chief will. We'll deal with the Committee."

Emma looked grim and said, "I hope so or they will deal with us." Smith returned the firm look, attempted a smile, quickly turned and, with the other officers, left the room.

Budnick turned to Susan, "Do I pay you time and half for overtime?"

"It's gonna be double time this time." She took him by the arm. "Come on let's go to Flo's and get lunch. Coming guys?" She tossed her hair as she forced a smile at Conway and Eiger. "But maybe I better go with you to see Diana."

Eiger got up, and put down his coffee cup. "Thanks, but I'd like to see her alone right now. I'll tell her you're OK."

Conway put his hand on Eiger's shoulder to reassure him, "We'll be at Flo's for awhile. Then I gotta sleep," He put his arm gently around Susan's waist and squeezed her, "Just wish it wasn't alone."

Susan kissed him on the cheek, "Don't you ever give

up?" She then turned and kissed Eiger. He walked out of the room, and out of the station, got into a police car and headed for the hospital.

Two paramedics came in as just Eiger left, pushing a gurney and asked where the casualty was. They were directed to Marcel as Pierre complained loudly that they had taken their sweet time. They took a look at his leg, put him on the gurney, connected him to an i.v. and headed back out. One of them asked, "Who's going to the hospital with this man?"

Pierre said, "Me," and looked at the detective who nodded that it was OK. The medics wheeled Marcel out of the station, put him into the ambulance, helped Pierre sit in the back, beside the stretcher, and left both men talking in French, mainly about Susan, as they closed the doors and carried them off to the hospital.

Budnick looked at the detective, "The Blochs should go home but they need protection too, same as Eddie. And take care of Starkey's situation for me. He saved us." Smith shook his hand and said, "Don't worry about it. I'll send a team to relieve him, no questions asked. Just let 'em know were coming."

Eddie broke in, "I'm going to the paper. Make sure nothing gets screwed up. Can I drop anyone?"

Budnick's shoulder twitched, "Yeh, if you're goin' near Flo's you can drop us there, get some breakfast or lunch, what ever time it is. Conway, Susan, you up for it?"

Conway looked dog tired, unshaven, suit rumpled, but feeling Susan's arm next to his the energy returned and he said, "Yeh, why not, can sleep later. Susan?"

"I just wanna go home. I'm so tired. I don't even know what's happening, but I'm so hungry I could eat an elephant. Ok. Let's go."

Budnick went over to the Blochs. "Quite a night, professor. Emma. Quite a night."

Emma walked up close to him and put her lips to his

cheek and said, "A terrible night, a terrible night Mr. Budnick, but perhaps all this violence and death was worth it."

"I don't know Emma, I don't know. What do you think professor?"

The professor picked up a pack of cigarettes from the table and put one in his mouth and lit it with a match handed to him by a young police officer standing nearby. "We will know that tomorrow when the reaction sets in. Maybe we'll have a real democracy for a change, maybe it'll be worse."

"Eddie, you?"

Eddie shook his head. "That depends on the people, Walter. It all depends on the people. I'm not expecting much. But it's a chance."

He walked out of the building followed by a man in plain clothes. Budnick, followed by the others, went outside onto the sidewalk and watched them get into the F10 and quickly drive away.

A black unmarked car drew up in front of them. There were two men wearing jeans and windbreakers inside. They asked for the Blochs. Farewells were exchanged; warm embraces, earnest words, reassurances that things would be alright and soon, they were whisked away from the station back to the grace and beauty of their home. They followed the car with riveted eyes.

'Cool as cucumbers. All the way through. They're something, they are.' He took Susan's arm, 'Come on beautiful, let's take Budnick for a meal that'll make even him satisfied.'

Budnick laughed, 'Ok, come on,' and walked over to the Range Rover. 'The wife is going to kill me with questions.'

'Shouldn't have married a prosecutor.'

'Shouldn't' have married at all.'

Susan said 'Hah-hah, you guys really like women, I see.

So you don't want to marry me anymore Mr. Conway?'

'Conway put his arm around her and whispered, 'Just let me know when you've made up your mind.'

Budnick made a call on his phone and when Starkey answered told him what to expect and to stay cool, then started the car up, put it in gear and pulled into traffic. As he did Susan, sitting in the back, leaned forward between the two men. 'I sure hope Diana is ok.'

Budnick looked at her in the mirror, 'Me too, and Johnny. He didn't look too good.'

Conway's eyebrows raised, 'Yeh, well, I can't feel a thing. Not a goddam thing.'

~

Eiger walked into the hospital with a policeman trailing close behind and was led to the emergency room where Diana lay, eyes shut, both arms connected to tubes and a heart monitor to one side of her bed. The cop stepped back and talked to the nurses at their station while Eiger sat down on a small chair and stroked Diana's forehead. She opened her eyes a little and saw him.

'Hi, Johnny', she whispered, her voice weak and distant. Her face was pale. She tried to move an arm to touch him but could barely move her fingers. A doctor wearing greens came in, said hello, and looked at her chart, then her neck, then lifted the blanket to look at her side.

'Husband?'

'Friend.'

'She lost a lot of blood internally. We almost lost her. But I think she's through the worst of it.'

Eiger nodded silently and then asked suddenly, 'The

man that was with her...'

'Wainwright? He left as soon as we took over. Don't blame him after what they did to him. Formally we could make a complaint but I'm not going to do it. He was a good doctor. Let her sleep. She really can't talk. She's still doped up from the anesthetic and very weak. You look whipped yourself. You could be in shock. And your face looks like someone took a good couple of shots at it. Here let me take a look.'

Ten minutes later after examining his jaw, his eyes, his teeth he said, 'You're going to have some bad bruising for a week or so. Need a couple of stitches in that cut on the side. I'll be back with a kit.' He walked out of the room.

Eiger sat there for a few minutes, staring at Diana who had fallen back into unconsciousness, then waited with resignation as the doctor returned and sewed up the cut in his face. Then he stood up, signaled to the cop standing near the nurses station and said, 'You can go back, I don't need the protection...

The cop protested, 'But I've got orders...'

'It's fine. You have better things to do. I'll look after myself.' They looked at each other, 'Ok, suit yourself. Good luck and hope the lady is ok.'

He walked down the corridor to the elevator and disappeared from view.

Eiger leaned over and kissed Diana on the forehead, touched his hand to hers, said, 'I'll be back tomorrow, sweetheart.' He got up, said goodbye to the nurses, shuffled to the elevator, walked slowly out of the hospital and got into a cab parked outside.

'Where you wanna go buddy?'

'Flo's downtown, you know it?'

'No but I'll find it.' He started up the car, moved out of the hospital grounds, and pulled into traffic, as he punched in the name on his GPS system.

'If you don't mind me saying so, you look a little rough for wear. What happened?'

Eiger leaned back deep into the back seat, closed his eyes and said, 'You wouldn't believe me if I told you.'

*   *   *   *   *

34

Flo's was still there. The city, the streets strangled by cars and trucks pushing and shoving for space, everyone at each other's throats, worried about the bills, the job, the future, haunted by the past, the present vanishing as fast as it appeared. Everything was the same as the day before. The cab stopped outside, Eiger found enough change in his pocket to pay, got out, took a deep breath of the still cold air and walked in.

Peter looked up from the cash, 'Hey my friend, you all right? Shit what happened to you, man?' Eiger said, 'I'm better than I look, thanks Peter. Need a coffee.'

Then he saw Budnick, Conway and Susan sitting in a booth over in the corner near the windows. Susan saw him and raised her hand to catch his attention. He made his way past the tables and a few people having coffee, eating. He slumped down exhausted in the booth next to Conway, opposite to Budnick and Susan. They were all quiet, exhaustion setting in. No one said anything. Peter brought over a pot of coffee and a mug for Eiger. 'Bacon and eggs, steak and eggs?'

Eiger looked up, bleary eyed, 'Steak, Peter, need a steak.'

Peter still looking at his mangled face said, 'Coming

right up,' walked briskly back to the kitchen and yelled out the order.

Susan asked, "Diana?'

'Not good but they say she'll recover. How are we?'

Conway sipped on a cup of coffee. 'We're back to where we were yesterday. At worst the Committee will have us silenced, at best we're back to trying to make a living.'

Budnick's shoulder twitched, 'I told you we have to get the Aldarizine file going. It's our only hope. It's back to the daily grind for us. Johnny, what you gonna do? You're welcome to stay with us.'

Eiger took the cup of coffee that Peter brought over and replied, 'I still have nine months to kill. I think I'll stick around. Bit more exciting than I bargained for but I like the company." He managed to form a smile but winced as he did. "But I've still gotta finish the General's case. After that, well, I don't know.'

Susan smiled and put her hand on his. "If you stick around, I won't complain."

Eiger smiled then leaned into her, picked up his coffee mug and asked Budnick "You think things will change after all this?"

Budnick shook his head, "I don't know. Whatever changes? We gotta try but I'm not optimistic. Too few like Emma and the professor, like Frank, and Marina and Tommy, like Eddie. Too many like Agius and Marko and the fat man. I'm so goddam tired of it all. Really goddamed tired. Fighting assholes all my life and they just seem to multiply."

"That's why the world needs us," said Susan, her face brightening. "We just gotta get back to the office and do what we do best."

"And what's that, sweetheart?" asked Conway.

"Defending the weak from the strong, what else?"

"An endless task."

"Then the sooner we get back to it the better."

The three men smiled at her simple statement of fact and lapsed into silence as they ate and let life flow back into them. Two hours later, they were still sitting there, downing the last dregs of coffee when Budnick suddenly stopped breathing and scowled as he saw two men walk into the café and stand silently, looking over at them. He said quietly, 'We've got company.'

They all turned and watched as the two men, wearing long grey coats and sullen faces, sat down at a booth behind them. Just then a news flash appeared on the TV screen by the bar; 'Free Press chief editor fired after publishing fake story of foreign control of government. Publisher apologises. Story removed from website. Mystery surrounds several shootings in the city overnight. Police Inspector suspended for incompetence.' It was quickly followed by another news flash, warning of a late season ice storm.

No one said a word. Budnick looked at the two men behind them, his face grim, and said, "Well, looks like we have another client or two. I don't know about you, but I'm going to Eddie's place. Sleep can wait. Anyone else?"

Conway and Eiger exchanged glances, put money on the table, stood up, put on their coats, and waited for Susan and Budnick to join them. Then one by one they filed past the two men sitting in the booth.

Just as Budnick walked past he looked down at them, said "Fuck the Committee," and gave them the finger along with his penetrating stare. The two men were startled but before they could react Budnick joined the others and said, "Susan got it right. Let's do what we do best. Let's go fight these bastards. That's what it's all about isn't it, for Eddie, for all of us?' Whadda ya say?"

In answer, Eiger and Conway linked arms with Susan and, with a nod to Budnick who lead the way, stepped bravely out onto the cold streets of the city that was, like them, threatened by dark and gathering clouds.

* * * * *

About Author

Christopher **Black** is is an international criminal lawyer based in Toronto, Canada.

He writes essays, articles and papers on international law and other issues. Some of his poetry has been published in both Canada, United States, and Russia.

With Andre Vltchek and Peter Koenig, he wrote *The World Order and Revolution! - Essays from the Resistance*, a compilation of essays (thoughts, analyses, and dreams) by these three outstanding authors: an international lawyer, a philosopher, and an economist.